RIVER AVENUE

RIVER AVENUE

A NOVEL

Jan M. Walton

RIVER AVENUE

Copyright © 2021 by Jan M. Walton

Printed in the United States of America

ISBN 978-1-7370022-0-8 (paperback)
ISBN 978-1-7370022-1-5 (ebook)
Library of Congress Control Number: 2021910381

Edited by Paula Stahel

Cover design by Roy Marshall (royboytn@gmail.com)

Interior design by Robin Brooks (thebeautyofbooks.com)

Photographs: Darkroom by iStockphoto.com/Maxiphoto
Fire reflection in water by Stockphoto.com/Oleg Tkachev
Sunset by iStockphoto.com/Jamie Tuchman
1929 Ford Model A stake bed truck by iStockphoto.com/Stan Rohrer
Children and house courtesy of the author

Author photograph by Joy Hmielewski

Windcove Publishing, Clearwater, Florida
windcovepublishing@gmail.com
www.janmwalton.com

*This novel would not have been written
without my sister, Jill Robinson,
who started me on this journey
and talked it out with me so many times.
I am eternally grateful.*

CHAPTER 1

Fayette County, Pennsylvania, 1930

On that Sunday, hope fooled me into thinking my mother walking down the stairs wearing her hat was our rescue.

"You've cut your hair," my sister Jane blurted out.

The six of us froze, coats and scarves and boots half on, as my mother gripped her way down the banister, her hat pulled over her bobbed hair. Tugging at a strand, she tilted her head. "I let it go too long." She looked upon us with the warm eyes that had always felt like a compass pulling us in the right direction. "Let's bundle up."

I masked my surprise by grabbing her coat and holding it out for her. Over her shoulder, I glimpsed her in the framed photograph that my father took when Lonnie was the baby. In it she was looking straight at the camera with a shy smile, arms clasped behind her, wearing a fancy sleeveless dress with a ruffled skirt, and the same Sunday shoes.

She turned to me. The grief had warped her smile into a grimace. "Put Addie in the pram, Dan, and walk with me."

That Sunday was the first time my mother had gone with us for dinner at Grandma's in the seven weeks since our little brother Alonzo passed, only five years old, the son my father gave his name to. My mother fended off this naming with me and George, telling my father she wouldn't give any of the girls her name, Lillian, and the boys should not have to carry his. But with the third boy, my father insisted, and she let it be. My mother called him Lonnie from his newborn days, and the nickname stuck.

Addie balked when I lifted her into the pram, cold from standing overnight on the front porch. My mother pushed the blankets around her and tucked Addie's hands underneath. Addie yanked an arm out and sucked on her thumb, staring into my mother's eyes as if to dare her to tug the thumb away. My mother hesitated, then straightened up and wrapped her scarf closer around her neck.

"She does that now," I said. Addie, going on two, had slept in my parents' room in the baby crib before we lost Lonnie. After the funeral, the crib was moved to the girls' room and my mother shut her door on us. Addie fussed through the nights, passed between Jane and me, rotating our sleeplessness with hers.

My mother shrugged. "It will pass. Lonnie got over it."

Jane disagreed. "She's doing it on purpose. Don't let her."

My mother answered Jane by grabbing the push-bar of the pram and propelling it through the gate into the road. George,

Ruthie, and Annie—eight, ten, and twelve then—trotted after her. My mother glanced over her shoulder and I moved to catch up. Behind me, the angry crunch of Jane's boots. My sister, at fourteen, stood six inches taller, on our father's stocky legs, than my mother. The two of them paused their skirmishes in the neutral territory of Grandma's sewing room, both delighting in copying the latest styles from the ladies' magazines to make their dresses. In our house, they battled over almost everything else.

On River Avenue, the chill March wind blew strong enough to glimpse the sun poking through the haze. Coke-oven smog hovered over the clusters of houses that dotted the surrounding hills, and the farm fields further out. Our town burned day and night. The furnaces of the Pittsburgh steel mills craved the coke roasted from the coal buried under our corner of Pennsylvania. For a century, dome-shaped brick kilns, oversized beehives with holes in the top, were filled with the black rocks and set on fire. The smoke escaping from the burns in hundreds of smoldering ovens was the everyday sky.

My father dreamed our house on River Avenue during his seven years of laboring in the coal mines. Bunching into the cage in the early morning dimness, descending into complete darkness, rolling trams in the underworld caverns for hours of grinding danger, had taught him respect for the men who would do it all their lives, and that his fate was not going to be theirs. Five of us had been born in a two-room company house before he saved enough to buy the piece of land up on the hill. Drawing the plan for the house, he calculated the height so the back windows on the second floor captured the vista of the slope down to the Monongahela River. Grandma and Papaw, my mother's parents, followed us to River Avenue, moving into the old farmhouse left standing at the crest of the hill when the surrounding acreage was sold off.

While he was a miner, my father's talent with a baseball bat built his reputation in town. Following tradition from the old-time mining days, every neighborhood organized a baseball team. My father had been one of the best hitters around since his teen years. He still played, his big personality showing off for the crowds that were entertained by counting his many hits in a game. His strut to the plate, swinging the bat, advertised him as a risk taker, and predicted he would ignore the signs and swing when he saw his pitch, more often crossing home plate than called out. When we watched my father fouling off fastballs until he got the big hit, Papaw would say, "Your pa's a cocky one, sure has the bluster, no matter what."

My father built our house while he waited for his older brother, Uncle Charlie, to fix a place for him in the gas company. Now, my father left us for weeks at a time, supervising crews hewing ditches and laying piping for the gas further and further into the surrounding counties. But he was home that weekend. He had walked into our house late Friday evening, saying he caught a ride with the supply truck and would go back to the dig site on Monday morning. My mother, quiet to his greeting, let him kiss her cheek.

When he was home, his stubborn resolve forced his way over ours. My father strode through the house, pointing to things out of place that we had missed in our scramble to hide stuff before he entered. We had learned to manage around his dictates, relaxing our guard when he was away. One-by-one we stood before him answering questions about school and chores. It was a ritual like the ones my sisters acted out playing with their dollhouse, scolding, manipulating the figures, posing his family as he liked until the next time he attended to us. We endured, knowing his attention was short term.

He had a second business as a photographer. Intrigued by observing an old shutterbug hired by the gas company, my father discovered his eye for the ball could also capture faces in a pleasing way with a camera. At first he practiced by commanding us into positions at various locations, experimenting with light and backgrounds. He shot photos of all the teams in his league, and the boasting around town created demand. Shooting at civic ceremonies got his photos into the papers and developed his relationships among the bigwigs in town who enjoyed promoting themselves. To print the photos, my father constructed a darkroom on the old wooden workbench in a corner of the cellar. Behind a curtain, he submerged exposed images in chemicals poured into shallow trays. The wet black-and-white prints hung like bats clinging to a tree branch, clipped with clothespins on rope lines that crisscrossed above the bench.

Scheduling most of his picture making on Sundays, he as

usual excused himself from dinner at Grandma's. "I'll be taking pictures of the choir at the Episcopal church, soon as they finish their service." He had left the house before us.

As we walked, I reached for the pram handle and my mother slid her hands away. We fell in step, my stride matching hers. As a little boy I had followed whatever she was doing like her shadow. Though I was only toddling when Jane came along, my mother made me her helper. With me perched on a stool and wrapped in an apron, she guided my hands in learning to measure flour and stir puddings, reading aloud to me from *Mrs. Norton's Cook-Book*. When the family grew, my mother assigned us paragraphs for reading aloud from the chapter about setting a formal table. The rest practiced the instructions while she coached. "When you move away from here, you must know how to do things properly," she insisted. At Feeke's store, she devoured the newspapers and magazines from New York, Chicago, and Pittsburgh. Lillian expected us to rise above this town to a sophisticated world, to want more than what she said most people settled for.

"We didn't make our cake." My mother's wistful tone, looking down at her shoes, hands shoved into her pockets, startled me.

Our birthdays had been forgone in the sorrow of Lonnie's passing in February. The circling dark moods of her grief pushed her under the bedcovers for entire days. The few times she had appeared in the kitchen and put on her apron while I cooked, I stayed quiet, afraid of scaring her away.

"I don't mind."

She let out a sigh. "It was my eighteenth birthday when the pains started, your father down the mine. The next morning, the midwife handed you to me." She bumped her elbow against me. "Sixteen now. Look at you."

Blushing at her attention, I thought of her frailty after Lonnie's birth.

Lillian had the short, small-boned build of her mother, five feet tall, trim at the waist and filled out in her hips and legs, so she seemed firmly planted where she stood. She had spent her childhood among boys, more than able to hold her own despite her size. There was a lot of energy in that petite frame, spirited with organizing the chores of raising a large family.

But with Lonnie, the pregnancy and labor left my mother so weak with anemia that lifting his seven pounds was too much for her. When he cried, Grandma or Jane lifted him from the cradle and laid him in place for my mother to nurse him. I pictured those early days of Lonnie's short life, how my mother rested curled around him, and when she was stronger, bound Lonnie to her while she cooked. She kept him close until his kicking forced her to give up the wrapping and let him push up on his arms.

George, running ahead of the pram, tossed a baseball over his head and missed getting under it for the catch. It hit the ground hard ahead of the girls, making them scream.

"Stop scaring your sisters, George!" my mother called. He grabbed the ball and pretended to lob it again. "I said, stop that!"

George winked at her. She winked back. There it was, her loving us, like the air, no thinking about it. The surety, though she was less generous with hugs and kisses than Grandma, her often distracted mind in a realm all her own.

Papaw saw us approaching and came outside to greet us at their gate. Our grandfather was the steady hold of the family, his grip on calamity as firm as when he wrangled a mule pulling a plow in his farming days. He met his daughter's eyes. "Lily, good to see you."

My mother bent to take Addie from the pram and transferred her to Papaw's arms, then hooked her hand over his elbow and turned him toward the porch. Papaw smiled at me as if to say, *We're on the right track.*

Inside the door, Grandma threw her arms around the bundle of my mother, Papaw, and Addie, and muffled her sobs into Papaw's shoulder. Then practical Grandma pulled herself up, wiped her eyes on her apron. "Is that the roast I smell burning? Come on, children, hurry off with the coats."

The usual clamor of all of us warming up in the kitchen raised a level in giddiness, as if it was a holiday. Grandma bustled about with a quicker step. My mother stood in the doorway with Addie grabbing at her dress, listening to Papaw tell her gossip he heard at Feeke's. Grandma called me into the pantry.

"Set a place, get a chair, next to mine," she whispered, shoving an ironed napkin into my hands, then pulling a dinner plate from the shelf. She squeezed my arm. "She'll be just fine."

During dinner, my mother did not say much. She smiled at our jokes, tended to Addie, listened to Grandma's plans for altering Jane's old dresses to fit Ruthie and Annie. A calmness in the way she held herself kept me smiling at her, made me believe Grandma's reassurances. I've gone over that meal a million times in my head and can't draw any clues from it.

When did my mother change her mind about us?

After pie, I left Grandma's house, eager for time alone at home to listen to my favorite music program on the radio. On Sundays after dinner, I claimed a small space in the week to pass time in my own way. The Sundays when my mother had huddled in bed, I had lain on the floor in the parlor below her, the music low. That Sunday, the symphony blaring, I mimicked the conductor with an imaginary baton. After a while, Jane brought back a sleepy Addie to nap, and I assumed my mother and the girls were washing dishes with Grandma.

From the parlor window, I saw my father walking around the house to the back porch. When he entered the kitchen door, left his jacket on the hook, shouldered the camera bag, and went down to the cellar, I tensed. I turned the radio sound lower, waiting for him to shout his displeasure about dust George and I missed sweeping after we refilled the coal bin. Hearing only the clink of bottles, no shout of my name, I eased the dial higher.

That Sunday, the fire gong rang late in the afternoon. When an old house in the coke patch caught fire, it always burned to the ground. Pine trees milled thin made cheap boards for walls and roofs that dried into tinder after years of settling coke dust. Kitchen stoves, kept burning with charcoal, sucked moisture from the wood grain. Icy Pennsylvania winter winds seeped through the cracks stuffed with old newspapers that passed for insulation. If kerosene dripped from a lantern, a candle tipped over, someone left a dishtowel too close to the flame, or a pail of kitchen coals smoldered, once a fire caught the house charred in no time. Fighting the fire was a matter of keeping it from spreading to nearby houses rather than saving the one where it started.

Shouts alerted neighbors and someone would run to an alarm box and set off the gong. Men answering the call first held the spread as much as they could with a bucket line while waiting for the water trucks with hoses. The fire chief qualified the strongest miners for the brigade, men muscled and quick to react from years working underground amidst the potential for deadly fire through every shift. Neighborhood men and boys joined in when more hands were needed.

When our neighborhood fire gong continued ringing, echoed by multiple nearby gongs, it meant a serious fire. Jane, upstairs, heard the neighbor men shouting to each other to get moving. She bellowed at me from the stairs just as our neighbor Roy's boy ran onto our porch yelling, "Get your pa, my dad's getting the truck." George was outside with the younger boys, gathering bikes to ride toward the excitement of the smoke. My father, bounding up the cellar steps, called for George to cap the chemicals he had not put away in his rush.

My father and I met out front as Roy pulled up, and the men and boys in the truck bed made room for us to hop in. From the top of the hill, we saw smoke billowing on the other side of town. Roy pulled the truck up as close to the burn as he dared. The blaze was coming from a warehouse of lumber awaiting loading onto train cars bound for Pittsburgh. Smoke and falling ash made our eyes water and started us coughing. Members of the brigade had fire helmets and goggles. Other men brought masks from the mines. We boys covered our noses and mouths with wet kerchiefs tied around our heads. I pulled my baseball cap low to deflect what it could from my eyes. It was grab what you could to protect yourself and get in there to help.

More men were arriving on their own and in fire trucks. The smoke blocked any light from the weak late-afternoon sun. It was like entering a rain cloud on fire, water spraying in all directions and hot ash falling. Smaller boys ran water buckets to wet a perimeter, hoping to slow the spreading flames. Older boys formed lines to manhandle the hoses from the water trucks, stretching the hose taut to position the water burst as close as possible to the fire. Grabbing onto a hose, I got into the rhythm of the line. My skinny frame handled the weight, my arms muscled from my after-school job loading mail bags at the post office. The postmaster ran past my hose line in a group of brigade men.

One water truck after another pulled up, the hose line easing only long enough for men to disconnect the snaking tube from the empty tank and fast-twist it onto the next to restart the flow.

When flames visibly burned in only one corner of the warehouse, the chief called for the hose lines on our side to stand down. We redirected the line to fill water troughs for the men to bathe the soot and ash from their heads and arms.

My father, Roy, and other men emerged from the cloud, covered in grime. Peeling off their shirts, they stooped forward, reaching into the troughs like thrashing ponies, scrubbing the soot off their skin. Trucks from Feeke's and other town storekeepers arrived, the drivers throwing open the bed gates for the men to grab bottles of root beer and soda to flush out their mouths.

When we had rested enough, we dragged ourselves to Roy's truck. Roy and his son swiped their filthy shirts across the ash-covered windshield until he could see his hand through it.

Later, I learned that after the clamor of the gong and of the men leaving, Jane had dozed off in the quiet house and was startled awake by Addie pulling on her leg; she had climbed out of her baby crib. When Jane led Addie to the kitchen, George and the girls were in the backyard with Roy's daughters from next door, playing within the faint light from the back porch. The girls told Jane that our mother had left them at Grandma's when she took pie to visit a sick lady who had cooked for us after Lonnie passed. Jane sent George next door to see if Mama had gone inside with Mrs. Feeke on her way back. After George came back to say that she had not been there, Jane went ahead with preparing supper.

It was fully dark when my father and I returned. In the kitchen, Addie, in her baby chair, and the girls and George sat around the table eating cake amidst their supper leftovers. Jane gave me a confused look when we came in and headed to the cellar.

As we shed our grubby clothes under the dim bulb at the bottom of the stairs, my father scanned his darkroom and grunted approval—for once George had done what he'd been told to do. The chemical bottles were capped and the drying photos hanging undisturbed.

I lugged my heavy legs up the short flight to the kitchen. Addie was whining to get out of her chair and I reached for her, feeling the ache in my arms from the pull of the hose lines. Setting Addie on my lap, I noticed Mama was not there and turned my own questioning look to Jane. My father slumped into a chair, asking for water. After drinking some and sitting up to take in the scene around the table, he asked, "Where is your mother?"

"She left Grandma's, took pie to old lady Carson, and hasn't come home," Jane answered him, her eyes meeting mine.

Checking his pocket watch, my father asked the girls, "Did she come back to Grandma's?"

Ruthie shook her head. "No. We stayed there a long time talking, then walked back, and we didn't see Mama."

My father nodded at George. "Get the torch and run down the road to Grandma's. Tell your mother we are back from the fire. It's time she came home."

George rolled his eyes, made a show of putting on his jacket, took the torch, and slammed out the door.

Soon a worried Papaw stepped through the kitchen door with George.

"Evening, Alonzo." Papaw hesitated at the sight of the children's faces, then forced a smile. "Walked back with George, on my way to ask Roy to drive me up to the cemetery. Guessing Lillian took a walk up there after she left us. There would have been time for her to get there on foot before dark, but not back."

My father pushed back from the table and stood. "If she's somewhere on that road, it's too dark to walk now. I'll get Roy's truck and drive up there. You can go on home."

"I would just as soon go with you. Her mother is expecting me to find Lillian."

Taking one long stride, my father had his jacket off the hook by the door. "Well, then, let's go and you can report that Lillian's husband brought her home." He slammed out the back door.

I exchanged looks with Papaw. He tried to make light of the situation in front of the girls and George. "Nothing to worry about. Your mother probably lost track of the time is all, and we'll bring her home."

After my father and Papaw left, Jane took the girls upstairs to read and sing, then tucked them into bed. Addie quieted down faster than usual, lulled with the singing. I settled George in his bed, keeping a light tone in answer to his speculations about our mother, wanting him to fall asleep without worry.

Jane and I met in the hallway, and with a glance at her face I saw she shared my intention to sit in the kitchen and wait for the truck to return. After putting the last of the dishes away, we sat on opposite sides of the table, fiddling with coffee cups.

"Did anything happen after I left Grandma's?"

Jane twisted a button on her sweater. "What do you mean?"

"Did something upset her?"

Jane shrugged. "No."

"You argue with her?"

"Why would you ask me that? This is not my fault."

"I didn't say that. I just wonder what happened after I left. She was better today, going with us."

"Grandma asked Mama if she should leave Addie home with her tomorrow. Mama pulled Addie out of her chair, and Addie hit her in the face. Mama started crying. Grandma hugged Mama, tried to calm her." Jane crossed her arms. "You know Grandma, her cheerful voice, telling Mama not to worry. She asked me to bring Addie back, and I did. I don't know what they did after I left."

About eleven, the sound of the truck out back roused us from slumping over the table. My father came in alone. Jane hovered as he sat on the bench to take off his boots.

"Where is she?" Jane, impatient for him to speak, crouched down to unlace and pull off his boots.

"Papaw talked to Mrs. Carson. Since your mother left there, we don't know. We drove through the cemetery, along the roads, checked the church, circled around town a few times. Papaw wouldn't quit until we stopped at the police station to ask them to watch for her. Your mother must be staying with someone and didn't tell us."

I couldn't have imagined her doing something like that before the grief took over.

"There's no more to do tonight."

"What about in the morning?"

My father ignored my question and left us in the kitchen, trudged up the stairs.

I checked that the front door was unlocked. Jane flicked on the lamp on the table inside the door, our eyes meeting in a silent hope that Mama would come back during the night. Upstairs, she whispered, "How are we supposed to sleep?"

I shook my head. She tiptoed into the girls' room. From my bedroom window I had a view up and down the road. The moon cast shadows across the patches of snow left in the yard. I expected to see my mother hurrying back to our house, her scarf drawn around her face in the cold, flushed from the fast walk, telling us time had gotten away from her. Upright on my pillow leaned against the iron bedstead, I fixed on the moonlight glinting through the frost on the window. George snored.

The door handle turned and Jane peeked around the frame, wrapped in a quilt. I nodded to her and she eased herself onto the end of my bed with minimal creaking. She whispered the question again, "How are we supposed to sleep?"

I threw up my hands. Jane curled up and closed her eyes.

I remembered something. A few weeks earlier, I forgot a schoolbook when I left in the morning and walked home at lunchtime, coming around the side of our house to go in the back way. In the back alley, my mother was sitting with Roy in his truck. The windows were up and I could not hear, but I could see she was talking fast, and by the look on her face, seemed upset. Roy sat staring straight ahead, his hands on the wheel, and only shook his head. Then my mother jumped out, slamming the door, and ran from the truck. I moved back into the shadow of the house, out of sight. There was no obvious reason it was unusual—we all took rides with Roy since we had no car—so what made me back out of their view? What instinct told me it was different, not to ask my mother about it? If my mother wasn't back in the morning, I decided, I would find Roy.

Jane stirred, whispered, "What will we do in the morning?"

"She'll be back."

Jane shook her head, pulled the blanket around her, and tiptoed back to the girls' room. I lay awake, listening for my mother's footsteps on the porch below my window.

CHAPTER 2

A few hours earlier, I had hummed along to the music that buoyed my hope, now vanished with my mother. Since the day of Lonnie's funeral I had winced at brushing against the scab of unhealed grief. During that Sunday night, my body bowed with the weight of sadness crawling atop me, as if I had been given my mother's sadness to bear with my own. I left my bed and curled up on Lonnie's cot, waiting for the ordeal to play again when I closed my eyes.

How did Lonnie get the diphtheria? No one close with any of us had been sick, and it was impossible to know who carried the bacteria and breathed it into him. Lonnie was the leader of the little children from surrounding houses who always gathered with him out back of our house. He loved digging roads and ditches in the dirt. When it snowed, he tunneled into the mounds of ice to carve out pretend mines, pushing piles of stones inside. Cold did not bother him, and he was outside so much he often had a runny nose. At first it seemed like he had only a chest cold, something one of us would get and all end up sharing in the bitterest part of the winter. My mother had me and George move our beds into the girls' room. Nothing was worse than seven sick children at once.

By the third day, the fever and sore throat intensified. On the fifth day, my mother was in Lonnie's sickroom before dawn, applying warmed compresses on his throat. Swallowing was so painful he cried and could not even sip water. The doctor's grim verdict panicked my mother.

My father had been on the road with the gas crew for two weeks, in the next county. He telephoned every evening around suppertime. My mother pleaded with him to come home. Reassuring her that Lonnie would get well, he said he would telephone the doctor himself, certain her alarm was heightened by lack of sleep. Maybe at the end of the week he could catch a ride with a truck headed for town. Mama hung up the phone crying and resumed her vigil at Lonnie's bedside.

The doctor put our house under quarantine to avoid spreading the sickness. No going out, no school, no visitors. Only my mother and the doctor went into Lonnie's sickroom. She waited behind the closed door when Jane or I brought up supplies or food, telling us to set it down on the floor and step away before she took it inside. The county health workers had given us older children the antitoxin a few years back when they came around to school, but she took no chances. Lonnie and Addie were too young for the inoculation. Grandma cooked and left the food and our schoolwork on our porch, talking through the window glass because she and Papaw never got antitoxin themselves. The only good news was that no one else developed any sign of the sickness.

Taking turns caring for Addie, sleeping next to her crib in my parents' room, making meals and washing clothes, Jane and I lurched from day to day. We tried our best to keep the younger kids from being bored. We had the radio and the run of the downstairs, which got cluttered with the six of us fending for ourselves. Still my father did not return.

In the evenings, my mother would not leave Lonnie to take my father's call, putting it on me to tell him Lonnie's not getting better, please come home. The crew was working so far out in the next county, they could spare no trucks, he said. I asked him to find someone else headed back our way; he said he would try.

At the end of the second week, light was just coming in the windows when I soft-footed to the kitchen. Mama was sitting at the table, head laying on her arms, skinnier than I had ever seen her.

She raised up at my step. "Your brother died in the night."

Burying her face again, she shook with dry heaving sobs. Kneeling next to her, I circled her back with my arm, let her shaking push into me. I looked around to see Jane standing in the doorway, tears brimming, and motioned her to sit on the other side. Between heaves Mama mumbled for us to call the doctor.

Hanging up after telephoning, I pulled on boots and slogged through the slush on the road to my grandparents' house. When I approached their gate, Papaw looked up from shoveling the porch steps and held my eyes with his.

"Your face tells me it's not good news."

Papaw grabbed me around the shoulders and squeezed my tears into the wool of his coat. Wiping both of our tears with his sleeve, he pulled me inside. Standing at the stove, already cooking our meals for the day, Grandma read the message on our faces, and folded me into her arms, whispering that getting sick didn't matter to her now.

Together we trudged to my house, going round the back. My mother was still at the table with her head down, Jane at her side, the others not up yet. Grandma was a small woman, but she took her daughter in her arms and lifted her out of the chair.

"We will get him ready, Lily, while we wait for the doctor. And we will clean you up."

Grandma and I half-dragged my mother up the stairs. I didn't know what getting Lonnie ready meant. Grandma told me what she needed as she shouldered the full weight of my mother at the sickroom door.

As Jane and I gathered things in the kitchen, the doctor stomped his boots on the porch and let himself in. Coat and hat off, he rolled up his sleeves, wiped his forehead with his handkerchief, readjusted his spectacles, and reached for the supplies I held. "I've called the undertakers." He made his way upstairs to the sickroom.

Jane came up behind me still standing at the bottom of the stairs. "Let's wake the others but not tell them. Get them into the kitchen and wait for Mama."

Though I was older, Jane often imposed order, me following her lead. Gripping the banister as I pushed up the stairs settled my trembling. As I dressed a wiggling Addie in my parents' room, Grandma came to find clean clothes for my mother. Kissing Addie, she murmured into her cheek, "Everything will be all right." Jane, in the other bedroom, was telling George and my sisters to pull leggings on and come down to the kitchen. After seating Addie in her baby chair, I stoked the furnace and the house began to get warmer.

The doctor came down for his hat and coat and left. We expected my mother, but it was Grandma who sat down with Annie, Ruthie, and George to tell them Lonnie had gone to heaven. The girls cried to see our mother. George grabbed onto me and I cradled his head. Papaw called my name from our back porch. I unpeeled George from my side and stepped out.

Papaw wanted my father back, as soon as possible. "Your Uncle Charlie can find a way. It's early enough to catch him at home." Grandma motioned to Papaw from the window. "Your grandma needs me. Make the call."

Talking to Uncle Charlie several times while Lonnie was sick was more conversation than I had had with him over several years. My father's brother and his wife invited our family for dinner only at Easter, when my aunt could reasonably expect the weather to allow the seven of us to stay outside her pristine home except for time at the table.

Hearing me stammer out the news that Lonnie passed, Uncle Charlie sighed. "I'll dispatch a truck to bring your father back."

Jane, listening next to the earpiece, hissed, "Why didn't he do that sooner?"

"Do you need your Aunt Letitia?"

Furious gestures came from Jane at the suggestion. With a polite refusal, I hung up. Jane folded her arms. "What was he waiting for?" We didn't know then that Uncle Charlie had tried to get my father to come back several times.

Grandma decided the younger children would stay at her house until the funeral. Jane bundled clothes for George and the girls and Addie. Papaw and I walked them down the road, Annie and Ruthie still crying for Mama.

When we got my brother and sisters settled in Grandma's front room, Papaw sent me home. "Let me know when your father gets home. And don't worry about us here—they'll quiet down with me."

I hugged him hard. My feet piloted me back along the road, my mind reeling. Dreading going inside, I paced our front porch until the undertaker's truck sidled along the fence to park in front of our house. Watching the men lift the short coffin out of the truck, I shuddered with the thought of Lonnie placed inside it. With the wooden box the men brought in two sawhorses, set them in the front room and covered them with a black cloth, then took the box upstairs.

In the kitchen Jane and I picked at food, waiting.

"Grandma prayed for him all these days, and it did no good," Jane muttered.

"Did you pray?" I asked.

"I don't know how to pray. I watch people do it in church but it never made sense to me."

"What are we going to do now?"

Jane shook her head. "We need to ask Dad."

"What about Mama?"

"When Dad comes, he'll know what to do."

My father walked in the door as the men shuffled down the stairs with Lonnie in the box. Jane and I huddled in the doorway between the front room and the pantry. My mother followed behind the coffin, watching her feet move from stair to stair, Grandma steadying her. Later, Grandma told us the men had been kind and patient for the time my mother needed before she let them handle Lonnie. Mama was dazed, her face swollen from crying and her eyes unfocused. In a soft tone my father called, "Lily." She raised her head and widened her eyes at him as she kept moving toward the bottom stair.

With the sawhorses adjusted and the coffin set in place, the undertaker removed the lid. Lonnie was dressed in white, his cheeks a blotchy red, his blonde hair groomed with pomade, hands folded over his heart. He lay on a bed of white satin, draped and tucked around him so we could not see his body below his chest. My father dropped into a chair at the sight of his youngest son. He watched my mother wait for the men to move away, then she bent over Lonnie and kissed his cheek. My father rose to stand behind her, encircled her with his arms, and buried his face in her shoulder. He was more than a head taller than she was and his frame overwhelmed hers, yet she stood rigid and did not turn to him. She waited for him to release her and then sat in the chair next to Lonnie. Grandma slumped onto the davenport and put her head in her hands.

Ladies from church had followed the undertaker, leaving flowers on the porch to adorn the coffin and the room. The undertaker placed some around Lonnie's face and tucked a nosegay under his hands. He placed other flowers in front and around the coffin, and handed a bouquet tied with black ribbon to my mother. I kept glancing at Jane for some sign about what we should do. When it was too hard for me to stand there any longer, I moved into the kitchen and Jane followed. Through the doorway we saw my father on his knee at Mama's chair, talking low to her. Not speaking, her sad eyes blinked back tears. When he took her hands, she pulled away from him and stood to grasp at Lonnie. Grandma coaxed her back to the chair.

After a quiet word with the undertaker, my father telephoned the Methodist minister to arrange the funeral for the next day.

Raised Baptist but not caring much for church, my father did not object to the Methodists. Our family was not among the every-week churchgoers but my mother got us there often enough that the minister knew all of us by name.

Grandma shuffled into the kitchen and lifted her coat from the hook by the door. "Can you bring me church clothes for the children? I'll keep them for the night." When she got outside, we heard her sob.

Relieved to have something to do, Jane and I slipped up the stairs to the girls' bedroom we had all been sharing. Jane handed me a satchel, expecting I could do no more than hold it open. Sorting through the jumble of clothes, Jane pulled out an assortment of tops and skirts and pants and shoes to pack for my sisters and brother.

I walked the satchel to my grandparents' house. Papaw and Grandma left me to be alone with George and the girls, who whispered their fears.

"Did it hurt Lonnie?"

"How does he look?"

"Will we see him?"

"Can he hear us?"

Grandma had made them her special tea that worked to make them sleepy. I carried home a thermos-full of the soothing brew for my mother.

Not able to face the scene in the front room, I went around the back. Jane had laid out a cold supper that she and I nibbled at but neither of my parents left Lonnie. Close-by neighbors brought pans of food and bundles of flowers to the porch. My father opened the door long enough to thank them for their kindness and condolences. Uncle Charlie called to say he had arranged cars to take us to the cemetery the next day.

My parents passed the night in the front room with Lonnie. Upstairs, Jane curled up on her bed across the room from mine, neither of us sleeping but not talking, until at first light I went down to stoke the furnace and make coffee. Grandma arrived to persuade my mother upstairs to wash and dress. My father washed in the cellar.

Word had passed around the neighborhood and people trickled into our yard all morning. The quarantine still on us, everyone understood we could not go to the church. Most of the neighbors were Catholics, their practices varying with the countries they came from. The women took turns coming to the windows on the porch, some crossing themselves with rosaries as they looked at Lonnie through the glass, nodding to my mother. The men and children stayed on the road outside the yard and my father spoke from the steps to thank them for coming.

When Papaw brought my sisters and brother to the back door, the girls ran inside to my mother. I took Addie from Papaw and he followed me into the front room with a hand on George's shoulder. Mama hugged the girls and whispered in their ears, then took Addie from me and led us over to Lonnie. Jane and my father and George joined the cluster around my little brother's coffin. Grandma and Papaw stood at the foot of the box, Grandma leaning on it for support. The girls watched Mama pull blossoms from the funeral bouquet to lay on Lonnie's chest, and at her nod each did the same.

Extending his hand to neighbors as he crossed the yard, the minister entered. He offered condolences to my father and asked if we were ready to begin the prayers. We moved back from Lonnie's side to give the minister room to stand over him. My mother's tears flowed as she passed Addie to Jane and put her hands over Lonnie's. The murmur of praying among the women on the porch passing rosary beads through their fingers accompanied the mesmerizing cadence of the minister's voice. For a moment, the spell let me believe that he could bring Lonnie back, like Lazarus. But when the minister asked God to take the angel Lonnie to his side, the grief of never seeing him again washed over me. At the end of the prayers the ladies on the porch were the only ones able to say Amen.

My father put his hand on Lonnie's forehead for a moment, and then slowly unclasped my mother's fingers from Lonnie's hands.

"It's time, Lily."

She bent and kissed Lonnie's cheek, then let my father walk her back a few steps.

With a grip on our mother, my father spoke to us. "Say goodbye to your brother."

My sisters cried and clutched at Jane. George touched

Lonnie's arm with one hand and reached for mine with the other. Grandma and Papaw laid their flowers in the coffin and guided the girls to step back. The undertaker and his man took the lid from behind the coffin, positioned it over the opening, and hinged it closed. Mama closed her eyes.

The neighbors moved aside as the men carried Lonnie out, standing mute as they slid the coffin into the coach. Two sedans, driven by men from the gas company, had parked behind the funeral coach. My father got my mother into one car and motioned for the girls to come with them; my grandparents and George and I slumped onto the back seat of the other car. Trailing the funeral coach, the drivers kept the slow pace for the five long miles to the town cemetery, spread across one of the taller hills.

Getting out of the car, a sudden break of bright sunshine on the snow blinded me. I shaded my eyes and focused on the gravel underfoot. As the undertaker and his man were taking the coffin out of the funeral coach, the cemetery caretaker whispered to the minister, pointing toward the burial spot. With only a day's notice and the ground still part-frozen, the cemetery caretaker and his men had dug a baby grave to fit Lonnie's small coffin. Some neighbors who had followed us in a few cars and pickups gathered nearby. I nodded to our next-door neighbor Roy and his wife Marion among the mourners, and a teacher from school, and Uncle Charlie and Aunt Letitia who stood with my father's sister, Aunt Hattie.

Walking behind the minister, my mother fixed her stare at

the coffin perched on the men's shoulders, my father guiding her steps with an arm across her back. Papaw held Addie now and Grandma had my sisters at her sides. Joining hands, Jane and George and I made our way along the path cleared in the snow to stand at the graveside.

The minister started the burial prayers. The cold wind shivered through us. My father propped my mother against his bulk and braced her upright. When the minister nodded at the undertaker, the men lowered the coffin into the grave with two straps underneath it, and when it touched the bottom earth, pulled the straps out. The cemetery man offered the shovel to my father, who scooped one shovel of dirt and dumped it over the box. Grandma and Papaw, who was holding Addie, came closer to the grave and threw flowers on the coffin. George and I grabbed some of the flowers the undertaker's men had brought from the house. Leaning over the hole together we let the flowers out of our hands. Jane moved the girls to do the same and, for a moment, the five of us stood there.

The gravediggers lingered nearby, smoking, leaning on larger shovels, waiting to finish the job of filling in the grave. Our neighbor Marion and Aunt Hattie had positioned themselves on either side of my mother, to steady her near the grave as the mourners passed by to add a shovel of dirt or more flowers. Catching Jane's eye, I motioned to the cars. Together we got my sisters and George back down the path. Addie and Grandma and Papaw were settling into one car, and we got into the other.

Watching, I could see it took coaxing by my father to guide my mother away from the grave. She did not want to leave Lonnie. From the car window, we could see him speaking to her and taking her elbow, yet she would pull away, tears rolling down her face. My father stood with her for a time, edging her along the path to the car. Her stricken look made me feel colder.

George kept his head under my arm during the silent ride home. Jane clutched my sisters. It felt like the first disorienting moments waking from a bad dream, when you are telling yourself it wasn't real, but it is still so vivid you can't shake it off. When the cars left us in front of our house, Grandma asked Jane and me to pack more clothes; all of us children would stay at her house for a while, letting my father and mother have time alone.

Inside, Mama was already upstairs in bed. My father stood in the front room, looking at the empty spot where Lonnie's coffin had been. In silence we packed clothes and books. He said nothing to us as we left the house.

Every day for a week Grandma walked down the road to check on her daughter. Listening to Grandma and Papaw talking, hearing that Mama was not getting out of bed, I wanted to talk to my father. But Papaw discouraged me from going to the house, saying my parents needed the time.

Early one morning at the start of the second week, my father came to my grandparents' house, catching Papaw outside. After they talked a while, Papaw brought Grandma into it, and the three of them called us children together.

You had to know my father to understand how we could line up to sit on chairs in front of him, seeing him for the first time since the graveside, and not say anything. My father's general approach was to keep control. With him, it was best to do as he said, and hold our thoughts to ourselves. We were to go home, he told us, and help our mother get the family routine back in place, go to school, get busy doing normal things. What was normal? How could we go back to the life we had before Lonnie died? None of us could put those feelings into words.

At our house, the official contagion sign was gone from the front door. The sickroom bedding had been burned, Lonnie's clothes were gone, the disinfecting and cleaning was done. My mother remained in bed, the door to her room closed. Addie's crib had been moved into the girls' bedroom.

My father said we should wash the clothes and get the younger children ready for us all to go to school the next day. Grandma would watch Addie for those hours. On the way home from school, Jane would bring Addie back.

For the next week, my father left early each morning and came home after we had eaten dinner. When he went upstairs to change clothes, he sat with my mother for a while, then stayed downstairs and slept on the davenport. A pot of boiled dinner or a pan of ravioli was left on the porch in the afternoons by the good neighbor ladies who acknowledged our mourning with a sign of the cross when they saw me come out to bring it in.

George and the girls knew better than to cry or talk about

Lonnie in front of our father. We went through the motions of going to school, taking care of the chores, making meals, doing what Grandma and Papaw asked. My father left grocery money in the pantry as usual and, with Grandma's help, Jane and I kept the kitchen stocked and meals cooked. One of us took plates up to my mother and later brought them back down after she had picked at the food. Sometimes she asked about what we were doing and how the girls were feeling, and sometimes she lay silent in the dark room.

At the end of the second week my father called another meeting with Grandma and Papaw, Jane, and me.

"The crew is working in the next county, and I have to get back with them. Dan, you're in charge, with Grandma and Papaw's help. I expect your mother will feel better soon."

Like a tiny splinter rubbing, Jane had a way of prattling at him that annoyed me. "Don't worry, Dad, we will take care of everyone. Your job is important; you need to be there."

That was not how I saw it, but his intention was clear. My father staying with the road crew, with short intervals at home dipping into our lives, our daily needs handled by my mother, was normal for him. He wanted that more than he was concerned about us.

He left the next morning before we woke.

The weight of my mother's grief shocked me when the force of it landed on me and on Jane. Before, we had our independence outside the house, at least for the school day and the hours before dinner. Now the girls and George looked to us for everything. Our mother never acknowledged the burden on us. Grandma did her best to fill in the gaps and was the one who would go into my mother's room during the darkest days. I don't know what passed between them, as Grandma would come downstairs looking grim and my mother's behavior remained the same.

Neither of our parents recognized that we grieved for Lonnie. With my father gone, there was more open crying. Soothing the girls as best she could, Grandma listened to their fears that any illness would mean one of us dying, trying to ease their worrying over every sneeze or cough. We missed Lonnie's laughter and playfulness. George being closer in age to Lonnie than to me, the two of them had shared a strong big-and-little brother relationship. At night in our room, Lonnie's bed empty, I sat with my hand on his shoulder while George sobbed in his pillow.

Grandma sent word to my mother's younger brother about his sister's condition. The late winter storms had kept Uncle George from getting to the funeral. When Papaw had moved their family to town, selling most of his country acreage to a mining company, he kept a parcel of his of farmland. Uncle George restored the farm and made a life of it. It was over twenty hilly miles outside of town, some of it traveled on rutted cow paths. My mother and George were close, three years apart in age, having shared their early years on the farm where they roamed pretty much as they wished, making up games and exploring. They confided in each other, relied on each other, and she trusted her brother. She used to say he was her longest friend.

After hearing from Grandma that Uncle George was on his way to visit, Mama came downstairs while I was cooking breakfast and Jane was setting the table. Jane put a cup of coffee in front of her. The two of us stayed quiet, glancing sideways at her, one hand on the cup and the other holding her head. Jane went up to wake the others, warning them to stay quiet, not upset Mama. They smiled, kissed her cheeks, and were a little shy around her, like they weren't sure if she would embrace them or push them away, but she reached out to hug each one. She had no words for us, watching us get ready for the day as though the routine was unfamiliar to her.

It was almost dark that evening when Uncle George knocked on the front door. Mama had paced the front room waiting for his truck. At his knock she yanked open the door, falling into his arms. He was taller than she was, hefty in build, and held her like a sturdy tree. Resting against him she looked small and fragile. She stayed wrapped within his arms for some minutes, while he patted her back and whispered to her. Greeting us, he told Jane and George to run out to the truck for the boxes packed with jars of the fruit and tomatoes from the farm. Also in the boxes were comic books, a new set of checkers, and sets of paper dolls for the girls.

Leading my mother to the davenport, he sat with his arm around her while asking us about school, baseball, and our favorites among the comics. Mama nestled her head against Uncle

George's shoulder and closed her eyes while my sisters cut out the doll figures, George read the comics, and Jane and I made supper.

Uncle George stayed for two nights. During his visit, my mother tried to be present for him, coming downstairs dressed in the morning. What they talked about while we were at school, he didn't say. When he was packing up the truck to head back to the farm, Mama stayed outside with him for a long while, sitting in the front seat talking before he started the engine. She got out and came around to the driver's side window to hug him, and then he pulled away.

After that, she floated through the days like she was watching us carry on but not joining in, not caring about things like she used to. We were used to Lillian's tendency to get lost in reverie in the middle of chores or cooking, but now Mama was like a sleepwalker, startling if touched, not responding to questions. When my father called, not every evening, she was already upstairs in her room with the door closed, and he stopped asking for her.

"We've got enough spring thaw I can push the schedule. The crew has to make up time lost to the last storms."

"When will you be back?"

"If we get ahead, I'll find a few days to come home soon."

Hearing this from me, my mother turned on her side. "Your father could get Uncle Charlie to arrange for him to be close to home any time."

It felt like I was between them. I talked to Jane about their tension and my confusion. "What am I supposed to say? Ask him to come back? Tell him we need him to come back?"

Jane sniffed. "His job is important. Mama is making things worse for herself."

If we had not had Grandma and Papaw to help us through those seven weeks, I don't know what would have happened to us.

Curled on Lonnie's cot as the hours ticked toward dawn, what I thought I knew about my mother, feeling close to her, evaporated. My mother's absence from our house that night felt like the tremble along the walls of a mineshaft, just before the cave-in.

CHAPTER 3

When the gray light of morning overpowered the moon on Monday, I crept downstairs and found Grandma in our front room, frantic with worry. She hurried my father from his coffee into his coat to go with her to the police station to report Lillian still missing. An hour later Grandma came back alone to tell us what happened.

Hanging around the sergeant's desk when they arrived was the town newspaperman, waiting for confirmation that the warehouse fire was an arson. Hearing my father's name, he perked up. "You asked the police to look for your wife last night, if I read the blotter correctly, didn't you, sir?"

Never one to pass up attention, my father verified he had. "I'm an auxiliary brigade man, and she disappeared when I was out fighting the fire. No word from her since."

Recognizing what Grandma told us he called the "human angle" to the fire story, the man pumped more details from my father. When the late-morning edition hit porches and storefronts, the headline read, "Fireman Saves Building, Loses Wife."

The publicity unleashed a flood of concern, mixed with gossipy fascination. Neighbor ladies came to our porch asking if there was any news, and did we need them to come in and help. Grandma, at the door, shooed them off with firm refusals. If my father answered the door, the ladies lingered, since all it took to get him talking was to say how sorry they were, and how hard this must be on him.

My father had insisted we go to school that day. As the paper circulated, the gossip about my mother being missing spread as fast as the fire the day before. Sympathetic teachers in the elementary school shared their lunch with George and the girls so they would not have to go home for the noon meal. Jane and I accepted the sad looks and quiet support from our friends and the taunts from the rougher kids implying our mother was a crazy lady. My mother's walks around town had long been the fuel of whispers.

Townspeople that Papaw called chinwags named it strange that Mama liked to be outside frequently, amidst the relentless smog from the coke ovens blurring the sky. Rough footpaths worn into the sides of the rutted and hilly roads made for slow going. When it rained, water sluiced down the hills into mudslides and formed huge puddles in the low places. But my mother had walked every inch of our small town in a hundred different ways. The aim of making her way to a certain destination took unexpected wanders into a long meander, forgetting the original end. As soon as I was steady on my toddler feet, she took me roaming with her, matching her pace to my short strides, point-ing out what she wanted me to notice along the way. When I got older and the family busier, we walked together less often, but if we happened upon each other somewhere in town we would fall into the habit of striding home together by way of a rambling path.

After Lonnie passed, if my mother got up from her bed, she was gone from the house when the girls and George returned from school. When she came in with muddy boots and brambles on her coat, sometimes after dark, we guessed she walked to the cemetery to sit on the ground at Lonnie's grave. Grandma's cronies reported the times my mother had appeared at the church during funerals, asking to ride to the cemetery with the mourners, then standing at Lonnie's grave until they brought her back.

Not caring about the gossip, the only person I wanted to talk with about Mama was Roy, to ask about that afternoon in the truck.

After school on Monday afternoon, the postmaster greeted me with a clap on the back when I arrived for my job. Wondering if they needed me at home, Mr. Kegg accepted my argument that it was best to keep busy, and maybe someone would come in who had seen my mother. Starting on sorting the bags and packages, my eye was on the door, waiting for Roy to pick up his mail in the late afternoon as usual. But ten minutes before closing, Roy's wife, Marion, stepped in.

Marion and my mother were friends, as much as my mother

was friends with anyone. Women in our town had organized practices for befriending each other—the ladies' guilds at the churches, sewing circles—and my mother was not a joiner of those groups. Marion was too busy to participate. Marion managed the accounts for Roy's store, Feeke's, where she tended the counter, and kept house raising their three children. My parents had been friends with Roy and Marion since before we lived on River Avenue, even going camping together. One of the few photographs I have of my mother shows her standing in front of the tent while Roy and my father practiced putting it up in the yard before a trip. Lillian and Marion chatted in the yard while hanging wash, and shared rides in the truck to bring groceries back from town. An avid reader of the ladies' magazines, my mother kept up with the styles and the prominent women whom she admired for their positions on issues of the day. She would talk about these things during rides in the truck, showing Marion the articles, and Marion would nod politely, glancing at Roy to judge his reaction. I never heard Roy object to Lillian's views, but he was not much for making conversation while driving. Maybe he had words with Marion when they were alone.

A few years back Marion had asked my mother to teach her to drive the truck, saying Roy refused. Lillian was a good driver, having learned from Papaw at the farm, and she gave Marion a few lessons. But during the short times they could take the truck and practice driving, Marion did not get the hang of it, and my mother told us Marion was too timid to be a driver.

While Lonnie was sick, Marion sent Roy or her older son over every night with a pot of something for our dinner. But Marion had kept a distance since she and Roy were at the funeral, not coming over or asking after my mother. If I saw Marion in the yard, she waved, and I took that to mean that she was there if we needed her. Roy talked to my father if they happened to pass each other in the back alley, but their schedules were different, with Roy leaving before dawn to manage the deliveries coming and going from the store, and my father on the road.

Seeing Marion in the post office when I expected her husband, I blurted out, "Where's Roy today?"

"Roy's driving the town roads one more time before dark, looking for your mother."

The look on my face seemed to puzzle Marion. "She's not back, is she?" she asked.

"No, I would have heard from Papaw if she was."

"Roy had to make the regular deliveries today, figured he could ask about her at all the stops, do that much to help."

Hearing Roy was out looking for my mother made me want to get home and wait for him in the back alley, where he parked his truck. Reaching into the cubby for the Feeke store mail, I handed Marion the bundle, deciding not to mention I wanted to talk with Roy, instinct telling me he would not want her to know. Why did it feel necessary to cover for him?

"Dan, you know you can send George over any time if you need anything."

"Thanks, appreciate that."

As soon as Marion left, I locked the entrance. The postmaster waved me off when I mumbled an excuse for leaving before tying up the bags. When I got to the alley behind our houses, Roy's truck was parked, empty. For the next two days, neither Roy nor Marion came to the post office for their mail. I thought about taking it home with me and looking for Roy, but Mr. Kegg didn't like mail being handled unofficially. If Roy or Marion came in on Thursday, I missed them when Mr. Kegg sent me to the train station with the outbound mail for Pittsburgh.

The week had dragged on with no news of my mother and Grandma fighting to contain her tears in front of us. Giving Jane a break, Papaw now fetched Addie in the mornings and brought her back in the evenings. Staying in town rather than returning to the road crew, my father made a daily trip to the police station. One report made by a couple in our town, who had been out driving on Sunday, said they had seen Lillian walking in Uniontown. They had not stopped or spoken to her, and when questioned about her attire, became unsure it was her. No one else came forward with any information. The police depended on someone giving them a tip or my mother returning on her own, telling my father they had seen cases like this and the wife always came home after a few days. Unless they had a lead or evidence of a crime all they could do was alert the police in surrounding towns and wait.

Uncle Charlie and Aunt Letitia came to the house on Thursday evening. My aunt brushed off the davenport before sitting, then announced she would read with the girls. George and I played catch in the yard. Uncle Charlie smoked with my father on the porch, and I heard him say they could send a man to Uniontown to make inquiries.

After school on the fifth day, Friday, I was behind the post office counter when Uncle George walked in. Surprised to see him, I assumed Papaw had enlisted him.

"Are you here to help us find my mother?"

He didn't answer. Instead, he asked, "Can you take a break outside with me?"

The postmaster was in the back and we had no customers, so I led him outside. I scanned the sky and saw no sun, just the persistent grey of the coke clouds and, against the murkiness, the outline of the one stick-like little tree that managed to grow in the hard dirt patch separating the post office from the road.

Uncle George came right out with it. "Lillian came to the farm late on Sunday afternoon."

I froze. "What are you saying?"

Looking me in the eye, he went on. "On Monday, she took a ride to Uniontown with one of the vegetable traders who loaded up at the farm."

"Where did she go, where is she now?" Forcing words out, my voice took on a pitch like Addie screaming a demand.

He shook his head. "I don't know, but I know what she means to do." He took an envelope from his jacket, showing me it was addressed to Grandma and in my mother's writing.

I felt cold all over. Uncle George took my elbow and steered me to his truck at the edge of the road. Leaning against it, I shivered.

"She wrote this letter to explain that she is leaving your father and doesn't want him to know where she is."

"Why didn't you take the letter to Grandma?" My voice was louder now, a more offensive tone than I had ever directed toward an adult, never to Uncle George, my mother's beloved brother.

"I promised Lillian to hold the letter for five days, to give her time to get away safely."

"Safely? *Safely*? Alone?"

"I tried to talk her out of it—believe me, I did—but the most I could get her to agree to was that I would wait until the fifth day to deliver the letter. If she changed her mind and came back before today, I would have torn it up."

The fear and frustration of the past days rose in my voice, passing over the meaning of what he said. "Why did you wait all this time to give this to Grandma? Why did you let her worry so much? Why did you let us *all* worry?"

"Grandma and Papaw can't know I helped Lillian get away. When Papaw came looking for her, I let him believe she had not been at the farm."

"You let him believe…"

"If they know I helped her, it could mean trouble for her, for me, for all of us. More trouble than we have now."

"More than we have now? Who did she go with?"

"Look, Dan, there are things you don't know, things you would never have needed to know, but Lillian can take care of herself."

"*Where* did she go? Why are you telling me this?"

"Because she and I both trust you. I need you to pretend that this letter came to the post office, that you found it, and you take it to Grandma. She will believe you. You keep our secret. That way, if I hear from Lillian, I will send a message. If you can just not let anyone know I helped her."

Anger churned in my stomach, with confusion and fear. But somehow in the space of a few moments, I convinced myself that if Grandma read the letter, she would find a way to get my mother to come back. Wherever my mother was, she knew it was the fifth day, that we would find out she had left on purpose. Leaving my father? If I took the letter to Grandma, maybe she wouldn't tell him.

The secrets and lies gathered like the coke clouds, a grey, oppressive mass that lowered the space between me and the heavens, too low to stand straight up.

I took the letter from Uncle George's hand.

It was near dark when I stepped on Grandma's porch, lights in the kitchen and the front room. Opening the door, calling out her name, walking through to the kitchen, I found Grandma stooped over the oven, putting the lid on her big roasting pot of beef with potatoes and onions. She had been cooking for us all week. The busywork kept the worry confined to her mind and freed her hands to be useful.

Banging the oven door closed, she looked at me, waiting. Grandma knew me to be one to speak when there was something important to say, not a chatterer like the girls. I handed her the letter. Grandma knew the handwriting.

Tears rolled down her cheeks as she read. "Where did you get this?"

I was sixteen and the oldest of the six surviving children of Lillian and Alonzo and now I knew my mother had run away. Stepping into the quagmire of lies, in that moment I invented a reason there was no postmark on the envelope. "It came in a bag of mail from Uniontown, and they were shorthanded up there. Someone must've forgotten to stamp some of the letters in the bag. When I sorted them, I found it."

I was lost in the situation and I lied, protecting Uncle George, for what? What if I had told Grandma the truth on the fifth day—could she and Papaw have followed my mother and talked sense into her? Would my mother have listened if I had gone with them to tell her how much we children needed her? Did my mother stay away thinking we didn't care?

Sitting there, both of us crying, when Papaw came in. Grandma handed him the letter. After he read it, Papaw sighed. "We best go see Alonzo."

"No, no," I protested, "we have to get her back before he finds out."

My grandparents looked at each other and then at me. They knew their daughter's state of mind, would do anything not to lose her. They also knew my father.

Papaw was firm. "We have to work together to find your mother. We'll talk with him after supper, no need to upset the children."

The family expected Grandma to bring the dinner to our house, so I helped her wrap the pans and arrange them in a big market basket to carry with us.

Before we left their house, Papaw put his hand on my shoulder. "Dan, we will make this right for you children, don't worry."

Dreading what my father would say when he saw the letter, I couldn't imagine what making things right meant.

When we stepped inside the kitchen at my house, Jane and the girls were setting the table and my father's voice from the cellar was demanding that George explain the mess down there.

Jane gave an exasperated sigh. "The coal man came and George did not tidy up after."

Papaw went to the cellar door. "Supper's here."

My father came upstairs wiping his hands. "George will eat when he's finished in the cellar. We can start."

Grandma pressed her lips together. "We're not ready. Jane needs to help me with the gravy."

It was obvious she stalled to give George a few minutes, and the tactic worked. George came up as we sat down and took his seat between Papaw and Grandma, my father scowling at him across the table.

There was so much tension among us during that meal it's a miracle no one broke down at the table. My father ate. The girls moved food around on their plates, too afraid to say anything in front of him about their turmoil over five days of Mama being missing. Grandma patted Ruthie's leg from one side under the table and Jane squeezed Annie's arm on the other. George ate with sullen eyes on his plate, his upset combined with anger about the bawling out in the cellar. Unaware, Addie sang softly, kicking a leg in rhythm against her baby chair. Papaw tried commenting, "The roast is tasty, Ma. They're saying rain tomorrow." Grandma's look silenced him.

Wanting to tell Jane about the letter, the only chance for me to warn her was when she stepped into the pantry for plates before the dessert. Following her, I whispered, "Something happened today." She moved closer to hear more, but we had to go back to the table.

Grandma hurried to end the meal and get the girls and George clearing the dishes and start the washing up. She motioned me to keep everyone in the kitchen when Papaw asked my father to step into the front room with him and Grandma.

For the first minutes it was a calm talk, the murmuring voices audible in the kitchen, but not the words. Ruthie, washing, clattered the dishes in the sink. George, as he dried them, was explaining to Annie what the teacher said about a book he lost. Trying to overhear the talk in the front room, I moved closer to the doorway and Jane came next to me. "Grandma got a letter from Mama."

Her eyes widened. Then my father commanded, "Dan, come in here."

My father waved the letter in his hand. "When did you get this?"

"Today."

"Why didn't you bring this to me?" His voice rose. "Why did you not bring this letter directly to *me*?"

"It's addressed to Grandma."

"Addressed to Grandma," he mocked me, "addressed to Grandma."

Papaw tried to calm him down. "Alonzo, Dan did right to bring it to us, and we came to you."

My father turned on Papaw, yelling, "How do I know you didn't plan this? Maybe you helped her. A letter for you, not me? Full of nonsense about leaving me? Lillian is not herself, she can't make decisions, and I am her husband."

The shouting drew my brother and sisters to bunch in the doorway, George and the scared girls staying back of Jane. Addie, still in her baby chair, screeched to get out. George swung her to the floor, and Addie got free of his grip and ran to Grandma. As Grandma reached for her, my father stepped between them.

"Do not touch her," he growled.

Grandma fell back. Addie started to cry and plopped down on her behind in the middle of the floor. Papaw grabbed hold of Grandma and lifted her up.

"I want you both out of this house," my father yelled. "Get out of my house."

Tears ran down Grandma's face. The girls screamed for her. George ran to Papaw's side, like he meant to go with them.

Papaw tried once more to calm my father. "Alonzo, you need our help. Let us help."

My father stomped to the door and thrust it open. "I told you to get out!"

Grandma grabbed her coat from the davenport and ran out the door. Papaw took his time, hugged George, put on his hat, and stopped in front of Alonzo at the open door. "We did not help Lillian do this. We love these children."

He walked out and my father slammed the door.

My father realized we were staring at him. Addie still sat on the floor sniffling; Ruthie and Annie, sobbing, backed away from him into the kitchen. George clung to my shirt. Jane and I stood transfixed, not able to take in what had just happened.

My father barked out orders. "Dan, tomorrow morning you will get the breakfast, and Jane, you will keep watch over them while Dan is at work. On Sunday, we are all going to Charlie's house. On Monday, you will take Addie over to Marion before school. I will fix that with her. Directly after school, get Addie and start the supper. I expect all of you to come straight home from school. Do not go over to Grandma's house. Do you understand me? There is no more help from Grandma and Papaw."

We stood in shocked silence.

"Do you understand me?"

Mumbling, we answered. "Yes."

"This is how things will be done until I get your mother back here."

He picked Addie up off the floor. Handing her to Jane, he softened his tone. "Don't worry, your mother is coming back." He nodded toward the stairs. "Up with all of you now, Jane will tuck you in. Dan, I will speak with you."

George and my sisters started up the stairs. Following my father back to the kitchen, I clenched and unclenched my fists, steeling myself for his anger, aghast at how he had treated Grandma. He poured himself a cup of coffee with shaking hands, steadied the cup on the table.

"If there are any more letters, you bring them to me and only me. No going to Grandma with anything." I did not react.

"Your mother's mind is weak since Lonnie died, too weak to know what she is doing. When I get her back here, this house will go back to normal." He slapped his hand on the table. "I know they helped her because she would not have been able to do this by herself."

I opened my mouth to speak and then thought better of it, but he saw me stop myself.

"What have you got to say about it? Do you know something more?"

"No, no, just that they are worried about her, and I don't see why they would have helped her."

"She never would have done this any other way. They always wanted this."

"They don't want this."

"You don't know anything about it. Go to bed."

Upstairs Jane, in the hallway, motioned me to step into the bathroom and closed the door, indignation written all over her face.

"How could Mama do this? She can't run off, leaving Dad, leaving *all* of us! She's gone crazy and Dad has to get her back."

Jane usually spoke her mind. Her personality strode into a room with a commanding presence. That she got from my father, the ability to make everyone feel he was taking over the conduct of any business taking place, hard to disagree with, hard to go against. He acted like his will could make us behave as he wished. Jane had a much easier time with my father than I did. Now she was defending him.

"What is Dad supposed to tell people? She has brought shame on us. He has a position. She's ruining things for him."

This was not what I expected to hear, and not what I felt. My worry for my mother was greater now, competing with my nervousness about George's and the girls' reactions to the scene with Grandma and Papaw.

"She is so sad, and to go off alone like that, well, I can't explain it, but she needs help."

"Help?" Jane's voice was sharp. "Dad needs help—he has to find her, and get her back here, and try to keep this from becoming a scandal."

"What about how she feels?"

"She made this mess. She didn't care how we would feel."

"We have to take care of the little kids. They're still crying over Lonnie. And now we don't have Grandma and Papaw."

"Dad is right—they helped her and that means we do not want them here."

"They did not help her," I insisted. "Why would Grandma show Dad the letter if they wanted her to get away? They would have kept quiet."

Jane folded her arms across her chest and turned up her chin. "Maybe they didn't help her that day, but they are on her side. Dad's right."

She flung open the bathroom door and stormed out.

CHAPTER 4

The hunt for my mother was on, both my father and me determined to bring her back, going about it separately. My father meant to get her home with no one knowing his wife had left intentionally. When she disappeared, people sympathized with him, and maybe with her, understanding they grieved for a child, that she had long been melancholy, that they relied on her parents to see after us. But if people knew she had left him, my father's reputation would be in jeopardy of the talk and speculation that would ignite rumors. When he banished Grandma and Papaw, he had no fear they would say anything publicly, believing they would be shamed if folks knew about the deterioration of Lillian's state of mind. With the police looking for her, the story of a mysterious disappearance suited his purpose.

There were only a few ways for my mother to leave town on that Sunday, the most likely on the train, but the police had already looked into that. The stationmaster verified she had not purchased a ticket; only one train passed through the station on

Sunday and she was not among those who boarded. If not on a train, she must have gotten a ride from someone on their way out of town.

My father set his plan in motion, getting Uncle Charlie to direct the resources of the gas company toward finding the ride she must have taken. There were company stations along the gas line in the towns and outlying counties surrounding Pittsburgh, outposts to monitor the flow and pressure in the web of underground lines. Posts along the main roads were mostly built next to filling stations. Meter men could have seen my mother in a motorcar that stopped for gas, men camped along the pipeline trenches might have noticed her in a passing car. The office put the word out along the lines, in all directions. Her likely destination would be Uniontown, the closest city big enough to disappear into, and a major hub for trains and buses going east or west.

It was a marker of my father's position—superior to tradesmen, elevated above miners—that he could command the gas workers to be on the lookout for his wife. After Uncle Charlie fixed the way into the gas company, my father detached himself from the gritty side of our town, one of many so-called "coke patches" created in the western Pennsylvania hills. Alonzo hated the mines and the coking, though he respected the old-timers who did the filthy, dangerous work, day after day, year after year.

Yet it was because the mines spit out tons of the soft coal—bituminous—that burned hot into coke for making steel, that towns like ours had thrived. Work in the mines and the beehive-shaped coke ovens that multiplied across the landscape had drawn immigrant laborers, disembarking from the ships in Philadelphia and piling into trains that distributed them around the coal-seamed valleys. Thousands of men coming alone, followed by brothers, wives and children, and parents, indentured to the coke companies that owned the houses and stores. Half the adults in our town were from Italy, Poland, and Czechoslovakia.

Rough, hard labor—mining, coking, loading freight, clearing land, laying pipe—and the harsh living in the Pennsylvania hills toughened men in form and temperament. Gruff and sturdy, willing to do whatever was before them to make a living, they formed a collective attachment—the man next to you might be your lifeline in the tunnels and furnaces. They survived through the mining strikes, the struggle for the unions, the pay cuts, lock-outs, and food shortages. By 1930, the mines were closing around them, with fewer men working in the still-producing pits, machines taking their places to increase the pace and output.

My father held himself in a different appraisal. He fueled his ambition with adoration of Henry Clay Frick and Andrew Carnegie and their visions of the self-made man, one who designed his own success and set out to achieve it. Focused on admiring how they started from little to produce so much wealth, Alonzo overlooked the contempt that Frick had for the working man and the distance that Carnegie kept from the realities of the human toll of coke production. My father would carry on over dinner about the importance of where we lived, in the hub of industrial progress, essential to America's prosperity and growth since the National Pike had been established between Maryland and the Ohio Valley a hundred years before. His belief in his ability to make his own way corresponded to what he saw as opportunity before him. Where miners saw loss, he saw what came next, and that was piping and storing natural gas. He and his brother Charlie allied their futures on gas when Charlie got into the gas company first and paved the way for my father.

My father always said a man should take advantage of his connections. In the search for my mother, I had the lead of knowing she had left from Uncle George's farm with someone he let her go with. And there was her mysterious encounter with Roy to follow up on. Papaw was another source of help despite my father's decree we have no more contact with our grandparents. I would not openly defy my father, but I would talk to Papaw.

What I seemed to have lost was my alliance with Jane. After she stormed from the bathroom, I tried to understand her strong reaction against our mother. Maybe she was right about Mama acting carelessly, but Jane's defense of my father was unexpected. I had always thought of Jane and I as a joined force providing soft resistance to his rules and the flare-ups of his anger. It was just as well there had been no opportunity for me to tell her about Uncle George giving me the letter before my father's outburst against our grandparents.

Given Jane's reaction to Mama's letter, I decided not to tell her about my search, adding to the growing cache of secrets I was keeping. But I needed to strike some understanding with Jane so we could protect our brother and sisters. She had to be as nervous as I was about how hard the loss of Grandma and Papaw in our daily lives would fall on them.

Jane greeted me the next morning with an even tone. Taking that as a sign of truce, I started in on how we should organize the Saturday for George, the girls, and Addie.

"Why don't I take George with me for my shift at the post office this morning?"

"Good. There are plenty of chores here to keep the girls busy until lunch time."

"When we get back, I can take over with Addie for the afternoon. You might want to get out for a while."

Jane traveled in a social circle of girls and boys from school, with invitations most every weekend. She had stayed home in the weeks since Lonnie died, and I hoped my offering a break from our house would work in my favor.

"Fine, I will."

No chance that she would tell her friends what we found out about my mother. As angry as Jane felt, like our father, reputation was paramount to her. By saying nothing about the letter, she could maintain her sympathetic position amidst her friends. Both Jane and my father took out into the world only the portions of their lives that put them in the best light, leaving the rest within our walls. How did she learn this, I wondered, and was I schooled in this, too, so that lying or not telling the whole truth was easy?

Annie and Ruthie came down for breakfast, and when they saw my father was gone from the house, unleashed their questions. "Where did Mama go?" "Why did she leave?" "When will she come back?" "Will she call us on the telephone?" "Did she take her clothes?"

Jane cut them off. "We don't know."

They were so unsettled by what they had seen the night before, they could not let it go. "Why did Dad make Grandma cry?" "When can we go to see her?"

Jane clattered dishes in the sink, her back to us. To quiet them, I said something I did not believe.

"You have to promise not to go to Grandma's house until Dad calms down. He'll change his mind about them; we have to wait."

My father never went back on something he decided, even if proved wrong. He adjusted his reasoning to make his previous decision seem part of his logic.

I had to find Roy. The more I thought about the look on his face that day talking to my mother in the truck, the more I believed he knew something that might lead to her. Roy was always at his store on Saturdays, and if George and I finished early at the post office, we could stop there with enough time to see him before I had to get back home to relieve Jane.

As we walked on the way to the post office, George had

something on his mind. "That day Mama left, it wasn't me that cleaned up in the cellar."

"What do you mean?" I flashed back to my father running up from the darkroom when the fire gong sounded, calling for George.

"I heard him yell for me to close up the bottles, but I ran down the road with the boys. I got back just before you and Dad came in. I didn't do what he said. When he checked them, the caps were on the bottles. But it wasn't me."

When my father and I had gone down to wash up, the darkroom curtain had been open, the light left on. The holding pans for the print bath were full, and the prints he had processed were hanging across the line. The bottles, sealed.

"Don't worry about it; it doesn't matter now."

He shrugged. "I guess you're right—he didn't blame me, for once."

Looking at his profile, the set jaw, the slim nose, hair brushed off his forehead, for a second I saw my mother's face in his. George was a hardy boy on the outside, more sensitive than my father knew on the inside. My mother could find her way to the part of George that needed care, not with fussing but by being close when he wanted to say something and encouraging him. My father went the other way, no babying, as he called it. He tested George regularly, taunted him—not fast enough, not orderly enough, not silent when given punishment.

I had not been paying enough attention to how George felt,

and now I wanted to be a better brother to him than I had been. I put a hand on his shoulder and gave it a quick squeeze. "Don't worry, we'll be all right. I'll make sure of that."

He half-smiled at me and we picked up our pace.

Entering the post office from the back door used to load in the mail deliveries, we found Mr. Kegg sitting at his desk in the office. He was a kind man, always good to me, and offered George cookies and a stack of unclaimed funny papers while I started the routine for opening the counter.

Saturday was the busiest day of the week. Most people had telephones, but letters were the primary means of communication, and businesses sent their official correspondence through the mail. Every household had to visit us to fetch their mail, and many folks left stopping in until the end of the week, though we had our daily regulars. Letterboxes were built into two of the lobby walls, and the counter filled the space between them. Each box holder had their own key, but older folks and those who just liked to chat would come to the counter and ask me to go behind the boxes and retrieve their bundles.

It was my lucky break to have the post office job. Mr. Kegg knew my father— everyone knew my father—but Mr. Kegg promoted the post office services with my father's photography. Every year when the new two-cent red stamps were issued, the town paper featured my father's photos of a smiling Mr. Kegg holding the freshly printed sheets. During one of the shoots I had handled the lights, and Mr. Kegg asked if I wanted to haul mailbags after school. Now, a year later, Mr. Kegg was teaching me the operations.

I could see a future that suited me in the postal service. The flow of information coming and going was ordered, the connection to the outside world essential for the people of the town. In the post office we were privy to the highs and lows of everyday life. Letters opened in the lobby generated reactions of joy, sorrow, worry, regret, pride, shame, scorn, anger—it was all there to observe. Mr. Kegg ran an efficient operation and had a friendly word for everyone coming in. He taught me to step back and wait when news upset people, giving them a moment to collect themselves. We protected the confidences of the post office, mindful of the postal history each person had experienced, keeping a mental ledger whether hearty greetings or quiet hellos would be appropriate the next time they came in.

Townspeople returned that respect while we mourned Lonnie and now during my mother's unexplained absence. Everyone I saw that morning wished us well and reviewed the prayers they continued to say for my mother's safety as I handed over the mail bundles and postmarked their bill payments and letters. Moving at a fast pace so I could finish early, I made just enough small talk to be neighborly. Neither Roy nor Marion came in, not unusual, as Saturdays were their busiest mornings at the store. By half-past eleven the lobby was empty, and though we were open for another half-hour, I asked Mr. Kegg if I could run out. Since George was there to help with the cleaning up, he was agreeable, and I told George I would be back to walk him home at noon.

With a quick trot along the few blocks to Feeke's, I saw the truck and Roy sitting inside. Facing my approach, Roy lifted the fingers of his left hand off of the steering wheel in a half-wave. He was a tall, lean, wiry guy, his dark brown hair shaggier than the miners would grow it. People used to say he and Marion made a handsome couple, and he was the handsome part, strong looking, with alert eyes that lighted on you when you were close to him. I had seen him in a suit only once, at Lonnie's funeral. His everyday outfit was a clean plaid work shirt, dungarees, and boots, ready to haul stock in the warehouse or work the store counter by pulling on a canvas apron.

Roy was a Feeke brother, one of four sons of Ernest Feeke. People called their family real Pennsylvanians, like ours, those who had been in the county since the 1700s or earlier, arriving among the waves of settlers that pushed out the native tribes and took over the land. The Feeke family had long been merchants, and Roy's older brothers expanded their stores with the growth of the county, now moving into car sales, putting the first auto dealership into the town. As the youngest, Roy was in the habit of doing what his brothers planned and that had worked out into a good living for him, Marion, and their children.

I stopped at his open window. "Hey, Roy, can I talk with you for a minute? I need to ask you something."

Roy jerked his head to the right. "Okay, Dan, get in."

I walked around the front and got into the passenger seat. Roy was always on the move and the grimy truck showed the wear of miles logged over the country roads. I had ridden in it many times, usually in the back bed, and Roy let me drive once. Lillian got Uncle George to teach Jane and me to drive, practicing in his truck at the farm. My mother's enthusiasm for driving ran up against my father's tendency to hold on to his money. She never gave up lobbying for our own car and he never gave in. He saw no reason to spend for a family car when we could easily walk wherever we needed to go for necessities, though he made frequent use of the gas company cars. A few times, my mother had borrowed Roy's truck and taken us riding, or she had gone with Grandma to the farm, while my father was away. Instinct about his disapproval kept us from telling him.

Now alone with Roy, I was unsure how to begin, but he started. "Dan, it's just a darn shame that your mama is gone."

"Have you got any idea where she is? I was thinking you might know something."

He looked at me in a puzzled way.

"Because Marion said you'd been out looking."

"Well, I asked around at all the market stops but nothing came of that."

I put my cards on the table. "I was thinking you might know something she said to you. A few weeks back I saw you talking, sitting together in your truck, out back of the house."

Roy put both hands on the wheel and stretched out his long

arms, staring straight ahead, then sighed. "Lily knew her own mind, always did. I never could change it."

He looked over at me and half-smiled. "I wish I knew where she was."

His tone was one I had never heard from him, soft, sad, like when Mr. Kegg talked about his late wife, whom he had loved very much. Staying quiet, I listened for where Roy was taking this. Out of the corner of his eye, he saw the opening I was giving him.

"When you saw us in the truck, it was just one of those days when I gave her a ride back from the cemetery, and she wanted to talk." He lit a cigarette and blew two or three smoke rings. "I've known Lillian since we were in primary school, and sometimes she let me listen." He paused. "Your pa don't need to know that."

It came easy, hearing from a second man who talked with my mother and wanted me to keep a secret of hers. It sunk in that Mama kept me close and both Roy and Uncle George believed I was more my mother's son than my father's, loyal to her, as they were. Of the two, Roy's interest and mine seemed more aligned, yet I felt that there was something he was not saying.

I told him what I knew. "Uncle George helped her get away from the farm, and he gave me a letter Mama wrote to Grandma, saying she is leaving my father."

Roy tossed the cigarette out the window. He winced. "That fits, that fits all right, she would go to George. Leaving your father … does Alonzo know?"

"Grandma and Papaw showed him the letter. He's mad. He doesn't want anyone to find out. Uncle Charlie's got the gas men looking for her, trying to get her back."

"If her brother got her a ride from the farm, any of those guys she rode with, they aren't going to be seen by no gas man."

He read my confused expression. "Those guys working for George, they know your mother. Don't worry about that, she's fine with them. It's just that they don't travel the main roads."

"Can you find her? We need her to come back."

"I might find her, Dan, but I can't say what she aims to do. I can't say."

"Tell her the girls are in an awful state, tell her we need her."

Roy shook his head and gripped the wheel. He gazed out the windshield and blinked back tears.

"Lily told her mama she's leaving Alonzo." He shook off the emotion and faced me. "She's already gone, Dan, and you might have to live with that."

"She might not mean to leave us. If you find her, I think she will come back."

Roy shook his head. "I can try. But she knows her mind."

I opened my door. "I have to go back to the post office. If you find her, or hear something, tell me there, not at home."

Shaking his head, Roy started the engine, and with the lift of the fingers, pulled away.

During my run back to the post office, Roy's words about having to live with her gone nagged at me. There was no real reason to feel hopeful but at least Roy wanted to find my mother. Considering telling Jane that I had spoken to Roy, I decided against it, remembering her anger at our mother. Telling Papaw about Roy could ease Grandma's mind, but they might question why Lillian confided in him. The secrets weighed heavier. If Roy could bring my mother home, I could just let the secrets go.

The next day, Sunday, Uncle Charlie drove over to pick us up for dinner. At their house, my father holed up with his brother in the small room with the piano off the parlor that Aunt Letitia called the music room and Uncle Charlie called the smoking room, where he kept his cigars. Aunt Letitia and my father's sister, Aunt Hattie, cooked and whispered in the kitchen until they put the meal on the table. It was obvious to Jane and me that the conversations in both rooms were about my mother. Even though she was furious about our mother leaving, Jane shared my discomfort with her being the subject of the whispers among my father's family.

Charlie and Hattie were both older than my father, by eight and sixteen years. None of us knew their father, our grandfather Andrew, who had died a month after my parents married. We'd known Grandmother Cora, who had passed five years earlier, although we had seldom seen her during our young years. Charlie had no children and Hattie's were grown. Neither one was close to us. Their interest was always polite and caring, but not loving. We spent much less time with them than with Grandma and Papaw, who had been a daily presence in our lives. This all to say we had almost nothing to talk about at the dinner table, even in good times, and in our present turmoil it was all the five of us could do to sit quietly and eat, taking care of Addie, hoping no one would speak to us.

It was not to be that easy. Aunt Letitia singled us out one by one, with commentary on dress (Ruthie's too small, George's dirty shirt), hair (Annie's unkempt), manners (me too slow to pull out the ladies' chairs), language (Jane using slang), and that it was clear our household lacked the proper organization and supervision. She admonished my father, saying his expecting us to manage on our own would not do, that banishing Grandma and Papaw had been a hasty decision.

Aunt Letitia had no concern for our feelings or theirs but the arrangement with Lillian's parents had kept her from having to take an active part in our lives. She viewed our presence at her Sunday dinner table as my father's tactic to get Uncle Charlie to persuade her to oversee us until my mother returned. This was not working out as he thought it might, because Aunt Letitia saw no reason for her to take on the care of six children in our house, and there was no possibility of us moving to her house. Our current situation was my father's doing and his problem to solve, she informed him. When she finished her critiques, Uncle Charlie gave a look to my father that said he would not fight her.

Aunt Hattie was silent throughout the discussion. As a guest at Letitia's table, she did not feel it was proper to cross her with another opinion. But before we left Charlie's house, she took my father aside to offer an alternative. She would take Ruthie, Annie, and Addie to her house for as long as necessary, leaving Jane and me to look after George. Hattie lived on the outskirts of our town, too far for them to walk to school, but her neighbor's children rode in each morning on the milk truck, and the girls could do that, too, then come back in the evening along with their neighbor on his way home from the mill.

The girls cried when my father announced the arrangement to them on the way home. Uncle Charlie waited with the car while Jane packed their clothes, the girls wailing the entire time. I promised to come and see them when the mail truck went out that way. Aunt Hattie had a telephone, and Jane told them to call home every day. Addie kicked and squirmed, not wanting Hattie to hold her. Ruthie and Annie knelt on the backseat of the car, their teary faces visible through the rear window, still begging not to go as the car pulled away. Jane and I exchanged looks.

Jane told my father, "This might cause more problems."

Jane was the only one who could direct a disagreeing comment to my father without him getting angry. Not that he would tolerate an extended lecture from her, but he seemed to give her view some consideration.

"It won't be for long. They can manage."

It did not go well.

By Thursday, Aunt Hattie had her son, our cousin Oscar, drive her and the girls back home. They had cried for the better part of three days and she could take no more. She announced that she would stay with us in our house until my mother returned. Addie's crib came into George's and my room to make enough space for an extra cot in the girl's room for Aunt Hattie.

She had her ideas about our daily regimen and set about getting the house into what she called a proper order. It had been years since she had cared for young children, and she had never taken care of us. The girls held back some crying but they were no less upset, whispering their longing for our mother and Grandma to Jane and me. Addie became fussier than she had ever been, refusing most foods, and her fitful sleep had one of us up with her several times each night. My father was on the road again, coming back for only one night the first week Aunt Hattie stayed with us. When she asked him for news of my mother, he said there was none.

I wanted to have another talk with Roy. Hattie's presence at home gave me brief time to myself. I had not seen Roy or his truck in the alley between the houses since the day I talked to him at the post office. With school and work after school, the hour after closing the post office and before supper was when I roamed around town to spot him.

During one of these walks, a strange woman approached me. She was about the same age as my mother, with short curly hair under a wide-brimmed hat angled on her head to allow the front curls to frame her face. She wore a navy day-dress, long-sleeved with white lace trim at the collar and cuffs, and pumps with stockings. The late afternoon weather was brisk, and over the dress she wore a wool cape, with slits for her arms to extend just to where her gloves ended at the elbows. The smart clothes set her apart from the everyday plainness of most of the women in our town. I assumed she was waiting for someone, until she came up next to me.

"You're Lillian's boy, aren't you?"

I was unused to talking with unfamiliar people. My shyness and the surprise of her declaration kept a response stuck in my throat. She motioned with her head for me to follow her into the vestibule of an office building in the middle of the block.

"I am sorry if I surprised you, but I am a friend of your mother's."

I found my voice. "You know she's missing?"

"Your mama had a big shock." The lady drew her cape closer around her. "She needs some time."

"Have you seen her?"

She shook her head and took a cigarette from her handbag, turned away to light it. "Not since she left town. I used to see her every week."

"Where? At the cemetery?"

"No, on the route my husband drives for George. Lillian would meet us to collect."

Confusion and curiosity clambered inside my brain. Not understanding what she meant, yet feeling that if I heard more, it would take me to a place of no return. Already on that path, having lied for Uncle George and conspired with Roy, I used the tactic Mr. Kegg taught me for handling times when people confided personal information—nod and wait without speaking.

"Look, a woman like Lillian, seven children, mourning one, finding out like she did—it was too much. The men look the other way, seems like that's how it could go on so long, none of them going to risk saying anything."

The wind whipped into the cubby where we stood, and I shuddered.

"What did she find out?"

Taking a long drag on the cigarette, she blew out the smoke.

"Your father has another family, and that woman had a baby."

It hit me like the spike end of a pickaxe. Seeing me sway, the woman steadied me against the wall with one arm, and with the other opened her handbag. She drew out a small silver flask and nudged it against my hand.

"Take a sip. It'll help."

What was she offering? Gulping air, I shook my head, forced out words. "Who are you? How do you know my mother?"

She put the flask back in her purse, watching me. "I told you, my husband and I work with George."

"It's not true."

"If you don't believe me, see for yourself, look for what she found in his darkroom."

I pushed off the wall and moved around her toward the street. Cooler air found its way to my lungs.

Clutching her cloak around her, the woman stepped out. "Sorry your mama's gone." With that she strode away, holding her hat against the wind.

Jumbled thoughts ran through my brain like the oversized headlines in the movie newsreels. My father had another family? Where? Could there be photos? If the story were true, would my father leave evidence in the cellar of our house? And what did she mean about seeing my mother "every week to collect"? Uncle George was connected to this somehow.

Was I going to look in the darkroom, see for myself? Then what? I did not let myself go there yet.

Pushed by the wind and some inevitable propulsion, I rushed toward our neighborhood. At the house, the lamps were lit in the front room, and walking along the side windows gave me a view of Hattie and the girls in the kitchen. It was not quite dinner time. Entering the cellar from the outside would give me a few minutes before I had to see them.

The hatch door creaked open and I got a footing on the dark steps, feeling my way along the wall with one hand until my foot touched the earthen floor and I found the string pull for the light.

Ruthie called down from the kitchen, "Dan, is that you?"

"Be up in a minute."

Their chatter and the scraping of chairs on the floor over my head went on.

The dim light cast shadows around the cellar. The heavy curtain closed off the darkroom corner. Whatever I touched had to be put back as I found it. My father tolerated no interference with his set-up. If he detected something out of place, he would take it out on my brother. I pulled on the curtain from the right side near the middle, trying to open it enough to get through without shuffling the curtain over. I squeezed through and reached for the string attached to a light bulb in the middle of the space. My hand found it and pulled, light revealing the workbench.

My father had built the workbench in an L-shape, about a yard deep, with one shelf underneath. On one side, he stored the processing chemicals, and below those, wooden milk crates held envelopes full of prints. On the workspace, metal trays were lined up to hold prints as they went from one chemical bath to the next. Above, clothesline strung side-to-side held clips for air-drying prints. After drying, he laid the prints between special paper that further set the images and flattened them by laying a brick on top of the pile.

Nothing hung from the clothesline. As far as I knew, he hadn't been shooting over the last chaotic weeks. Running back the days in my head, I remembered that my father checked the space when we came back from the fire and saw the chemicals were closed. George told me he had not capped the bottles. My father could have left the curtain open, photos hanging from the line, others in the dry pile, when he ran out. When Jane was upstairs while Addie napped, had my mother come back into the house? Had she come down here that day? Assuming she did, what would she have seen?

A dry pile lay under the brick. They would be the last photos my father had printed. With shaking hands I lifted the brick away from the black paper covering the pile, about ten prints in all. The top photo showed two surveyors along a roadside, a cleared field in the background, a typical shot my father took on the road with the gas line crews. Lifting the thin tissue paper separating the prints, I saw the next was like the first. Breathing easier, flipping through three prints of laborers digging trenches for the gas lines, the work pictures of the regular doings of the crew lulled me into hoping for nothing unusual.

At the bottom of the pile, two smaller photos.

In one, a small boy, no older than Addie, stood next to an armchair where a baby swaddled in a blanket was propped against a pillow. In the other, a smiling young woman sat in the armchair holding the baby, the boy leaning on her knee.

The stark black and white of these two photos jerked me back to the reason I was snooping in my father's darkroom. I imagined my mother stepping in here to close the bottles and glancing up. If they had been hanging to dry in the second row of clothesline, they would not be obvious. The space was so small you had to hold the front row aside with your hand to see those pinned up behind it. Did she do that, or were these still in the bath where she could see these faces floating up to mock her?

If what the strange woman told me was true, I was looking at my father's other family. But what if my father had taken these photos for one of the crewmen? He had done many favors with his camera— people asked him all the time, this could be one of those favors. Why were they still here, then? Maybe he forgot, with the distress of the days since my mother left, and when he had time to come down here, get back to where he left things, he would remember that he promised to print these and send them to the man whose family this was.

Or maybe he meant to hide them, and he had hurried when the gongs rang, knew what he left hanging in the darkroom, had just put them up, too wet to take down, and he thought he could get back and hide them, no harm done. Except that my mother came back, and went down to the cellar, maybe for a jar or some potatoes, or to wash her boots off. And there was the curtain open, lights on, and she stepped into his corner.

Even if she saw the photos, would they have alarmed her? Couldn't she have figured they were for a workman? Or was she already wondering why my father was on the road more than he used to be, making her feel like he stayed away when he didn't have to. Wondering why he had not come back as soon as Lonnie got sick, leaving her to go through the misery of his final hours alone. Had she thought about his excuses when she saw the photos?

Our understanding of what he did away from home rested on what he told us. Most of the week he operated outside of our family circle. He announced his departures and where the crew would be, and it was implied we had no basis to question him. When he left, the air cleared with silent relief.

He insisted on our gratitude for the life he provided, demanding we be thankful for all we had because of his work. I hadn't thought about my mother missing him or needing him more, not until Lonnie got sick. That maybe his being away so much was not the life she wanted. If my mother discussed her feelings with him, it was in private.

George yelled my name, startling me. I reassembled the photo pile, taking care to place it back within the frame of the dust that had settled around it, and placed the brick on top. Pulled the light off and edged out of the curtain, straightening it. Stepping out of my boots, I ran upstairs to the kitchen.

Everyone sat at the table waiting to eat, and I washed my hands, then took my chair. The girls chattered about something that happened at school and George joined in, with Jane encouraging them to explain to Aunt Hattie what their teachers said. Sitting next to Addie, I busied myself with cutting her food, and the conversation went on around me.

The faces in the photos loomed in my head. Addie pulled on my sleeve. Turning to see what she needed, the eyes of the little boy in the photo looked into mine.

CHAPTER 5

I had let the woman walk away without asking her name. What she said about her husband driving for Uncle George and seeing my mother every week to "collect" made no sense. Uncle George had drivers making runs from the farm, supplying the markets in the coal towns with fruits and vegetables in season, but my mother had nothing to do with that. If I could talk to Jane, she might right my confusion with another explanation. But since her outburst against my mother, I hesitated to share with her what I had learned from the woman and seen in the darkroom. Not enough to go on to risk telling Jane.

Uncle George was key to the mystery of the woman's information. He had asked me to lie for him, or at least not tell the whole truth, and if he trusted me for that, he would have to tell me what my mother had been doing.

Figuring out how to get to the farm took planning. I would have to leave as soon as the post office closed at noon on Saturday and get back by Sunday evening. Explaining where I was going would require a story, and I again confronted both my willingness and my comfort with making things up. Justifying the ruse, I told myself was I protecting my family in the temporary circumstances. Hattie would believe what I told her since she knew so little about what we normally did. It was Jane's scrutiny I worried about. Either my story would convince her or I would have to take her into my confidence and get her to keep quiet about it. Using my post office duties was the best cover.

I concocted the story as I helped Hattie clear the table after supper.

"Hattie, Mr. Kegg asked me to run a special post up to Uniontown on Saturday, and wait there to bring one back on Sunday, so I'll stay up there in the postmaster's station."

This had happened before, always with Mr. Kegg or one of the regular carriers taking the run, but she wouldn't know that.

She studied my face for a moment. "We can get along without you for a night, Dan, but going up there alone? Will Mr. Kegg get someone to meet you?"

"Yes, the postmaster will be there. I'll stay at the station post office, just wait for the bags, then come back. He's not sure which train they will be on."

Jane walked back into the kitchen and heard the last part. "When is this?"

"Saturday, overnight."

She shrugged. "I guess that means I have to stay in."

Hoping to get away with little discussion, I stayed quiet, but Hattie read Jane's disappointment.

"You can go for a few hours. We'll work that out."

Aunt Hattie, although strange to us, was finding her way to understand us. I had observed her sensitivity to the girls, and her manner of taking George aside for a quiet talk. Jane appreciated her gesture, nodding with a smile as she collected dishes to put away in the pantry.

My story accepted, I had to get a ride to the farm. Luck was with me. When I took the trash out back to the alley, Marion was there, trying to gather up the mess of garbage spilled out of her overturned cans.

She slammed a top onto a can. "The critters have been out here almost every night pulling the cans over."

"I can find some rocks to put on top of the lids. Say, Marion, do you know if any drivers from George's farm will be at the store on Saturday afternoon?"

Bending toward a clump of potato scraps, she said, "There's usually one after lunch, bringing in what holds us 'til Monday morning."

"If I get there right after noon, can I catch him? I need to ride out there."

"At noon he's likely to be ready to leave. I can send a word ahead with one of the others if you want." She stood up. "You're after George about your mama, aren't you?"

"Yes, but if you would not send word to him, I'd rather just show up there."

"You're worried about her, I know that. But if George knew

anything, don't you think he would have told your papaw, or the police?" Marion didn't know we had the letter.

"I need to try. Can you ask the driver to wait for me on Saturday? I will be over to the store as soon as the post office closes."

She sighed, hands on her hips. "I will ask him. What does your pa know about this, or Hattie?" She gestured toward the house.

"They don't."

"That's how it is, now? You're on your own?"

I slammed the lid tight on the last can. "That's how it is."

"I don't know why your mother's causing all kinds of upset. I saw your papaw yesterday, looking as bad as I've ever seen him. Your pa isn't right thinking, now, either, making them stay away." Marion wiped her hands on her apron. "I'll make you some sandwiches for the ride. See you on Saturday."

When I hurried into the store just after noon on Saturday, Marion was busy with customers at the counter. Seeing me, she nodded her head toward a man standing near the potbelly stove that sat in an open space amid the shelves and bags of goods. Marion pushed a bag across the counter toward me with the sandwiches she had promised.

The trucker put down the coffee he was drinking. "You going with me? Let's get movin'."

We established at the outset that he knew I was George's nephew but he did not know my mother, and he otherwise seemed indifferent to my presence. He drove chewing on a big plug of tobacco, spitting it out the truck window, and refreshing the plug. The April breeze blew through, cold in the hills and warmer when we got to the valley.

George's land was far enough out in the countryside to escape most of the fumes we lived with in town. The coke and coal companies had bought up much of the farmland, either to dig mines in the coal seams running through them, or to harvest the lumber for charcoal and furnaces. Papaw had sold a good part of his original acreage when the price was high, keeping the crop fields. It turned out the mining company didn't find much of a coal seam there, and the intention to mine coal changed to keeping it as lumber stock. Since the land hadn't been clear-cut like most other former farms, George's spread was undisturbed and isolated.

Before George took over, tenant farmers had kept up the orchard and the canning crops—tomatoes, corn, peas, onions, and such—along with some goats and pigs, making cheese and curing hams. George had been running the farm for about ten years and expanded the operations and the markets he sold to. Most farm people who sold out ended up in the towns working coke or iron or lumbering as laborers on the land that used to be theirs. When George needed workers, he had no trouble finding the old farmhands who welcomed getting back to the land. The growing populations in the mining towns needed larger quantities of food. Farms like George's had a steady business, trucking the produce to local markets, and the bulk crops loaded onto train cars bound for canneries in Pittsburgh.

Keeping my trip a secret seemed easier as the miles went by. If no one in my family saw Mr. Kegg between my leaving and my return, the story would hold up. He went to a different church than us and lived on the other side of town. Only Marion knew where I was going, and I trusted her silence. Eating a sandwich she made, I realized that I had seen her twice and not asked where Roy was. She had not mentioned him so I assumed that, wherever he was, it was not out of the ordinary. Maybe he had given up looking for my mother, but I doubted that. He seemed intent on finding her.

The rumble of the farm truck on the rutted roads kept me alert and thinking about what I wanted from Uncle George. The details I knew about my mother's leaving compounded into blaming him for letting her go. How could he have let one of the truckers give her a ride? If she had seen the photos, he could have made her stay on the farm until she calmed herself. I wanted to take the photos to the farm but couldn't risk my father coming home and finding them missing. Had Roy come back out here to question George after our talk? And why had George let more than a week go by since giving me the letter without checking in on us? Maybe Papaw told him to stay away because of my father, but I was not ready to let Uncle George off the hook for anything.

My mother used to say I was slow to boil, not one for letting strong emotions take me over. I learned that from dealing with my father. When he got worked up about something, it was best not to put more fuel on the fire. Meeting his upset with quiet responses and ample show of respect for his authority smoothed out most situations. I would tell my brother George, "Give him no reason to get angrier," trying to help him avoid the worst punishments. But dealing with my father like that over so many years had heaped my own strong feelings into a hidden burden. Now, angry with Uncle George, I wanted to go in sharper, make him deal with me, not back off. I worried I was an amateur at this.

When the truck crested the last hill before the cut-off onto the farm road, the vista of Uncle George's acreage spread below us. Spring plowing was underway in the acres of dirt fields. Clusters of smokehouses, poultry sheds, barns, and workshops were arrayed between the fields, with people and trucks moving among them. The farmhouse was further away from the outbuildings at the end of its own branch of the farm road.

The trucker stopped at the fork, my cue to get out. As he pulled away toward a barn, I walked about a quarter mile to the house, thinking about the many summer days we had spent here. It was a classic farmhouse, two stories, wood-frame, made from planks harvested on the timberland. A porch extended across the entire front. Up the middle steps, the front door was center, entering a hall where we left coats and boots, with the stairway to the second story hugging the back wall. Turning left from the front door led into a parlor, and directly behind that was a big kitchen that ran the width of the house and was twice as deep as the front room. Upstairs there was a small alcove that was the sewing room when Grandma lived there. Bedrooms off the center hall were outfitted with iron bedsteads and feather mattresses. On muggy summer nights at the farm, we children slept in a tent out back, which suited us fine, as we spent all our time outside anyway unless it was pouring rain.

Letting myself in the front door that was never locked, I didn't expect George to be in the house at this time of day and planned to wait for him in the kitchen. The trucker might tell him I was there if the man ever spoke.

The big farm table in the middle of the room had eight chairs around it. Along the back wall were three large windows and the door to the rear porch. Standing at the sink, the gaze over the fields was soothing. Uncle George didn't keep house as well as Grandma. The kitchen was untidy—dishes in the sink, glasses and bottles on the table, chairs pushed back like a group of people had recently jumped up and left. I sat down at what looked to be the cleanest place at the table, unwrapped the last of Marion's sandwiches and took a bite, thinking about my speech to Uncle George.

From my seat, I had no view of the approach to the house, and the heavy step of a boot on the porch alerted me to someone coming. George's upper body appeared through the pane of the door. He pushed in with force so it slammed back.

"Did something happen? Are the children all right?"

I rose from the chair. "They're fine but something happened. I'm here to hash that out with you."

He kept his eyes on me as he slipped out of his jacket and hung it on a hook by the door.

"You came without telling your pa, I'm guessing, because he wouldn't have let you do this. Where does the family think you are?"

I explained the story about the mail and reminded myself to be forceful. "My mother left for a reason and I want you to tell me what she told you."

"Dan, have a chair. I don't know her mind."

"Where is she now?"

"Why are you coming here with these questions? What happened?"

"Did you think you could ask me to lie and leave it like that? Do you know how many lies I have told since you handed me my mother's letter? You owe me the truth."

George ran his hands through his hair, pulled out a chair, and motioned for me to sit down. "Let's talk, okay? Calm down and talk. Tell me what happened."

Anger mixed with the loneliness of the speculations that had been churning in my mind. I wanted to talk to someone about what I had seen and heard, and Uncle George was my best option. But I did not want him to treat me like a boy who would accept whatever he said. I had changed since my mother left. Uncle George would find that out.

I looked directly at him. "Start with the people who drive for you, and what my mother was collecting."

Running his hands back and forth along his thighs, he stared at me. "Who talked to you?"

"A woman I've never seen before stopped me on the street. She and her husband drive for you." I held back what she told me.

Uncle George leaned toward me. "I don't know what made her talk to you. That woman and her husband are distributors of mine."

I waited. He jiggled one leg. "I have lots of small truck operators working regular routes for me."

"How is my mother involved?"

"We arranged it so they could tally up with your mother after the runs. She counted the cash, kept the records and held the money until I could have it picked up."

"She was collecting money for the deliveries?"

He sat back. "We're not talking about vegetables, Dan. They distribute a special product we supply." He waited, our eyes locked, and then he kind of smiled. And I realized what the product was.

Uncle George was bootlegging. And my mother helped him.

"Are you telling me...?"

Uncle George waved his hands. "We don't do the hard stuff, not the poison that people are putting out in Pittsburgh and Chicago. We make a good Pennsylvania beer. It's all local people working for me. Seven years, never lost a truck, never robbed. If any of the lawmen know about it, they're looking the other way—probably enjoy our brew as much as the working men do."

I could not believe he was boasting about being a lawbreaker. Uncle George, who Papaw was so proud of, for expanding the farm, for making it possible for his parents to live well in town. Could they know what he was doing?

"How could you get my mother involved in that?"

"She was never in any danger, there was never any trouble. And, telling you true, Dan, most of it was her idea. She introduced me to a Belgian fella who came out here from Philly looking for land to try growing his wheat. He had a whole big brewery back home before the war. He got over here and wanted to start it up again. I had the land, he had the know-how, a starter yeast, and the wheat strain. The wheat grows well here. Might've let him go on his way with a thanks-but-no-thanks if it hadn't been for the demand. All these men in the mines want a beer or two at the end of a long day, and what used to be on the shelves, they couldn't afford. We make what they want and sell at a fair price."

"You gave her money?"

"She took a share; we're partners. We expanded the truck routes based on her telling me where the gas company was sending out their crews. Every time the gas lines broke new ground, we got a farmer or a storekeeper or an old miner to set up a barn or shed out of the way, where we could stash the supply. The word spread, quietly. Men on the crews all knew to look around for it, wherever they went."

"You're telling me that my mother was a bootlegger for seven years?"

"Pretty much, yeah. She's smart. I couldn't have done all this without her."

My heart thumped like in one of those movie cartoons where it comes flying outside the character's chest. Everything that had happened since the day Lonnie got sick crushed me. I blanked on how to yell, cry, or keep breathing, anything to help myself. It was like the panic old miners who lived through cave-ins described coming on at the moment before the scaffolding broke loose. Me trapped with my dead brother, my mother's ghost, and my father's secret family. Where was there to go?

Head in my hands, elbows on my knees, I struggled to take in air. My scuffed brown boots, high socks, woolen knickers, the schoolboy clothes I wore almost every day, seemed to compress against my skin. Hooking my thumbs under my suspenders, I pulled them and my shirt away from my clammy chest, tried to unbutton the neck. Ripped it when it wouldn't give.

Uncle George was saying my name, asking if I wanted water. The anger that carried me into the conversation lit a pathway in my brain.

"You couldn't have done it without her? What are *we* supposed to do without her?" Then I blurted, "Did she know about my father?"

"What do you mean?"

"The day of the fire—did she tell you what she saw? Did she know? Did that make her leave? Or did she stop loving us?" Tears clogged my eyes. I had not cried since the funeral.

"When she got here she was freezing, not steady on her feet. I couldn't get much from her, took a long time calming her."

I had no patience and didn't care if he thought me too bold. Polite uncle-and-nephew conversation was over between us. I raised up and dragged my sleeves across my eyes. Never again would I let anyone see me crying.

"George, level with me." He leaned back, lifted a brow. I propelled on.

"Everything that held us together as a family has blown apart in the last two weeks. Before, there was not a day without Grandma and Papaw walking in the door. We had never been without my mother. The girls couldn't tolerate three nights at Aunt Hattie's house because we had never been apart. Now, my mother is gone, my father threatened our grandparents to stay away from us. I'm the one left holding the pieces. Trying to keep the girls from crying, holding a fussing baby who has no mother, pretending as best I can for my sad little brother who has no one else to turn to."

He kept eyes on me, clenched fists at his side, a muscle twitching in his cheek. We had no history of confrontation, had to feel our way toward what we wanted from each other. Would he talk man-to-man, or hold back like the protector he thought he was? I gave him a verbal shove.

"I'm taking no more lies from you, Uncle."

Alert to the sarcasm, he held out his open hands. "Dan, the truth: I don't know where Lillian is."

"Did she tell you why she came here that day?"

"She had nothing with her but the clothes she was wearing,

talked about going someplace where no one would find her. Between bouts of crying, she talked crazy, about things we used to do when we were kids here on the farm, about before she married Alonzo. Wishing she were lying underground instead of Lonnie. Jumping around like she lost her right head."

He stood and paced the kitchen floor.

"I sat with her until she wore herself out. She kept saying her mind was made up to leave. She wrote that letter for Grandma. I argued with her. Like I told you, I could get her to agree only that I would wait five days before taking it to the folks."

"You didn't refuse to take the letter."

"No. But only because I didn't want to upset her more."

Scanning Uncle George's face, I believed him. I figured he supposed it made no difference now, and I deserved the truth.

He came back to sit in the chair near mine. "She dropped asleep on the kitchen table. I carried her upstairs to a bed and covered her. When I got up at dawn, I found a note saying she was getting a ride to Uniontown, and that letter for Grandma. I figured she had cleared her head, would get on the train from there and go home with some story for you all."

"Did she tell you about my father?"

"She rambled about a lot of things. Nothing I didn't already know. His temper, his being on the road so much, his excuses—she was all nerves."

"And what about the trucker she rode with? What does he know?"

"He says he dropped her off at the train station. That's what made me think she would get the next one back home. She didn't say much, as he remembers it."

"Look, after I heard from Papaw she was missing, I couldn't risk the police or anyone coming here looking for her or asking questions. The men who work for me know to keep quiet—I don't worry about them. The best way to get the letter to Grandma seemed to be through you. I'm sorry I pulled you into it like that."

"Could she still be in Uniontown?"

"I don't think so, at least not with any of the people we know there. If she *is* there, she's lying low. She'd read in the papers the police are looking for her. My men have their eyes open, but no word has come that she's there. They would tell me. There's no benefit to my men to keep it from me." He ran his hands through his hair again. "She's got her money in a bank there."

He left that hanging in the air.

I got the point: my mother could pay her own way, whatever she wanted to do.

The sadness in his eyes told me he wrestled with the damage from my mother and his lying. He had told me the truth, but I wasn't ready to trust him again. And after this he would ask me to lie again, or assume I would keep the farm's business secret, for the family. Asking me outright would mean he owed me. Either way, Uncle George and I had to move forward together. If my mother came back or not, my brother and sisters and I would need him. If he expected my silence, then I would give him a burden to carry, too.

"That woman who works for you—she told me that Mama left because she found out that my father has another family, that on the day of the fire, my mother saw photos in the cellar. I found them, just like she said. Photos of a woman with a baby and a little boy."

Uncle George shook his head, closed his eyes, and whispered, "Oh, Lily, oh, dear Lily." Opening his eyes, he leaned in and put his hand on my arm. "I don't know if it's true, Dan, but I know how to find out."

"So, you think it *could* be true? My father *could* have another family. How can that be right?"

"It's *not* right. For Alonzo … it's possible." He heard my breathing quicken again. "Look, you want me to level with you, you have to accept some hard facts about your father, and about your mother. You didn't know she had another side to her life, things she was carrying on separate from you all, outside your house. But she did. Lillian was a good businesswoman, and the business she was in is illegal—for now, not forever, this Prohibition will end."

He rose and went to the sink, rested his hands there as he looked out the window over the fields. "And maybe your father had another side to his life, too. Alonzo is a forceful man, you see that. He wants what he wants, and he goes after it." Uncle George turned around. "I don't know if there is another family.

You hear stories, from time to time, a man moving between two families, two lives. You know him, what he's like."

In my mind's eye, memories played out. The times when my father would show us close-up black-and-white photos he took for the police at crime scenes and wait for us to cry out in shock. The sly grin on his face said he tried to upset us on purpose, delighted in our fear. Me holding myself tight and freezing my face, not satisfying him with a reaction. Him taking his dinner while reading the paper, the rest of us eating in silence, my mother looking over us, her mind elsewhere. Scene after scene where George came up from the cellar hanging his head after a tongue-lashing. The girls begging my mother not to show him their school reports, Ruthie's low grades, Annie's misbehavior. My mother pleading with him to come home when Lonnie was sick. Only Jane wanted his attention; the others cowered away from him.

When had this become our story? When Jane and I were small, he played with us, taught us baseball, had us giggling with one of us on his knee, the other on his ankle, pretending to ride a horse. What changed? What kind of man had he become?

"I need to know the truth. How can you find out if he has another family?"

"I can get someone to follow him."

"How do you know where he is?"

"My men know where the crews are. It won't be hard to get eyes on him."

"How long before you know?"

"Couple of days. When I have something to tell you, I'll send someone to the post office. I'm staying around the farm these days."

I nodded my acceptance of the plan. "What about finding my mother?"

"If she's still in Uniontown, somebody will see or hear about her. But I'm thinking she's gone from there. It's two weeks now, and if she meant to leave, that's not far enough to go." Uncle George leaned toward me. "Dan, she could be gone for good."

"You're giving up."

"No, no, not giving up. Just know that there's no forcing her to come back."

I stuck my chin out. "If she means to leave us, I want to hear that from her."

Uncle George squeezed my arm. "We'll keep looking."

"Did my father know what my mother did for the ... business? Did Papaw know?"

"Lillian didn't want Alonzo to know, and we didn't tell Papaw but he might have figured it out. He talks to a lot of folks around these parts, sees the drivers when they go in for their supplies. He's never asked me about it."

I considered how much their business staying under the legal sights depended on many others tolerating the wrong. What if I had found out about my mother bootlegging before she left? How would she have defended what she was doing? Uncle

George rationalized breaking a law he saw as going against what people want, and all signs did point toward Prohibition coming to its end. Still, my mother had risked breaking the law. For what?

Uncle George called her a good businesswoman. At home she organized us in chores according to age and talents, methodical, always with a plan. She quoted the principles from Frederick Taylor's factory efficiency experiments, got us making dinner like an assembly line. Jane and I carried on without my mother because of that training. Now I had to wonder, did she teach us to be self-sufficient so she could have more time for what she was doing with Uncle George? And what about the time—when did she do all that business?

Tangled up in how she managed it, I could not release her from wrong. And how much wrong there was to deal with depended on adding in my father's transgression.

The wind stirred the trees outside, branches tapping on the tin roof of the porch.

"I've told you the truth, Dan, and I'm asking for your confidence. You've got too much on you now, I know that. But I'm asking for your confidence."

"I will keep quiet while you follow my father and look for my mother. That's as far as I can go right now."

"Fair enough."

It had gotten dark outside. Uncle George glanced at the clock. "You set things so no one is looking for you to be home tonight?"

I nodded.

"All right, let's make supper, then get some rest. You'll ride with the early truck out of here, before first light."

Upstairs later, Uncle George made up one of the bedsteads in the front bedroom for me. I caught sight of my torn shirt, knickers, and high socks in the mirror.

"Can you lend me a pair of overalls and a shirt?"

He chuckled. "Yes sir, it's time for those knickers to go, my boy. We can find you some overalls."

Just before dawn he knocked on the door and left me a pair of farm pants and a work shirt. I stuffed my old shirt and knickers into the trash barrel outside.

Uncle George saw me off with a tin mug of coffee. I climbed into the passenger seat of the truck, not thinking about what might be in the back. As we drove, the sun streaking weak light revealed vegetable crates packed tight in the truck bed. Was it all produce back there, or was I riding in a truck hiding bootleg beer? If the truck got stopped, I'd be part of it, too.

Wanting to know the truth about my parents required both evasion and straight-up lying. I may not have gotten myself into this but getting out of the mire of the situation seemed less possible. I felt a sick submission to whatever might happen.

The plug in the driver's cheek moved up and down. A different man than the one who brought me to the farm, but like the first one, driving in silence punctuated by tobacco spitting. Maybe that's how George picked these men—ones who don't talk much will not give away the details of what they're doing. Quiet men driving regular-looking farm trucks would have an easier time blending in as they did the business. They took a lot of risks making it look normal. What would make a man agree to run bootleg beer?

What kind of man did that? The driver looked ordinary, with the familiar rugged face seen on most men in mining country. But he was his own man, wasn't he? He must have intentions for himself, things he wanted, maybe a family. How did a man make the choice to do something wrong, something illegal? How was it figured out in Uncle George's mind to even ask them to do it, and then when presented with the job, for them to accept?

"Mister, do you know my father?"

"Yep, seen him out on the road with the crews."

"Does he ... get some of your ... delivery?"

"Nah, he's a boss. Only the crews in the camps come after what we got. The bosses ain't staying with them, and it's done all quiet."

"Where do the bosses stay?"

"You don't know where your daddy stays? They got regular rooming houses set up for the bosses, depending on which section the crew is workin'."

This was news to me, and another reminder that I was short of details about my father's habits.

"You think the bosses know what the crews are getting in your deliveries?"

"Oh, they know the men get beer, all right, but as long as there's no trouble, if the crews stay settled in the camps, everyone shows up every mornin' and it's all quiet, they let it be. They got to keep the men happy out there for weeks at a time. We help with that." He spat a big part of his wad out his window.

Did my father pretend he didn't know about the illegal beer, and the men who worked for him repaid the favor by saying nothing about what he was doing? Men worked it out so everyone could have their wrong if no one spoke about it.

And not just the men. My mother had secrets, too. It was worse knowing that my parents were each doing wrong before their wrongs backed up against each other when my mother left.

CHAPTER 6

Trudging to the top of the hill on River Avenue, I stopped at my grandparents' gate but saw no movement through their front window. Their house seemed too quiet even for a Sunday morning. I pictured them in a trance, laying in their bed, waiting for their daughter to waken them. Just as well not to see them; if I faced them while holding what I had learned from Uncle George about my mother, it would be impossible to say nothing. Moving on, I wished for the comfort of times when I loped onto the porch and opened the door to the smells of Grandma's cooking mixed with the aroma of Papaw's pipe.

I suspected Uncle George underestimated Papaw's ear to the town grapevine. Papaw was one of the old-timers, and they specialized in passing the gossip. In the post office it flowed as steady and murky as the river. I had overheard a lot of stories about townsfolk while sorting the bundles and selling postage for letters and parcels. Copying Mr. Kegg's diplomacy, I learned to block some out, not repeat the rest. If the grapevine was a marker, within a short time most people knew most of what was going on.

Papaw likely knew about the beer running, and he probably had figured out my mother's part in it. He would have told Grandma. Papaw and Grandma were like two sides of the same coin, together so long. They would have kept the bootlegging that their adult children had gotten into to themselves, even if they disapproved.

I missed talking to my grandparents, especially Papaw. He had always been our anchor, the one we could go to whatever the question. Now two weeks without seeing them, not hearing their practical wisdom about every little thing that arose in our days, compounded the losses of Lonnie and my mother. Every day one of the girls or George asked to walk down the road to their house, complaining that it wasn't fair, pouting or crying when Hattie said no. Jane, cozy with her anger at my mother, didn't seem to mind their absence.

Addie had become a worry I wished I could talk to Grandma about. While my mother grieved for Lonnie, she made sporadic efforts to cuddle Addie and talk to her in a loving way, though she couldn't care for Addie like before. The first few days after my mother left, Addie fussed, but we distracted her with Grandma's help. Since we lost Grandma too, it was harder to soothe her. She cried for her mama. Her budding vocabulary had collapsed to "*No!*" Most of the food put in front of her ended up on the floor. She squeezed Hattie's cheek and dug in her nails, drawing blood.

If she exhausted herself with defiance, she would sleep for a few hours.

When Addie awoke crying in the night Jane was the one to get up, because the sight of Hattie leaning over to pick her up made her scream more. Her fussing woke the rest of us, and until she settled down we didn't get back to sleep. Disrupted rest made for grumpier mornings and tiredness at school.

Before Lonnie died, we had been our own universe, a family solar system of brothers, sisters, parents, and grandparents, rotating around each other, sharing the same light and air. Would my mother and father have broken away from our family if Lonnie hadn't died? If the photos told a true story, my father had pulled away before that. Perhaps Lonnie's death was not when our troubles began, just the start of my paying attention. Lonnie's death was what our history teacher called a turning point, where things changed into before and after. I churned somewhere between, thrust into my parents' secrets, no sense of where they led.

As I reached the front porch of my house the sounds from inside carried through the glass. The scene in the front room when I opened the door: Hattie struggling to get Annie to stop smashing a doll against Ruthie's arm, who screamed in pain and retaliated by pulling Annie's hair; Jane holding a crying Addie and raising her voice over the din, yelling at them to stop; and a thumping sound that turned out to be George on the back porch throwing a ball as hard as he could against the house. Hattie gave up and stood over my two sisters as they continued to struggle, hands on her hips, moaning, "Lord, what am I to do with these children?"

I strode across the room and separated my sisters, holding them apart. "Stop this *now*."

I was not much taller than they were at that point, as all the girls in our family grew tall like my father and George and I tended to the small side, after our mother. My tone did the work.

"I want the two of you to go upstairs, and you come back down together when you are ready to act like sisters again. Go."

Ruthie and Annie exchanged glares and inched past me to the stairs. Jane started to speak to them, but I raised a hand to quiet her. "Leave them to it."

"Well, you have the magic touch." Jane's sarcasm was thick. "I guess that's all we need around here, you tell people to stop, and things calm down. Isn't that nice, Aunt Hattie, that Dan has such power?"

Hattie looked from Jane to me and shook her head. "If you two start up, I cannot cope, I tell you that for certain. The children arguing and fussing is more than I can take as it is. You two work yourselves out." She plied the squealing Addie from Jane's arms. "Come with me, Addie dear, let's get you some milk."

Jane and I faced each other. The rupture in our usual easy way felt raw. She lashed out at me again, now in a whisper.

"I saw Mr. Kegg last evening, strolling with his daughter. He didn't seem to know anything about you waiting for mail in Uniontown."

That was surprising, but I didn't feel pushed by the force in her manner. She expected me to bend to it. I held her gaze without answering. She gave in first.

"Well, where were you last night?"

"I'm not saying."

"I can tell Hattie, and I can tell Dad."

"I guess you can."

"What are you up to?"

"Look, Jane, we're all at loose ends. I'm trying to figure out what we're going to do."

"You want Mama to come back, and you think that will make it right again. Well, I don't want her back." Defiant Jane stood with arms crossed. "I don't know what you think you can do. It's not up to you."

"What about taking care of each other? What about George and the girls? They need us."

"They need their mother."

"For now, we're who they have."

"You go ahead, then, Dan, do what you want. Dad might have something to say about it."

We could have gone on arguing, something we seemed to have gotten practiced at in no time. Jane was the last person I wanted to be at odds with. Seeing her rigid back and clenched hands, I tried to smooth things out.

"How can I help around here right now?"

"Go make George stop that noise, get him to eat something.

I'll see about the girls." She threw her arms open. "I don't want to argue with you. But Mama did this to us." Jane stomped up the stairs.

After George and I ate some breakfast, I walked with him over to the ball field, where a group of the boys were taking batting practice, gearing up for the start of the season. Some stubborn patches of snow lingered here and there, but the earth was drying out and the April green was taking on its spring brightness. We never had much in the way of full sun, even in the height of summer, because of the coke clouds, but with the breeze it was pleasant to be out in the air.

The mining company's long history of a men's baseball team in every neighborhood meant the team rivalries in the coke patch went back two generations. The lore and positions were handed down as men coached their sons and grandsons to keep the rosters filled. George and his friends played in the boys' games at the field behind the school, where kids used coal dust to scratch the baselines into the hard-packed earth. My father's hitting reputation as a young man provided George with standing; my father could still hit to make the boys hang on the fence to watch.

With the boys warmed up to practice swinging, I took a position in the outfield to retrieve their balls and throw them back. George laughed with his friends, got some good hits, and after the practice he and I continued to play catch. Tossing the ball pulled us into an instinctive rhythm, let us coast for a time on the pleasure of it.

Roy's oldest son, Junior, and his cousin wandered over and the four of us played round-robin. After that we changed to me hitting grounders to the three of them, making the boys practice running to meet the ball as it skipped toward them and hop it into the mitt. George was getting much better than the year before, when he often waited in the outfield for the ball to bounce close, losing seconds by dropping to scoop it into his glove and throw it in. Aiming the balls to challenge the boys made me think about being ready for what comes. You couldn't stand still and let it drop on you. Running toward it gave you the best chance.

After a good hour, I waved them toward home plate. Flushed with the effort, the boys clapped each other on the back with their mitts and appreciated each other's catches. I was lighthearted for the first time in weeks. Junior thanked me for the workout.

"Is your pa around?" I asked him.

"Nah, he's on the road somewhere, dunno exactly. He's gone so I have to do stuff in the store today."

I didn't know enough about Roy's habits to judge if his being on the road on a Sunday was regular, or if it had something to do with looking for my mother. I let it go, judging there was no need to get Junior involved, and not wanting to upset George. We started back across the field for home just as the church bells in town rang for the noon services.

Reaching the back alley behind our house, my relaxed mood faded. Hattie stood on the back porch bellowing at Ruthie and

Annie in the yard. They had resumed their fight, now slinging mud at each other from the big puddle left by snow melting into the dirt.

"She started it," Ruthie screamed and took a handful of the mushy dirt and smeared it across Annie's back. Annie, who had left herself open to the attack by facing Hattie, whirled around and tackled Ruthie, who tumbled into the puddle. The girls fighting like this had never happened before my mother left. Disagreements between them had been short-lived and resolved with my mother mediating an acceptable solution. The most heated moments might require separation into different rooms until tempers cooled down. None of us went after a brother or sister, or anyone, physically.

George and I looked at each other, reading mutual reluctance to get into the middle of their mess. I walked closer to the puddle and George followed just to the perimeter, where it would be possible to jump back in a hurry if mud came our way.

"What is going on here, you two? Why are you doing this?"

My sisters sat in the puddle, crying. Extending a hand to Annie, I got her up, then pulled Ruthie out. Shivering, dripping mud and tears, not ready to make up, one shoved the other. Hattie came down from the porch and yanked open the cellar door.

"Over here, both of you. Down to the cellar to wash off. No going in the house like that." She threw up her hands to me.

I waved them toward the cellar. "When you get cleaned up, we have to work out what is going wrong with the two of you."

George and I stomped the dirt off our boots and took them off on the back porch. Hungry, we rummaged in the bin for the bread Hattie had made that morning, smeared it with butter and sat down with the milk. The front door opened and closed, and a moment later my father walked into the kitchen, hat off, wearing a work jacket and a smile for us.

"Boys, how are you today? Where is everyone?"

"Hattie is helping the girls wash mud off their clothes. Jane and Addie are upstairs."

"When they finish, I want to work in the darkroom." He sat at the table and peered over his glasses at George. "What do you have to say for yourself today, son?" His tone was milder than it often was, but for George, the words were enough to flummox him.

I got in the way of it like a cut-off man relaying the ball from the outfield. "George, tell Dad about our practice today."

That started George off on a better foot as his excitement about ball playing was an easy pickup for my father. While they discussed grounders and proper mitt adjustment, the girls and Hattie came up from the cellar.

My father's mood extended to the girls, whom he opened his arms to, and they nestled in his embrace, one on each side, still eying each other warily. Hattie offered him eggs, and he took coffee, saying he had eaten earlier. She did not ask where he had been for the last few days, as my mother would have. I hesitated to ask, supposing he would suspect the question from me. Addie came toddling in ahead of Jane. He scooped Addie up and set her on his knee, reached to pat Jane's arm in greeting.

Someone looking in the window during those few moments around the table might have thought we were a normal family having a pleasant Sunday together. My father was not home enough to understand how much we were hurting, or he blinded himself to it. Hattie edited her reports to him, omitting accounts of the fighting and crying to spare him getting involved. But that kept him more distant from our distress. And if he was spending time with another family, he was choosing to ignore us. I felt an urge to provoke him, stop the charade of hugs and concern. It was like edging close to the mud fight out in the yard, judging how near I could get and still be able to move out of the way of the splatter.

Setting Addie down, he was finished with us. "I will be down in the darkroom making some pictures. Hattie, I'm here for dinner this afternoon, and in the morning, I'm going back out with the surveyors."

She nodded from where she stood at the stove. "I hope you are planning it so's the men can get home for Easter."

"The men will get back by Saturday, most likely." He pulled the chain that lit the bulb over the top of the cellar stairs and started down.

I followed him.

At the bottom of the stairs he pulled another chain to light his way to the corner darkroom. I went to the opposite side and edged into the alcove where we kept canned goods and the jars of fruits and vegetables from the farm that Grandma had put up for eating over the winter. Looking over what remained, I made my voice neutral.

"We are low on potatoes and other staples Hattie will need. I want to get Roy and the truck to bring more in. Will you leave money in the pantry today?"

Pulling open the curtain that closed off the darkroom, he grunted. "Yes, every time I'm here, I leave money. Hattie seems to spend it all, too. She's not as thrifty as ..."

I saw my opening. "As Mama is?"

He turned and eyed me. "Your mother managed the house money well enough, yes." His tone was guarded.

I took the next step.

"You haven't been down here since the day of the fire."

My father turned back to the workbench and cast his eyes over the chemicals and trays. He moved to pick up the brick on top of the photos I had looked through, his face in the shadow.

"When we came back the bottles were closed up, remember? I'm sure Mama is the one who closed them that day." My father's arm froze in motion. "Because George told me later that he ran out of the house to see the fire instead of coming down here when you told him to. I figure Mama came back to the house and was down here, because no one else was."

A slow turn around to face me. "Is that how you figure it?"

I met his eyes. "It had to be her. If she came down here to

clean her boots and saw the curtain open, I bet she tried to tidy things up for you. Not the wet photos, she would have known not to take those down."

"No, not the wet photos—they still hung there when I got back." He grasped the curtain, ready to pull it across the corner, close himself off from me. Stepping forward, I stood before him. He tugged at the curtain, dismissing me.

"Turn off the lights down here before you go up."

I put my hand on the curtain below his. He stopped, brow furrowed, half-puzzled and half-stubborn, like he was about to wrestle the curtain from my hand.

"I am worried about the children. You're not here. It's been three weeks. Aunt Hattie does her best, but Addie and the girls need Grandma and Papaw—we all do. We lost Mama and then you took them away from us, and it's too much. I intend to take the girls and George to see them, and I think Addie should stay with them for a while."

I blew the air from my lungs with the last sentence, letting go of the frustration and the adrenaline that pushed those words from my mouth. Confronting my father tasted bitter.

"Well, now, Dan, standing up for yourself, are you?" My father spoke with that same sarcastic undertone Jane used for her pinpricks. "Not your mama's boy?"

I felt the sting of his taunt, pushed on. "Hattie doesn't tell you how much upset there is while you're away. The fighting, the crying that goes on. She tries, but she doesn't know us like

Grandma and Papaw do. They can calm the girls, help us get through this."

His face reddened. "They helped your mother to leave. They are not to come into this house."

"I won't say 'Yes, sir' to that. I think you know why Mama left. And it had nothing to do with Grandma and Papaw."

Pressuring him with implication, I flicked my eyes toward the photos, held back blurting out I had seen them, because if he made an excuse for them, what next?

He wrenched the curtain from my grasp. "I have a position in this town. I got us out of the hard life, into our own house, and my children will not work in the mines. I refuse to let what she's done ruin what I've built, the respect I have." He straightened up to full height, stared me in the eye, and spat out, "You will not use that tone with me again. Do we understand each other?" He dragged the curtain closed between us.

Leaving the lights on, I stomped up the cellar steps. He had admitted nothing, but he had not denied that he knew why my mother left.

Standing up to him, I proved something to myself. I may have become a liar, but I had left behind the meek boy who kept quiet and watched from the sidelines. Maybe I could recover from lying but I would not turn back to silence.

I wondered what my mother would have thought of my newfound boldness. She was bold enough herself; perhaps she would have encouraged that part of me, pushed me to get over the shyness. It crushed me to think she might never know me as a man, that she had walked off carrying a suspended memory of the boy I'd been. Jane's point about my mother's fault sunk in— she *had* turned our lives in a direction we could not reverse.

Finding the truth about my father might tell me why but would not change the consequences of what my mother—Lillian—did. Time would pass, the six of us would stumble forward, and what happened in our family would cling to us like encroaching vines encircling and squeezing the bark of saplings in a stand of trees, strangling their limbs.

CHAPTER 7

Hattie wanted to go home for a day. The constant care of the six of us and our house wearied her. She needed to check if her son, our cousin Oscar, had kept up her house as she wished. Reviving her large vegetable garden after the hard winter required her instructing him about the planting. Hattie trusted that Jane and I could keep the peace until she returned the next evening, and she promised to bring a ham for Easter dinner. Oscar picked her up early on the morning of Good Friday.

School closed for the day. The Catholics were obligated to spend hours in church reliving the agony of Christ. Protestants made their observances by closing their stores for the afternoon.

Sitting together for breakfast, a rare tranquility prevailed around the table. Just the six of us keeping each other company, the pressure of our situation floating somewhere above, letting us eat in peace. No need to pretend things were like they used to be. A quiet acceptance of Lonnie not being there. No questions about our mother. The heaviness on me relieved in sharing the unspoken understanding with my brother and sisters. Somehow we had an easier time with the absences when there was no call for explaining ourselves to adults. Left to ourselves that morning, leveled off in shared grief that was manageable, able to feel it without breaking, let me believe we could go on.

With both Hattie and my father not due back until the next day, it was the perfect opportunity to take my brother and sisters to see Grandma and Papaw. I didn't announce where we would go, to hold off arguing with Jane.

"When we finish, George, Ruthie, Annie, get dressed and ready to go out with me for a walk." For once, none of them complained, nods all around.

Jane eyed me with curiosity but avoided a question. "Addie could do with a ride in the buggy."

"I'll bring it round to the porch if you dress her."

Jane said no more, and I wondered if she would walk with us.

A weak sun competed with a brisk wind, keeping the temperature chilly. When I wheeled the buggy from the back porch to the front steps Jane led Addie out, ready in her woolen leggings and coat, hat pulled over her ears and tied under her chin. Addie protested the itchy feel of the strings and I retied them looser, persuading her to keep the hat on. We still feared any of us catching cold.

When George and the girls joined us, I turned the buggy toward the road, glancing over my shoulder to see if Jane would come along. Waving us off, she stepped back into the house, continuing to observe from the front window as we turned out of the gate. I caught on that she knew where I intended to go and appreciated her silent acquiescence to my plan.

The others kept pace with me pushing Addie's buggy. Almost anywhere in town we wanted to go meant walking past Grandma and Papaw's, and their eyes longed for it as we neared. I stopped and unlatched their gate. George and my two sisters halted, looking as if they were about to be pushed off a bridge.

"Come on, we're going in, it's okay," I urged, and pushed through with the buggy. They hung back.

Ruthie whimpered, "I want to go but we'll get in trouble. I'm scared."

Annie joined in. "Does Dad know you're taking us here? Because he's still mad at Grandma and he won't like this."

George pushed past me to hold the gate. "He's not gonna know about it."

Just like that we were conspirators. It astounded me how easy we inferred agreement to not tell. Annie and Ruthie walked through to follow the buggy. By this time Papaw was at the door, and if we surprised him, he didn't hesitate to get us inside. I sensed his willingness to override my father's decree but explained anyway.

"I told Dad I would bring them here."

He tilted his head into a question about that, then got caught up in the hugging and kissing that Grandma, running in from the kitchen, had taken up with each child. Soon coats were off and we assembled around the table near the warm stove,

Grandma doling out cups of hot chocolate, mostly milk for Addie. The talk flowed fast, with everyone speaking over and around the others, our usual way of talking with Grandma and Papaw. For us, the skill of taking part in multiple conversations at the same time was like riding a bike—once you got the hang of it, it came naturally. Our familiar rhythm settled in.

After a time, Papaw asked me to step out onto the porch with him. We put on our jackets and he grabbed his pipe. Grandma exchanged glances with him as she continued listening to George's description of his last ball practice. When we got outside, Papaw lit the pipe and smiled at me through the haze of the bowl's smoke.

"Your Grandma hasn't slept since the last time we saw you children. This visit is just what she needed."

"We needed it, too. It's been so hard for the girls, and Addie isn't sleeping well. No one is." I wanted to tell him all our troubles but held back to hear what he had to say.

"How will you explain this to your father?"

"I don't know that I will. I don't want to."

Papaw gave me a steady look as he puffed a few times on the pipe. He held the porch rail and eased himself down to sit on the top step of the stoop. I plopped down next to him.

"Dan, I know you were out at the farm and George told you about your mother."

"I had to ask him for help. I wish I didn't keep quiet when he gave me the letter. He didn't want you to know."

"I've had words with him on that, the worry it caused your Grandma, the time wasted. He's not proud of what he did, but it's done now."

"Did you know about the bootlegging before ... before Mama left?"

He sucked on the pipe stem and blew out the smoke. "I figured what they were up to, yes, but not at the beginning. Word moved underground and when it reached my ear, I put two and two together. Seems like I should have known sooner. But it's not like they would do any different by me saying so. Your Uncle George and your mother always went their own ways."

"But wasn't it dangerous for Mama? And still now, for Uncle George?"

"Yes and no. Enough people want what he's selling that it's easier to just let it be, as long as nothing comes out in public. Besides, the Prohibition will be over soon, and the state will want some of that money George is making. So they're content to let it run its course."

I got to the bigger question.

"Did Uncle George tell you why I went to the farm? What the woman who works for him told me about my father?"

Papaw turned to face me. "Yes, son, he did, and that was a heck of a thing to hear. And from a stranger."

"I saw their pictures in the darkroom."

Papaw kept his eyes on me, the pipe smoke moving around our heads.

"He left those pictures drying on the day of the fire. Mama could have seen them—I think she *did* see them. Somebody was down there to close up the bottles. He told George to do it when we ran out. But George told me he didn't go down—he ran out, too. Mama saw that other lady's picture, and the boy, and her baby."

Papaw sighed. "A hell of a thing."

"I need to know for sure. Uncle George said he could get someone to follow Dad, find out the truth."

Papaw took the pipe from his mouth. "He followed Alonzo himself."

I held my breath, but I knew what was coming. "Tell me."

Papaw didn't sugarcoat it. "Your father stays with a woman who runs a boarding house, a widow. She has two children, a baby, and a boy about Addie's age, maybe a bit older." He put his arm around my shoulders. "Alonzo is the baby's father. Maybe the older one, too."

Braced against Papaw, our faces so close, I saw the glimmer of tears in his eyes. Dribbles of mine fell on my sleeve. He pressed his shoulder tighter to mine, and we sat like that for a moment. My mouth was dry when I forced out words.

"How do you know for sure?"

"George sweet-talked one of the kitchen maids at the boarding house into conversation when he was making a delivery. She didn't know George had any connection to Alonzo, or even Alonzo's right name, called him the gas man. The girl said the gas man stays with the missus, that he was there when the baby came, waiting on the midwife."

"Did Uncle George see him there? How can you be sure it was my father she was talking about?"

"He made the delivery early, at first light. The gas company car was parked behind the house. George swung back an hour later to watch, and sure enough, your father came out of the house and got into that car."

"He might be just staying there, right? That doesn't prove anything."

"I know you don't want it to be true. But put what George saw with what the maid told him, and it adds up. I believe it."

"He has no right." I pulled away from Papaw and stood up. "He has no right to do this. What kind of man does this to his family? *We're* his family." My heart was fluttering in my chest like the hummingbirds that sipped at Grandma's summer flowers. "What are we going to do?"

He patted the step. "Take a seat, son. You're fixing to burst."

I dropped and clawed my head with my hands. Scenes from Lonnie's last days flashing through my brain again, remembering my mother haggard, keeping the vigil at his bedside, Jane and I pleading with my father on the telephone to come home, his arrival when the tiny coffin was carried down the stairs.

His cruelty made me sick. Dry heaves wracked me, and Papaw rubbed my neck through the gagging, waiting it out. When I could sit up, I moaned.

"Papaw, what are we going to do? How can we live with this?"

Papaw chewed on the pipe. "I don't know, son. I don't know that we can. A river's been crossed." That was one of Papaw's sayings, when things happened there was no going back from. "I wish I knew what your mother intended. That I can't figure."

"What does Grandma think?"

"Your Grandma thinks we can find Lillian, get her back here and take care of her, keep her away from Alonzo."

"You think that's what Mama wants?"

"I don't know what your mother wants. She's sick with the grief, got drowned in it, and before Lonnie passed she had her spells. You know the hard time she had after Addie came. And before that."

He was right about my mother's spells, but this was the first time we had spoken directly about them. Our practice of not telling was more developed than I realized, worn into us by living with her, getting through the bad days. The long recovery after Lonnie's birth, her preoccupation since Addie's, were recent chapters of her longer story. Grandma and Papaw helped smooth out the edges without discussing why my mother spent some days in bed in the dark, not letting any of us open the door. Other days she was gone from the house when we came home for the lunch hour, no food ready, and we tramped over to Grandma's, who fed us and sent us back to school with no mention of where my mother had got to. Evenings, she pushed more of the cooking over to me, the old enjoyment of working together on recipes gone, meals set before her barely eaten.

Early when she was pregnant with Addie, my mother sobbed telling us she was carrying another baby. In the first months after Addie's birth, it didn't matter to her one way or the other if we ate, went to school, wore clean clothes. Grandma and Papaw were the legs under our table, always there to fill in where my mother went limp. We became used to her not doing much, grateful if she sat at the table with us, heard us talking about our days, smiled a little.

We learned to lean on each other, stick together. Jane and I took on more responsibilities for daily rituals, taking care of Lonnie and Addie, both so small and trusting. I felt strong when I could fix things for those two little ones, them gazing up at me when I tied a shoe or buttoned a blouse or blew on hot soup to cool it.

Sitting on the stoop with Papaw, I imagined my mother walking alone on the rutted footpaths, searching outside for comfort that eluded her. Most days the coke smog blurred the sky into a low-hanging grey-black smudge. At the cemetery, there was some respite under the trees interspersed among the graves. She walked to the cemetery, sat among the dead. Was she looking for strength to live, or envying those who no longer struggled?

"Papaw, do you think Mama knew about the other woman before she saw the pictures?"

"Can't say."

"But that woman must know about us, right? How can she not know he's married and has children?"

"We didn't know about her, she might not know about you—it's another county, people don't get over this way. Just the deliveries going back and forth is how word travels. But maybe she knows. He's telling her something."

"He's a liar."

"Your pa is a lot of things. He's another one always gone his own way. Don't know how he's done this."

"He lies to everyone."

"It's a hell of a thing."

"I want to tell him I know."

Papaw put the pipe down. "How's that going to help you children? How will that make things better? Alonzo's temper is already up, he's forced us away from you, and there's enough upset in both houses to keep us from ever sleeping again." He slapped the pipe bowl against the side of the step to dump the ash. "Your uncle George will find Lillian and get her back here, and she'll leave Alonzo, take you children with her. We'll help her."

"That's what Dad thinks you've already done."

"We will do it. Soon as George finds her, we'll get you children, too." He grabbed the porch rail and hoisted himself upright. "We best get inside and see what they're up to." Papaw pulled open the screen door and held it for me.

Inside, Grandma held a sobbing Ruthie wrapped under one

arm. Grandma buried her face in Ruthie's hair. George and Annie looked close to tears, too, and Addie mashed crumbled cookies.

"It's just too much, Pa, it's just too much."

Brushing off the cookies, I took Addie from her seat and gestured to George. He got up and nudged Annie.

"We best go, we need to get back." Squeezing Ruthie's arm, my voice was gentle. "C'mon, get the coats on."

Hugging and kissing, with Grandma whispering in each of our ears, got us out to the porch, where Papaw stood with the buggy. Grandma whispered in mine, "Bring them back when you can."

Nodding on her shoulder, I said, "Jane won't come."

Grandma pulled back and patted my arm. "Stay close to Jane. She needs you."

While he tucked a blanket over Addie, Papaw gave me his last bit of advice. "Keep things running until George gets your mama back here."

My upset mixed with relief hearing Papaw had a plan to help us. Pushing the buggy forward, I waved, he winked, and we trudged through the gate and turned toward our house. George marched next to me, Annie and Ruthie linked arms and stumbled behind us. The short walk home was enough to calm us. It went without saying that we would not talk with Jane about the visit.

Jane had just finished scrubbing the kitchen floor and would not let us in the back door, so we traipsed back around the house to the front porch and together lifted the buggy up the steps. Addie pushed a leg over to climb out and George helped her down. The wind had moderated and the air felt warm enough to stay outside. George and I sat on the steps to watch the girls play a singing game with Addie. They clapped and stomped out rhymes that Addie didn't understand but she loved the part where everyone jumped.

A truck belonging to Feeke's store rolled down the road and stopped in front of Roy and Marion's house. If that was Roy, I was ready to jump up and get a word with him, but it was his older brother who got out of the driver's side and made his way onto their porch.

Jane opened our front door. "You can come in but no going in the kitchen yet. Leave those boots out here."

She was becoming as fussy as Aunt Hattie, never missing a chance to let me know how many chores she did, as if we had a scorecard and I was way behind. I brought Addie up to the porch and took off her boots, then mine, when we heard a commotion next door. Glass breaking, a woman screaming.

Junior ran out the front of Roy's house toward the truck. He kicked the metal door with his heavy boot and fell back. Getting up, he spotted us staring. He grabbed handfuls of gravel from the ground and flung them at us.

"Your mama's a whoring bitch," he screamed.

CHAPTER 8

At midnight, the house was quiet. Somehow the world was still turning, the clock still ticking, though a wrecking ball had smashed through what was left of our lives. Resting my head on the kitchen table, alert for crying from the bedrooms above, I prayed my brother and sisters would sleep. The illusions about getting my mother back that toyed with me during the walk back from our visit with Grandma and Papaw had turned into a sick joke, obliterated by the news Roy's brother brought that afternoon.

When Roy Junior pelted us with stones, Jane and I shoved Addie and the girls inside our front door. Instinctively, George lobbed stones back, yelling, "Shut your mouth!" It was as if the boys were acting out one of the pretend war games they had often played from yard to yard, but both were crying and they meant the stones to wound. Junior's pitching arm was stronger, with better aim, his stones landing hard, mostly missing George's head but intending harm to arms and legs. I lunged for

George and dragged him to the porch, crawled us to the door to get inside.

"Why is he saying that?" George sobbed. "Why is he saying that?"

Jane huddled the girls and all of us crouched at the side window, lifting our faces above the sill to watch what was happening next door. Stones continued to thump our porch. Exchanging glances with Jane, knowing it was no good to tell George and the girls to ignore the uproar, I tried reassuring. "Roy's brother is inside with Marion if she needs help."

The Feeke's front door opened, and Marion's two little girls stumbled onto the porch as though someone had pushed them, coats thrown out after them. The door slammed shut. Junior stopped throwing stones and went to them, helping his crying sisters get their coats on. Annie and Ruthie sympathized. "Ruby and Violet are crying! What is wrong over there?" On any other day, these were their friends and playmates. George, one cheek red-marked from a stone strike, eyes on Junior, knelt rigid with clenched fists.

"When things calm down, we can find out what happened. No fighting," I warned, tapping George on the shoulder.

George glowered. "You heard what Junior said."

I had no ready reply.

Marion's screaming went on. Her children slumped together on their front steps. Roy's brother opened a window and called out to Junior. We cracked open our window to hear the uncle say

Marion was so agitated he had called the doctor, who was at church for the Good Friday services. We heard that he had called the store to get a boy to run to the church; Junior should keep watch for the doctor's arrival.

Soon, another truck from the store pulled up and the doctor clambered out. Roy's brother gestured from the doorway for the doctor to hurry in. A moment later, the uncle came out and hustled Marion's girls into the truck bed, gave the driver instructions, and took Junior's arm. We could tell Junior argued with his uncle about leaving his mother, but the crying sisters holding their arms out for him persuaded him to get into the truck.

When the truck pulled away, I maneuvered my brother and sisters away from the window. "Hattie left a list of preparations for Easter and we need to get busy."

George persisted. "I want to know what Junior meant about Mama!"

"Mr. Feeke and Marion have to settle their own business."

Jane led the girls toward the kitchen for chores. George, not buying what I said, shrugged me off, stomped to the kitchen. We both knew Junior must have had heard something disturbing from his uncle. I wanted to find out what it was and kept an eye on Marion's house from our window. When Roy's brother stepped onto their porch to light a smoke, I hurried outside.

"Mr. Feeke, is everything all right?"

His shoulders sank when he looked toward the voice. He knew me from the post office and visits to Roy and Marion's house. Dragging on the cigarette, he made his way to the narrow alley between the houses. I met him on the muddy gravel.

Roy's oldest brother headed their extended family and the businesses. He was tall and lean like Roy but he carried himself upright and serious, looking like someone accustomed to people asking him what to do. Now, sweat broke across his forehead and his hand trembled when raising the cigarette to his lips. Mr. Feeke blew out the smoke and steadied his eyes on me.

"Your father is not home, is he?"

"No, we expect him tomorrow."

He shook his head and waved a hand at me. "Then I might as well tell you now. You have a right to know before it gets all over town. Which it will, very shortly. If it hasn't already." He stood straighter. "Brace yourself, son."

He flicked the butt and crushed it underfoot. "Marion is distraught because I told her that Roy is never coming home. He found your mother. They're together, and they are not coming back."

All the ground-level air circulating around us sucked through my windpipe in one huge vacuum rush, followed by the darker, murky smog that hovered above it, choking me. Mr. Feeke put his hands on my shoulders, bent me over at the waist.

"Take it easy, son. Breathe slow, breathe slow."

My brain beat out words like timpani: Roy left his wife and children. Mama left us. She left us and she meant to stay away. With Roy.

I pushed some of the muck out in a big blow to open my throat. Sweat dripped from my neck and face.

"How do you know?"

A tapping sound from inside Marion's window turned Mr. Feeke toward the doctor gesturing for him to come back inside. Mr. Feeke got me upright, walked me over to Marion's porch, and sat me on the step.

"Stay here, breathe easy. I will be back in a few minutes."

I clung to the side of the step and tried to stop my panic. For three weeks I had hoped for my mother to return, had faked calm and reassurance for my brother and sisters, had kept my fears back, pushed away nagging worries as the evidence of both my parents' troubles and secrets piled up. I saw that other Dan and his siblings who had trotted down the hill in the sun an hour ago, and imagined them crushed beneath an oncoming truck, never seeing it coming. Our bodies splayed across the road, our blood trickling around us, the truck having sped on, no care what happened to us. I shook my head to clear it but the image stayed in my peripheral vision.

Mouth full of dust, I had no spit. Mr. Feeke returned to the step, handed me a cup of water. Sitting, he took out another cigarette, then offered me one, too. Shaking it away, I tried sipping the water. He took a few puffs and leaned forward on his knees, holding his head in one hand, the burning wrap of tobacco in the other.

"The doctor gave Marion a sedative, and she's sleeping. He'll be out in a minute."

My breathing slowed, evened out. We sat like that.

Glancing over at my house, I saw Jane looking out our side window. Our eyes caught, but I gave her no sign. The doctor came out and Mr. Feeke stood to give him room to step off the porch.

"Someone should stay with Marion for the next few days. The pills I left in the kitchen will keep her calm but she must be watched." Scanning my face, the doctor nodded at our house. "Have more of that water, son. If you need me, call."

"I don't know what we need," I stammered. "I don't know how this happened."

Had he seen this coming, during the hours in Lonny's sickroom, hearing my mother's woes? I had no strength to ask. After a squeeze of my shoulder, he pushed his hat on his head and hurried up the road.

Mr. Feeke slumped back down next to me on the step. Sweat oozed on my face and neck, the clammy trickles tracing down my back. When the wind hit my shirt, I shuddered, expected to feel cold forever. Crunching his empty cigarette box, Mr. Feeke stood.

"I have to watch over Marion until her sister gets here. She's sleeping well enough that we can sit in the truck."

I was grateful he did not suggest stepping into Marion's house; I was sure I would never go inside that house again. Getting a grip on the railing, I pulled myself up and after a few steps toward the truck my legs were stronger under me.

When we settled into the front seats, Mr. Feeke spoke.

"I guess I know how this happened, though I can't say I knew it would happen. No, sir, I did not know it would happen."

I had little experience talking with Mr. Feeke outside the post office protocol of "Good morning, would you like your mail?" Roy deferred to him, and I thought it best to do that.

"You probably don't know much about your mama and Roy from way back, and I daresay your father doesn't know all about it. Seemed it was all in the past. Thought Roy put it to rest, after Lillian married Alonzo, Roy got with Marion, time went on, they had their lives, children. Never really ended for him, I guess we see that now. He hid it well. I didn't even think much of it when he moved next door to your house. Roy seemed so devoted to Marion. Now I have to wonder, was he pining all these years?"

I kept my gaze on him, trying to take in the meaning. Mr. Feeke grasped the steering wheel, flexing his fingers, brow tight in thought.

"When your mama's family moved into town from the farm, she met Roy on her first day at the school. None of the girls would talk to her at first, and Roy took her under his wing. He was eleven years old and smitten—your mama was the first girl to hit him like that. Hell, everybody remembers that first girl, don't they? The one who makes you feel all different, the one who starts you knowing what it's going to be like with women." He glanced over at me, as if to say, *You know the feeling, right?*

"Of course, he had no understanding of that. He just knew

he wanted to be around Lillian. We older boys could see the puppy love, teased him all the time. When he got mad, we knew it hit the mark." He kind of smiled at the memory, glancing over at me. "She returned the feeling, in her way. She spent time with him. They played ball together. Not many girls played but Lillian was always with the boys, was more than able to hold her own. Roy showed her the secret places he liked to go and hide out, forts he built in the woods. Had more woods around here then."

It was like listening to the minister during Lonnie's burial trying to explain the pain as part of God's plan but knowing at the end of the speech you would walk away carrying it. Mr. Feeke went on about how it took Roy a long while to get over Mama marrying my father, and then he met Marion, and he seemed happy.

What was the definition of happy, for Roy, for my mother? What was the happy part of their lives? Mr. Feeke was asking me to picture them when they were my age. When Lillian chose Alonzo, Roy became unhappy. When did Lillian become un-happy, and her unhappy and Roy's met back up again, and they somehow thought leaving all of us would make them happy? How could she decide to grab happy back for herself and not care about us?

Mr. Feeke had stopped talking, waiting for something from me. "I asked how old you are."

"Turned sixteen just after Lonnie passed."

"We put Roy to work full-time in the stores when he was sixteen, gave him a good life. The stores have done well with the household goods, and we've got hardware, harnesses, wagons, bicycles, tires, now we're selling automobiles. Did some tractor sales, but around here the farmers want trucks. Like your Uncle George—he needs a few trucks."

Mr. Feeke shifted in the seat but that last remark didn't seem to come with any special meaning. Probably he knew why George bought trucks and keeping quiet about it was good for his business. Roy's abrupt leaving would not be good for the Feeke business.

I had heard enough. I needed to get out of the truck, go into my house, talk to Jane. Get to Papaw and Grandma before anyone told them.

"Mr. Feeke, I need go. When my father finds out ..."

He waved his hand at me. "I'm calling Charlie at the office to get Alonzo on the phone with me. I should be the one to tell him. I spoke with Roy. You should not be saying this to your father—I will do it."

"Mr. Feeke, is there any way Roy will change his mind, that he'll come back, that *they* will come back?"

Roy's brother turned to meet my eyes. "Son, I just don't think so. Roy said when he found her, Lillian told him to go home, didn't want him to follow her. But he wouldn't leave, and they moved on together. They're heading to California."

"And even if they wanted to come back, the damage is done." He shook his head, gazing off in the distance. "They're not coming back. We've got the children to think about. Roy's leaving makes me responsible. I don't know when Marion's going to be all right. And you have your sisters and brother to think about, too. You're the oldest. It's going to fall on you, your father on the road so much of the time."

Our bloody bodies lying in the road flashed before me again.

"Yes, sir. And there's Grandma and Papaw."

We got out of the truck, and meeting behind it, Mr. Feeke held out his hand to shake mine.

"Son, speaking for the Feeke family, we hold nothing against you children. Come see me anytime. Can't say how things will work out with your father, but you children ... It's not your fault."

I thanked him and trudged over the gravel to my front yard.

Looking toward Grandma and Papaw's house, I could see Papaw standing in the middle of the road. The Feeke truck would be noticeable from there. He must have seen me get out, his eyes still sharp. He probably thought it was Roy I was talking to, wondering what we said. If I headed for the front door and went inside my house, Papaw and Grandma would have a little more time before they knew. It was no gift.

I ran the length of road to Papaw and threw my arms around him.

After an hour with Papaw and Grandma, we had only the shock to sit with, no plan, no way forward. For them, it was small relief to know Lillian was alive, but no other comfort. The church bells around town intoned the three-o'clock hour, the time of Christ's death on the cross. The Catholics were beginning the vigil awaiting the resurrection. We had nothing to wait for except the wrath of my father.

Papaw left to find Mr. Feeke, thinking he could get more details about where Lillian was headed. He and Grandma could not bear the thought of having no contact with her. Willing to overlook she left us on purpose, that she meant to stay away, Papaw thought talking would change that.

Grandma rocked, murmuring again and again, "Your mother's not well, she doesn't know what to do."

That day, they still thought she could take back the leaving. I knew she could not. As Mr. Feeke said, Lillian and Roy left a trail of damaged people. My father's way of rebuke would never allow for an apology, an excuse of grief or sadness—not when he found that she was with Roy. Maybe there would be a day when I would speak to her again, but there was no taking this back.

Promising them I would wait for my father to tell my brother and youngest sisters, I walked home. Although I had agreed it was up to my father to explain the situation to the children, I intended to prepare Jane with what I knew before he came home. It was likely that his anger at Papaw and Grandma would intensify, making it harder on George and the girls. My only option would be more deception, as I could not foresee a life for any of us without my grandparents. Not now.

I cornered Jane in the kitchen and asked her to come down to the cellar to speak privately. She knew from observing me with Mr. Feeke that the news was bad.

"I don't want to hear it." But she followed me.

Jane did not flinch, arms folded across her chest, knees locked, tight lips, while I talked. Then she turned on her heel and started up the cellar steps.

"I will not be trapped in this house because of what she did. I hate her." And she pounded up the steps.

At dinner, Jane refused to sit in the chair that had been my mother's, next to Addie, as if association with her place at the table would taint her. I sat by the highchair and saw to Addie. The tension from the scene next door unresolved, we ate with little conversation. George remained unsettled about Junior, and the girls questioned what happened to their friends. I deflected, saying Mr. Feeke was seeing to them. Marion's house was dark except for the kitchen and an upstairs bedroom, where her sister tended to her. With the children gone, there was no danger for the time being of my brother and sisters hearing anything from next door.

It took over an hour for me to get Addie calmed and asleep. By then the others were in bed, reading, and the house quieted down. Jane must have fallen asleep herself, or she didn't come back downstairs to avoid me. Nerves kept me alert, waiting for my father.

In the hour after midnight, a car stopped out front and I

went to the front window. My father got out of a gas company truck, grabbed his valise from the back, and paused at the gate, looking at the side-by-side houses. His grim expression, sad eyes, drooping shoulders—like the day of Lonnie's funeral—said he had talked to Mr. Feeke. As he approached the front door, I wished he would stay outside to keep back the torrent that was inevitable once he opened the door.

He turned the knob and came into the house.

Our eyes locked. With my finger to my lips and gesturing upstairs, I led the way into the kitchen. My father took a chair. I leaned my back against the sideboard. It felt safer on my feet to talk with him. We had not spoken since our tense words in the cellar.

He launched right in. "Feeke talked to you, and I hear there was quite a scene next door. I told him I understood that he told you, but I hope you have had the sense to not speak of it to anyone."

"I told Jane."

He grunted. "No one else?"

I took the risk. "I told Papaw and Grandma."

He focused his steely blue eyes on me. My father hardly ever looked directly into our faces, like he was truly seeing us. Mostly he flicked his glance over us while he gave orders. Holding his gaze, I anticipated his harder self to start in about my mother. He would test me, I figured, thinking me loyal to her, expecting me to defend her. Truth was, at that moment, I had nothing.

I was empty of plan or thought or excuse or reasoning. I wanted him to be our father and figure it all out, show us the way forward, give us a footing for starting the next day, and all the next days, without my mother.

Not able to read his intention, it was like the two of us were seeing each other for the first time. It might have been the moment where we could have found a way to talk with each other, a way to acknowledge the grief and the stress and the uncertain future, and be not only father and son, but man-to-man in our steadfastness, each keeping the other from losing himself. That wasn't to be.

He clenched and unclenched his fingers, the way he used to stretch them before a game to steady his hold on the bat. He shook his head, smirking.

"If I am generous to her mother, she must be relieved to know Lillian's not dead. But her father, well, he's satisfied Lillian's gone off with the one he wanted all along, now, isn't he?"

"They aren't like that. They're sad, and afraid for us. They want to take care of us, and they're scared you won't let them."

"Well, they are right about that. Sad, they may be. I'll even grant that they didn't help her leave, now I know the story."

"I took George and the girls to see Grandma and Papaw today, before Mr. Feeke came."

"Their daughter destroyed my family, and they will not get back in here."

"It's not their fault."

"That's for me to say."

"What about what *you've* done?"

His raised his clenched fist. "Daniel, leave this room before I get up from this chair."

If I had not admitted I told Papaw and Grandma, would I have had his confidence? If I had made another lie of omission, would he have talked to me, so that our ground changed enough for him to believe I was on his side? I had no trust that his anger at my mother would be kept in check. There had been that fleeting moment with him, and on the chance that it might brush by us again, and next time, perhaps catch, I wanted to remember. He was a liar, who I would have to learn to lie to.

"Liar." The word hung in the air as I walked away, and he let me go.

CHAPTER 9

My father tendered us no comfort when he informed us our mother was not coming home. Facing the six of us seated before him, already drawn down on the little mercy he had reserved for Lillian if she had returned, and now hardened by Roy's trespass against him, Alonzo stated the blunt facts: Mama left us, Roy found her, and together they were going to California. None of us were to speak of our mother again.

George kept his head down, and my young sisters held each other, whimpering. Addie sat on my lap, kicking her shoe against my shin, sucking both thumbs, a recent habit. Jane sat next to my father, patting his arm while he talked. It made me cringe to see her gaze at him, nodding, waiting for his acknowledgement.

Repeating his speech about the importance of his position in town, my father warned that no matter what talk we heard, none of us were to speak about our mother to anyone. We would hold our heads high. The orders to stay away from Papaw and Grandma stood firm. Hattie would stay until he made a longer-term arrangement. He spat out instructions like we were a work crew. Jane got a squeeze on the shoulder as he stood to leave us sitting there.

How like my father to order us to transform into the compliant children he decreed. Did he believe children were too insensible to care if a parent ran off, or that declaring our mother didn't exist erased our feelings? Or did he have no concern for our feelings? Knowing him as I did, I believed he acted in his own interest, which was to cut off our past, allowing him the space to do as he liked. My father had failed every test on my private scorecard of caring for us.

Hattie attempted to soften his harshness, telling us none of us had done anything wrong. Yet the life he intended for us was punishment: banishing the grandparents we held dear, ignoring the grief of losing our mother, and carrying the weight of the scandal. My father had no idea what it would be like for us at school once word got around. He commanded keeping our heads up and ignoring gossip, but the ratio of those who would sympathize with us versus those who would take any opportunity to taunt us was low. My father didn't care, or didn't stop to realize, that his position over working men—other kids' fathers—already created tensions for us; when men got fired, or were not hired, by him, those frustrations played out in the schoolyard.

Jane was rooted in a circle of so-called friends whose parents would take the lead in spreading the scandal, and the talk behind her back would be fierce. Like my father, though, Jane focused on positioning herself in the social order, and was adept at playing a top-tier game. Gossip could not knock her out unless she gave into it. If anyone could sail over the sea of malicious talk bound to churn around us, Jane could. I feared she would also shield herself against me.

Jane had become expert at manipulating Aunt Hattie's nervousness and reluctance to argue by overwhelming her with pouting and tirades. Complaining no one did as many chores as she did, pushing her demands for more time with her friends, she wore Hattie down. Since our mother had left, everyone's behavior had changed for the worse. George lashed out with fists, the girls with screaming, crying, and arguing. Addie seemed to have gone back to babyhood, insisting on being carried, kicking, refusing to learn words or use utensils or the potty. Hattie, in what she believed to be a temporary role, tried any tactic to keep the peace, playing one child against another, whiplashing between giving in and handing out punishments. Pressing the girls into more duties around the house was probably a good thing for keeping them busy, but it led to more quarreling each night around the supper table.

During the past weeks, my older-brother instincts had swelled with my aching heart, like a canker sore inside your gum that stings every time your tongue flicks over the painful spot. Watching George wipe his teary eyes with the backs of his hands, holding the girls as they buried their heads in their arms, I knew I would have to be their mother, father, and brother, and also a barrier between them and the harsh treatment that awaited us when word got around about my mother and Roy.

For George and me, the first public appearance was imminent. Unless the weather brought a late season snow, there was a town tradition of baseball played on the afternoon of the Saturday before Easter, a game for boys and a men's game, on the fields near the center of town. It was late April, snow had not fallen for a few weeks, and the ground on the fields thawed. For the Saturday game, two squads mixing ballplayers from the different neighborhood teams would play to warm up the rivalries that would drive the season starting in a few weeks. George was to play with the boys, with me as one of their coaches. My father had signed onto the men's roster.

In the cellar that morning, I was coaxing a reluctant George into his knickers and loading our ball bag when my father clomped down the basement steps dressed for the game.

"Let's get out there. We're walking together. Remember what I told you."

He grabbed his bag from a hook on the wall and took the stairs. George and I looked at each other.

"Whatever happens, let him handle it," I told George. He nodded glumly, and we gathered the gear and climbed out of the cellar door. My father was waiting for us in the back alley and, seeing us approach, he swung his bag over his shoulder and marched toward the fields, the two of us keeping a few steps behind.

Other players and a gaggle of spectators were milling around the side-by-side fields set for the games. My father forgot us as soon as he mingled into the growing crowd of men he would play with and against. Waiting for the morning air to lose its chill, the umpires organized the squads for fielding warm-ups and batting practice.

Checking the rosters posted on the fence, it was a relief to see Roy Junior listed on the opposing team from George, which meant he would pitch to my brother but not sit in the same dugout. When I caught the eye of Mr. Kegg, an umpire for the boys, he nodded with lifted brows, letting me understand word was getting around about Mama and Roy. We had Mr. Kegg's discretion to thank for the line-ups separating the two boys.

Neighbors waved to George and me before turning to murmur to each other. Off on the far side of the boy's field I saw Papaw standing with a group of older men but we didn't acknowledge each other.

"Papaw's here to root for you," I said. George half-smiled.

Papaw being out there steadied me; he had a lot of respect around town, a different type than my father, if not more, in the way older, wiser men are deferred to. If he could hold his head up out here, we could, too.

Scanning the grassy area where people sat to watch, no Feeke brothers appeared to be in attendance, though they were a main sponsor of the season, their advertising posters arrayed along the center field fence. Roy Junior was all the way back in the outfield warming up his arm with two other boys catching his throws. We settled into our dugout. The boys on George's team were intent on getting ready to play, all their talk about bats and gloves, pitches to watch for, the normal pre-game chatter easing some of George's tension. His mitt was stiff, and I put him to work kneading it around a ball.

I knew my father could still play a commanding game, but I was unprepared for the aggression he unleashed that day. His batting practice was a series of attacking slashes that sent balls rocketing into the outfield. The other players cheered him on, their adulation firing him all the more. By the starting time of the men's game, he was drenched in sweat and pacing the dugout.

At my coaching station on the boy's field, I had a view of the other field and followed the progress of the men's game. Waiting for his turn in the lineup, my father jumped his bat from hand to hand, rising up and down on the balls of his feet like a prizefighter anticipating the bell to launch him into the ring. At the plate, he slashed at fastballs, fouling off pitches until he got his bat on one for a long ride. My father carried too much weight around the middle to run at top speed, but the distance he hit the balls made the path from plate to base seem short. I could see Papaw watching my father hit, shaking his head at the blustery performance.

Alonzo's easy strength on the field was a picture of defiance. It was the perfect situation for him to assert his story of our family shame: it had nothing to do with him. He was dominant, powerful, his play so admirable, there had to be something wrong with Lillian to leave such a man.

Watching him made me wonder, is that how a man gets away with doing whatever he wants, his audaciousness daring others to challenge him? Does carrying a brazen attitude make it possible to do wrong, things that are not permissible for other people, with no consequences? And a harder question: could my father have been a different man? Was there a time when that personality was a good thing, an asset for making his way, not for hurt? Could he have been an honorable man?

And what about my mother? Her boldness, her appreciation for the finer life despite our dismal surroundings, her cleverness, and the restlessness—those qualities had pushed us forward, given us an outlook of the larger world we could inhabit, made us ambitious. Jane absorbed that, having long yearned to get away from our town as soon as she was old enough. My parents presented a teasing jigsaw puzzle; getting the four borders completed didn't give you much help for figuring out where the jumble of other pieces fit into the middle.

Someone yelling my name pulled my attention back to the boy's field. George sprawled in the dirt at home plate. He'd been knocked down by a ball thrown back to the catcher by one of the infielders, maybe intentional, hard to say. With Roy Junior on the mound and the rest of his team wary, the air around George became charged, and the catcher backed away from him. George got up rubbing his upper arm, sending a dirty look Roy Junior's way.

"Settle down, boys, this here's a friendly game." The umpire repositioned himself and resumed play.

George tapped his bat in the dirt more forcefully than usual as he took his stance to wait for the pitch from Roy Junior. The pitches came fast and hard, George swinging for three strike calls, keeping that hard look on his face the whole time. As he turned to walk back to the dugout, the catcher couldn't let him go. "Your mama..." was all he got out of his mouth before George was on him.

Roy Junior sprinted to the plate and jumped on George's back. The catcher jerked loose, leaving George and Junior locked around each other, their flailing arms trying to land punches. The infielders ran forward and the umpires with them, arms outstretched to keep more boys from joining the melee. They were outnumbered as the two benches emptied to circle around the fight. Backing off, the umpires let the two boys tussle. Junior was older and larger than George. George's team screamed for him while Junior's urged more punching.

When I pushed through the mass of waving arms to reach for George, my hands found Junior's leg and I yanked it with all my force. Dragging him off George, I pinned my arms around both of Junior's legs. He struggled against me. "Back off, George, *now!*"

Junior growled under me and tried to punch away my grip. "Stop, Junior! I am not letting you go."

George lay panting next to us in the dirt. The umpires pushed back on the circle of taunting boys. Above the hollering I heard a woman's voice. Junior heard it, too, and stopped struggling. We looked up into Marion's drawn, pale face. Only twenty-four hours earlier, she had gone to pieces, been sedated by the doctor. She loomed over us unsteady on her feet, her sister behind her for support. Her old yard coat, the one she wore while hanging the wash or burning the garbage, hung open over a faded housedress on her skinny frame. Her hair was brushed straight back from her forehead and tied with a bandanna.

Marion commanded Junior, "Get up." He scrambled to his feet, reached his arms out to his mother.

"No." Raising one hand, she fended him off.

The field had gone silent around us, both games in suspension. Getting up from the dirt, I could see through the backstop fence that most of the spectators had come forward, closed in around to watch the fight, Papaw among them. Mr. Kegg and men from the other game who had boys playing with us had run over to see who was fighting. My father stood near the edge of the huddle around us, holding his bat, watching Marion.

Marion drew herself up as straight as she could. "Shake hands with George."

Junior's eyes searched Marion's face as if he had heard her speak a foreign language.

"This is not your fight. Shake hands with George."

Junior studied her for another long moment, then turned. George was behind him, mesmerized by Marion. Junior lifted his chin and held his hand out to George. George looked ready to cry, but he held the tears back. He took Junior's hand, and they shook.

Mr. Kegg and the other umpires pushed and pulled the gaggle of boys around us to disperse them back to the sidelines. As the boys moved away, the men from the other game came into Marion's view. She and my father locked eyes. In one swift move, Marion grabbed the ball from the mitt of a boy standing near her and threw it at my father. He saw her motion, caught it with one hand, and stepped toward her.

Marion spat words at him. "You wrecked my home with yours." Her sister gripped Marion's arm to back her away, but Marion shrugged her off.

Alonzo kept his eyes on Marion but spoke to Mr. Kegg. "I'll walk Mrs. Feeke off the field so the boys can get back to their game."

He handed his bat over for me to take, but I kept my hands at my sides. I suspected he was reading Marion's mood all wrong, or he was thinking he could change it. Either way, she was having none of him.

"*Mrs. Feeke*! Do not come near me! You ran Lillian off. I know your lies." Shaking, her voice rising, Marion leaned forward toward my father, daring him. "Lie to the other woman, not to me."

Marion's sister grabbed her arm again and tugged her back. My father still had the bat in his hand. Mr. Kegg stayed close.

Alonzo's gaze swept over me and to his left, George and Junior side-by-side, Junior alert to any sign from Marion that she needed him.

Turning back to Marion, my father's voice hardened up. "No need for hysterics, Marion. Calm down."

She didn't flinch. "Go straight to hell."

He took the blow, face reddening, his eyes flicking right and left, conscious of the men around us. I moved close to Marion's side, my father watching me step over the imaginary line of demarcation between them.

"Marion, walk with me," I said. "Take my arm." I waited, and after a moment, she leaned back, let me slip my arm under hers.

The men peeled away in ones and twos, as if they could hear a dog whistle signal for retreat. Without another word, my father turned his back to us and, swinging his bat in the air, strode back to the men's field, holding himself at full height, looking straight ahead, undaunted. The people who had been watching the whole thing now had a clear picture of our situation. I could feel the gossip circulating in the dusty swirls twirling in the air.

"Don't leave Junior and George," Marion whispered. "They can't fight."

"Mr. Kegg is watching them."

Leading Marion in small steps, her sister on her other side, we aimed for the truck. Marion squeezed my arm, tears on her cheeks.

"I don't know what I'll do."

Settling Marion settled in the passenger seat, I pulled the coat around her. "Don't let them fight," she whispered.

Back at the field, George and Junior still stood on the side, not talking, stricken looks on their faces.

Mr. Kegg came over. "You boys want me to scratch you from the lineup?"

Junior shook his head. "I want to throw the ball."

George held up his bat. "I need to hit it."

Once more, they shook hands, and walked back to their benches. Mr. Kegg whistled softly. "Those boys showed some respect for each other."

"They're friends," I said. "Our mothers, too."

Mr. Kegg went about reorganizing the boy's game, giving me time to step away. Papaw, at the fence, had seen the whole thing without Alonzo seeing him. Papaw knew I'd find him, and he was waiting for me under the awning of a rickety shed that stood beside the path leading to the ball fields.

"How's George?"

"He's all right. Don't think he'll do any more fighting with Junior."

"It's a hell of thing for a boy to take in, both of them, a hell of a thing."

"I'm not taking it too well myself."

He grabbed my face in both his hands. "Dan, we love you children, and we won't let you go."

"Papaw, don't make me cry."

"No crying, son. We're just going on."

CHAPTER 10

Days later, Hattie called for me to come upstairs to my parents' bedroom. She ushered me in and closed the door.

"I need your help."

My parents' room was under the eave of the house where the roof slanted on one side, the iron bedstead placed against the wall's low point. The space allowed for a wide chest of drawers and an armchair on the longer wall. Two tall windows let in whatever sunlight there was, but a gloom from my mother's dark days lingered over the room.

My mother's old trunk sat at the foot of the bed. I pictured my petite mother sitting on it to put on her shoes. I had never looked inside, but Hattie had opened the lid. Nestled amidst the folds of muslin was Lonnie's burial box, as forlorn in the trunk as the little grave we left him in.

Lillian's dresses and my father's jackets and shirts clustered on hangers strung across a wooden rod in the corner wardrobe wedged under the opposite eave. Hattie had pulled open the

dresser drawers, exposing Lillian's undergarments, an embarrass-
ment like catching sight of nakedness if the bathroom door was
left ajar. On top of the oak dresser was the tin box where my
mother kept her few necklaces and brooches. Next to that, her
brush and comb, hair ribbons, the wrap she pulled around her
head while she did the wash. Above the dresser, the mirror hung
a bit low on the wall, an adjustment for Lillian's height. Every
morning my mother had looked into this mirror, made herself
ready for the day, even on the day she left, when she dressed in
Sunday clothes for the first time since Lonnie died.

The bed was made up lumpy with the quilt pulled over the
pillows. Blinking in the ray of sun that arrowed its way through
the crack in the curtains, I conjured my mother laying under that
quilt, only the top of her head visible, blonde strands poking out,
knees drawn up, the muffled weeping. Since she left, when my
father was away, I had lain in this bed with Addie, soothing her
cries until exhaustion took us both to sleep. The grief and sorrow
collected under the blues and yellows of the quilt was as deep as
Lonnie's grave.

We had gotten through Easter dinner at Uncle Charlie's
house by a scheme of separation, children eating on the porch,
adults in the dining room, the bare formalities of greetings and
goodbyes, none of us saying anything out of turn. Staying within
narrow channels of acceptable conversation suited Charlie and
his wife. In their house we were treated like the little ceramic
statues Aunt Letitia collected, moved about and placed according

to her idea of a proper tableau: expected to stay put and mute. Hattie had become attuned to our discomfort but she was subdued with Charlie and Alonzo, despite being older than they were. She did not cross them directly, preferring to work around the edges of what they decided when she had her own view of things.

My father went back on the road the day after Easter, leaving Hattie to enforce his regime. Since my mother wasn't coming back, Hattie's situation with us was changing from temporary to what? That was not explained. Hattie continued chattering about wanting to go home and her fears that Oscar's lack of attention to her house would ruin the place.

Hattie did not take a rigid stand of punishing our lapses on the order to never speak of my mother, but she was quick to cut off any mention of her by changing the subject. Hattie captained a steady following of the routine: breakfast, school, chores, supper, bed. We did as she told us and hardly spoke to each other. Numbness had set in. Less crying, fewer fights, more often sitting quiet side by side at the table, slogging together silently to school. It was like each one of us had crawled under the quilt, quivering there, making only the minimum necessary movements. Even Addie, who continued to refuse the potty and had slipped back from words to baby gestures and grunts, was more limp than cross.

The house closed in on our growing bodies. I was no taller, but George and the girls seemed to sprout more inches each week, his pants too short, their dresses too skimpy. Hattie and Jane let down hems and narrowed seams to save buying new clothes. We got in each other's way, competing for bathroom turns, space at the table, sprawling on floors and the settee. The bedroom arrangement of a girls' room and a boys' room was lopsided, with Hattie and my sisters in one room, and only George and me in the other.

Most nights, Addie woke up crying, disrupting the girls' sleep. Across the hall, I only half dozed, always expecting her to cry, hoping to pass one night when she slept all the way through, but it never happened. Exhausted, Hattie let George and me try keeping Addie in our room with the crib between our beds. With us on each side of her, she would calm down and drift off.

It got so my sleep was not deep, no dreaming, more like floating on the edge of consciousness, waiting. The moment she cried out, I jumped. Sometimes she would let me put her back under her blanket and she'd stick her hand out between the spindles for me to hold. Other nights she would settle on my pillow and I tucked myself by her side so she couldn't roll onto the floor. If Addie wouldn't sleep, I brought her into my parents' empty bed to keep from waking George.

I shivered, and heard Hattie saying my name. She was gesturing at the trunk.

"Your father wants me to pack away your mother's things, but he didn't say what to do with the trunk."

Lillian had left her clothes behind. Jane and I had scanned

over the room from the doorway the day after she disappeared, wanting to bolster our belief that our mother had not meant to leave by verifying that nothing was missing. The police asked my father if she had packed. Best he could tell, he told them, she took a satchel that she sometimes used when we went out to the farm. Uncle George also confirmed she had no traveling bags with her. The satchel could have held her money. It made sense to me now.

Her presence in the room overwhelmed me. Spending nights with Addie on the bed, I had pretended my mother's arms took us in under the quilt, grief and all. Now my father wanted every remnant of her gone. Was Hattie asking me to agree to this, or to arrange it?

"Leave it be."

"I was thinking her parents might want her things. I thought her brother could come and get it, take it to the parents."

Imagining Grandma opening the trunk was too much. "They've got enough upset."

Hattie sank into the chair and wiped her face with her handkerchief. "We can't leave it in this room."

"Are you helping my father pretend my mother was never here?"

That came out sharp and I regretted my tone with Hattie, but not the question. If Hattie emptied the drawers of Lillian's chemises, if she folded the over-washed cotton housedresses, stuffed paper in the shoes left under the bed, pulled the nicer frocks from in-between my father's serge and tweed, if she packed and closed the trunk, it would be a funeral. Did she expect that I would help to erase my mother from the house?

"No, no, but this is his house, and it's his wish that these things are gone by the next time he comes home."

I put my hands on the dresser and stared into the mirror, what Grandma called a looking glass. My mother once told me that mirrors give us a glimpse of ourselves, but not the truest picture. She said we decide who we are. The surface on my mother's mirror had rippled so the depth of my image changed if I moved. Day after day, what had my mother seen pass in herself as she gazed into the mirror? Had she seen a Lillian she did not want, flaws beyond what hair ribbons or powder could mask? What was her truest picture? And how she could have a picture of herself that did not include us?

My eyes met Hattie's in the reflection, and it came to me that she saw me differently than I was seeing myself. Who was I becoming, who was my truest self? As I studied my face, my illusions passed over the surface of the mirror, rushing me through the days in the old house—playing on the floor with my mother, the walks, the cooking—and the years before we lost Lonnie, to the man I now was. My mother was never going to know me. And I did not know who she thought she was.

"Hattie, can you do anything with the dresses for the girls?"

"Yes." She studied me.

"I will help you bundle my mother's clothes in the sewing

cupboard and you decide about remaking them. If the girls object, give the dresses away."

"What about her personal things and the trunk?"

"Leave me with it. I'll find a spot to hide it. Until we want to open it again."

Hattie nodded, sighed, and heaved herself off the chair. "I wanted you to decide," she said, patting my arm.

After shifting the dresses, hats, and other clothing from the closet and drawers, Hattie closed the door, leaving me to the trunk with the warning, "Just be sure your father won't see it again."

I set Lonnie's box on the dresser and removed the top layer of muslin from the trunk. Heady whiffs of lavender floated from the sachets tucked into the trunk's corners. My mother had not perfumed herself with anything other than the laundry soap, but the scent inside the trunk brought a wave of memory. Grandma coaxed a thriving herb garden behind her house where Lillian cut the bundles to refresh her sachets each season. She taught the girls to stitch muslin bags and fill them with the dried stems, tie them closed with ribbons.

Hesitating to undo the careful wrappings, I unfolded edges of bundles to peek at the contents. The baby christening dress, bonnet, and blanket we had all worn was placed between layers of white linen. After Addie's baptism, Grandma had washed and pressed the tiny clothes, stuffed the arms and torso with swatches of tulle to prevent wrinkling. The puffed-up shape made it look like a shrouded baby. When my mother dressed two-month-old

Addie in the baptismal gown and bonnet, she proclaimed her the last sibling to wear it. Seven children born over fourteen years had drained her. Did she know then she would leave us? Was she already thinking about it?

Below the baby clothes was an ivory dress folded around a crown of woven ribbons and lace, and a pair of ivory shoes. My mother's wedding dress. Underneath, at the bottom of the trunk, I found a wooden keepsake box, etched with my mother's name surrounded by painted-on flowers.

Placing the keepsake box on my lap, I studied the elaborate lid. Had Papaw made this for her? The engraving of her name spanned the width. It had been scored in cursive and must have required painstaking attention. Painted around the name were bunches of white lilies of the valley, delicate tiny bells of the flower hanging along green stems. This could have been Grandma's dainty handiwork. I tried to picture my grandparents as the young pair who brought this daughter into the world and designed a treasure box for her hopes and dreams. What did it feel like now they knew they might never see her again?

Opening the box felt more intrusive than seeing the contents of the drawers. But she had left this behind to be discovered. I unhooked the brass clasp and lifted the lid. Painted on the reverse side were the words, *From your loving parents*. Six birth certificates tied with a ribbon lay on top. Slipping off the ribbon, I read the names—Addie's first, mine last in the bundle. Lonnie's wasn't there; I glanced at the burial box.

Under the birth certificates was a packet of photographs. I recognized my mother and Uncle George as children in a few taken at the farm. Lillian's smile in those pictures showed her at ease and content. In one, posed with Grandma and Papaw on the farmhouse porch, the future woman my mother became was there in young Grandma's face. Time raced ahead in the photo array to my mother holding an arm around toddler me with Jane on her lap, sitting on the rickety porch of the old house. My father must have taken that. The look on her face brought her voice into my head, the way she admonished him, whenever he posed us, to hurry and take the picture before we wriggled away.

A cream-colored parchment folder opened to reveal my parents in their wedding photograph. Posed formally, rigid, each looking into the camera as though they have no connection to the other. She held a bouquet, he his hat. Were they too nervous to smile?

Tucked into the folder was a yellowed page from a newspaper. Unfolding it, I read the list of marriage announcements for July 1913 in Cumberland, Maryland. Fingering down the list, I read their names and the date of the wedding performed by a local judge. Why go to Maryland? I sat back in the armchair to grasp the understanding.

Because my mother was expecting a baby in July 1913. She had me six months later. They had never talked about their wedding with us. Grandma and Papaw did not tell us about it. If a couple eloped to Maryland, a too-young Pennsylvania woman could sign for herself, no waiting, and the record of the marriage was published in a paper no one in their town would see. Couples who married this way were welcomed home with outward congratulations and an undercurrent of nosy questions and gossip. Grandma and Papaw must have known ahead of time. They had not disowned their daughter. The wedding dress preserved in the trunk was Grandma's creation.

But nothing in the treasure box could tell me how my parents came to that wedding day. Did she love him then? Was he intending to be faithful to her? Or had they been trapped by their recklessness, neither of them wanting to stay with the other?

I buried it all back inside the trunk, placing Lillian's and Lonnie's boxes next to each other, and closed the latch. Pulling the trunk felt like dragging a coffin across the hall to my bedroom. My father would never find it there. Covering it with a worn blanket, I piled books on top, figuring George would take no notice.

Hattie soon started on reclaiming material from Lillian's dresses. Jane didn't say a word about the fabrics, unusual for her but in keeping with the lethargy that we drifted through. She and I had given no more energy to arguing about my mother or father. I wanted to reconcile with Jane but where was our common ground? The situation was starker in that we knew what our mother had done, but in the house it felt like we could barely manage day to day, that we had no sense of what would come next. It was like one of those movies where the shipwrecked survivors make it into a lifeboat, then weaken from days adrift under relentless sun without water.

When Lonnie died, one of the Catholic neighbors told me she would pray for his soul in limbo. I asked her what that meant. She told me the soul of an unbaptized child went to a place outside heaven but not in hell and had to spend eternity there. They did not have God's grace to enter heaven but had done nothing to condemn them to hell. Lonnie would not suffer but he would never see the face of God.

Now our house was limbo; we had done nothing to deserve our fate. Before, the six of us sorted ourselves into twos by age; Jane and me, Annie and Ruthie in the middle, George and Lonnie the little brothers, baby Addie passed around the circle. Since my falling out with Jane over my mother, she aligned herself with the girls, shifting back and forth between disciplining them and cuddling with them, fussing over their hair and clothes, or punishing them with chores. If Jane could succeed in reducing the crying and fighting, Hattie left her to it. And Jane was constantly primping, her hair not curly enough, or her face too long, one dress color brought out her eyes and another made her look dull. George had lost Lonnie and the girls ignored him. Having Addie's crib in our bedroom pulled George out of his silence. He would sing softly with her in the dark until one or both fell asleep.

Unlike Lonnie, we were not facing eternity in our house. Already sixteen, I could leave and few would question me striking out on my own. Plenty of boys, and some girls, were on the move, looking for work as fathers lost jobs. Since the stock market crash, money had gotten tighter for many of the families tied to coal, coke, and iron. Some of our friends had quit school to find work. My father's job seemed secure, but he warned Hattie to be frugal and stretch the weekly allowance further.

If I announced I was leaving home, my father might make a show of objecting but he would let me go with no regret. Uncle George would not turn me away from the farm if I asked for a job. Could I take my mother's place in the business? He would give me a try, I was sure of that. But I wanted to keep my post office job. It was work I liked to do, and Mr. Kegg depended on me. Even if I did not have the post office job, in my heart I knew I could not repeat my mother's mistake and leave my brother and sisters.

Lillian was guilty of abandoning us, and Roy of leaving his children; I would not acquit them with my forgiveness. My father was their equal in fault, and my distrust of him swelled each time we had to see each other. But I would not be like them. My brother and sisters needed me. I would stay and take care of the family as best I could.

There had to be a way the six of us could find our new life together. We didn't need to clear my mother out so much as decide where to place her. If we wanted to talk about my mother, we had to be able to do that without fear. The anger, sadness and confusion would have to settle, like the sludge at the bottom of the murky river, leaving us floating above it.

Yet how could we live differently with Hattie over us? Our aunt was a good woman and kind to us, but her deference to my father meant we could not trust her. Hattie wanted to go home; why not tell her to go? I would take over.

That would get Jane's attention. She was too bossy to let me be in charge. Our debates had usually produced good compromises, and I missed putting our heads together and figuring things out.

Jane would insist my father had to agree. I had the notion that he would be content to continue providing the money and stay away for long stretches, as he had done for years. Was it naïve to think that he and I could settle on such an arrangement? Wary of each other, we had taken to circling without words, not confronting what he had done. I counted on my father's need for order and public face, which I was willing to keep whole if he would leave us alone.

The scheme might work except for taking care of Addie. To keep my job and finish school, I would have to have someone to watch her from after breakfast until Jane or I got home each day. With Hattie gone, how would I pay someone to take Addie? Even with frugality, we didn't have enough money in my father's weekly pantry deposit to cover that. And who could I ask to help? Grandma, certainly, but that would enrage my father. Addie needed a lot of attention, too. She should have been learning more words, getting steadier on her legs, playing more than she was. And there was the potty issue.

With no clear answer, I mulled it over for a few days. The weather was warmer, spring blossoms appearing in patches around town where people scratched some beauty from the coal-dusted dirt. Longer light at the start and finish of each day, though little more sun than the winter, the perpetual clouds hovering from the coke ovens, the mines, and the woodstoves. Up on River Avenue, the clouds dissipated somewhat overnight; in the mornings, we could glimpse the valley around the town. The ball fields were active from the time boys ran there after school until dark. George went every day, usually with Junior. When I asked if Junior talked about Roy, George told me no; it was better not to.

Addie needed to practice walking longer distances, and with the warm weather I put away the pram. She had gotten lulled into laying back while someone pushed and protested going outside without it. On the next warm afternoon, I pulled a knitted sweater over Addie's head and got her arms into it.

"Addie, you and I are going walking. Show me the bonnet you want to wear."

When we got out on the porch, she looked for the pram, and not seeing it, said, "No, no." I started down the steps and reached back with both hands to take hers.

"C'mon down, Addie, we're having a walk."

She shook her head and pushed my hands away. I pointed to the street, to the other houses, talked about what we would see. She went to the door and tried to reach the handle, wanting to go inside.

Hattie came to the door. "If she won't go with you, I'll take her in for some milk and a cookie."

That was exactly the problem. Addie was babied. We had all done it, but Hattie knew no other way. Had she done this with my father? Hattie was sixteen when Alonzo was born. She referred to my father as "the baby of the family" and had doted on him as a little boy. Had he learned to be demanding because the family met his whims? Even now, Hattie would not directly counter him, doing what he said with meek compliance. Sometimes, like with the trunk, she modified the orders a bit, but never let him know.

My throat tightened at the thought of Addie learning his habits from Hattie's weakness. Determined to break the pattern, I marched up the porch steps and picked Addie up, not hurting or startling her, but my grip firm.

"We are out for a walk—here we go." And with that I sailed her down the steps and the walk, planted her legs in the road and took her hand, and started off. It surprised her enough she stepped along. Hattie watched us for a moment, then closed the door.

It was slow going and I didn't plan to walk far, just get Addie to the bottom of the hill and back. She stopped and started, toddling on her stout legs. When she saw something interesting, she would crouch from the knees, like a catcher's position, and lean forward with an outstretched arm to pick up the stone or weed she wanted, then lose her balance and fall back on her padded rear. I pulled her up a few times and reset her for walking. The next time I waited for her to figure out how to get back up on her own. She whined and reached for me, and I coaxed her to stand by herself. She rolled to one side, got her knees under her, and pushed up with her hands. When she managed to stand, she held her dirty palms up to me with a big smile on her face. Brushing her off, praising her for doing it all by herself, I saw Marion trudging up the hill.

Marion was pale and thin, dressed in a worn cotton shift with a sweater hanging off her shoulders, her hair wrapped in a scarf. She carried two burlap bags, bulging with groceries, tied with rope handles. Since Roy took the truck, Marion depended on the Feekes to bring her what she needed or she walked back and forth to town.

I started toward her but she shook her head. "Stay with Addie." We watched her come forward and plunk her bags down in front of us, giving me a wan smile.

"Whew, I am not used to climbing the hill. Brought too much with me." Then she leaned down to Addie. "What a big girl you are, walking on the road."

"If you take Addie's hand, I can take your bags the rest of the way," I offered.

Marion stooped down lower and talked softly to Addie. "Will you walk with me?" Addie let Marion lead her while I carried the bags.

Since the day on the field Marion had stayed out of sight. I had seen her come onto the porch with her children in the mornings as they headed to school. We nodded to each other from our own side of the yards, but the chance for a conversation had not presented itself until now.

"Marion, how are you getting along?"

She shrugged. "My sister says as well as can be expected."

Not knowing what to say, I nodded my sympathy.

"Sometimes I am so mad at Roy, and then I get mad at all three of them. I meant what I said to your father that day."

"I feel mad at him myself. He's a liar." That came out before I decided to say it.

Marion jerked her head at me. "So you've seen the side of your pa you didn't see before."

"Yes, and if my mother hadn't left, maybe I would have known anyway, but since she left, it's all come my way."

"Junior—he can't understand it. I can't explain it to my kids, just can't tell them anything that makes any sense. Your mother and Roy hurt us bad." She stopped walking, looked at me like she just realized it was me next to her. "'Course you know— you're one who would know what I mean. The ones left behind, you're one of those." She reached out and squeezed my upper arm, held tight to Addie with the other hand, and we walked a few more steps.

"What do people say in the store?"

"Roy's brothers don't want me working down at the store anymore. Seems the Feekes worry folks will feel uncomfortable dealing with me, like they have to say something. They'd just as soon keep the subject of Roy and Lillian running off out of the business. But they have enough decency to keep up Roy's income for us." Her eyes ran glassy, but nothing spilled over.

It came easy to speak thoughts to Marion that I hadn't shared with anyone, having no one close, since Jane took herself away from me and not talking with my grandparents. I told Marion how we struggled at home, that my father banned talk of my mother, that I didn't trust Hattie and wanted her to leave. "I can take care of this family if I get the chance." Declaring my intentions aloud for the first time sounded right.

Marion stopped walking and stared at me. I felt I should apologize for dumping my troubles her way when she was grieving too. I opened my mouth to say that when she gripped my arm tighter.

"Bless you, Dan, for being a good man. Bless you."

"I don't think I know what a good man is."

"You know what a good man does, and that's the same."

My eyes threatened to spill. At Marion's gate I set down the bags, wiped at my face. She picked Addie up and hugged her close.

"Addie, honey, you walked a long way like a big girl." Addie giggled. Back on the ground she tested how far her hand could reach through the fence to touch the straggly flowers on the other side.

Marion put her hands on my shoulders. "Your mother loved

you, Dan, and she'd be proud. I will always blame her and Roy for what they've done, probably never forgive them, ever. But she did her job with you. You're right to take care of the young ones. God knows Alonzo isn't thinking of his children."

She opened the gate, pushed the bags inside, closed it and turned to me. "We're right here, neighbors, like we always were. Except now we're joined in the shame. We've got to help each other."

Marion caught me off guard with her generosity. My mother had betrayed Marion's friendship. Marion, who had even nursed Lonnie along with her own baby girl for a time while my mother was too weak. How she could pull the strength together to manage on her own now inspired me. I smiled at Marion.

"Yes. But I don't want to ask anything of you, unless I can help you, too."

She looked down at my baby sister tearing her flowers. "Addie needs some mothering and Junior needs a big brother. Let's start there."

CHAPTER 11

The triangle of Lillian, Alonzo, and Roy generated the most scandalous gossip the town had chewed on in years. For all his talk about holding our heads high, my father avoided appearing in public by staying on the road. Spring was the busiest season for the crews, hustling to make up for the time lost to winter as soon as the ground in the mountain areas softened for digging. But he was staying out of town more than usual.

After the Easter ball game, my father was absent from the spring practices for the men's league but he knew they would keep him on the roster. If he showed up personally at our house to drop off the weekly pantry money, he stayed at most one night, sometimes leaving after the few hours it took to check in with Hattie, use the darkroom, and pack clean clothes. In May, we celebrated Addie's second birthday without him, and he never acknowledged it. His interest in how we were doing was confined to the spending. He listened to Hattie and Jane describe the need for new clothes for the younger children and increased the allotment. Hattie, to her credit, involved Jane and me in deciding who would get what.

In the post office, the townspeople treated me kindly, talking around our difficulty rather than coming straight out with remarks about my mother or my father. Hearing folks being careful about declaring an opinion, I gleaned which people feared my father, disliked him, or wanted to stay out of his way. Men would ask where my father was working this week and leave it at that. Or after tipping their hats, they'd wait for Mr. Kegg to help them at the counter, avoiding me. Most of the businesses in the area had an economic interest with the gas company, and between my father and Uncle Charlie, their web of relationships, legitimate or otherwise, was tangled. Alonzo carried his position over other men like a walking stick that rapped the ground with every step. Risking his anger could mean loss of a family's livelihood, even for those not working for him directly.

There were also those men who kept up friendly relations with my father for their prurient interest in his photography work for the police. He carried the equipment with him, and the sergeants found him wherever he was, to ferry him in police cars to crime scenes and accidents. He puffed up with importance when someone asked about what he saw in the aftermath of crashes, fires, fights, and the occasional murder around the county. Some people played a double game, engaging him about crime details so they could say they had talked to him when adding to the gossip and speculation about my mother and Roy.

No one discussed Roy Feeke in front of me. The Feeke family's growing enterprises also created conflicts of interest, as everyone in town dealt with them in one way or another. If Roy's oldest brother drove by the post office and saw me, he beeped a hello. Marion stayed quiet about Roy and Lillian, leaving her house only for church and quick errands. She let me know that the Feekes linked her public silence to continuing Roy's income. If she stayed at home, away from the fray, all the better for the Feekes.

Women who knew my mother were obvious in quizzing me. The ladies from church lingered at the counter, asked how we children were getting on, was Hattie still with us, how old was Addie now, questions of that sort, trying to get me to say more. Such questions made me wonder what Jane was saying to her friends that was being repeated to their mothers.

Those who did business with Uncle George or drove for him found ways to let me know who they were. Men I had never talked with before flicked me waves when I passed them on the street, and a few offered rides to the farm. I took the gestures as signs of Uncle George standing by us. Still, he had not been in touch with me since I visited the farm.

Gnawing at me was the suffering Papaw and Grandma had to be going through, knowing Lillian wasn't coming back. With her gone, I wondered what Uncle George was doing to stay close to them. I wished, too, that Papaw and Grandma, or at least Papaw, would be bolder in trying to see us. Papaw had never been fearful of my father, only respectful to the degree needed to keep family peace. My mother had intervened on those occasions when he and my father did not see eye-to-eye, but Papaw could hold his own with my father. Papaw certainly did not fear Hattie telling tales. With my father away so much, why did Papaw not come by, or find us on the way home from school?

Keeping my guard up around people and daydreaming about a way to change our home situation distracted me on the job. Mr. Kegg corrected my mistakes, never admonishing me. One Saturday when I was cleaning up in the back room, a large casserole sat keeping warm on top of the woodstove. Mr. Kegg pointed at it.

"Dan, would you like to share this lunch with me before you go?"

There was a chill in the early May weather, and the chair by the stove was welcoming.

"Sure, thanks. Which lady made this?"

He winked. Several of the widows in town would bring hot dishes to Mr. Kegg, hoping for him to ask them to stay and enjoy it together. Not much interested in the widows, he relished the food and was too polite to refuse it. When we had both shoveled in enough to take away our morning hunger, Mr. Kegg sat back and wiped his mouth.

"There's plenty, help yourself to more, son. Unless you have to get on your way."

"I have to get to the market and then home, so Jane can get out this afternoon."

"Where's your aunt?"

"She's gone home for the weekend."

Mr. Kegg was older than my father but not as old as Papaw, and he had lived in the town his whole life. He had a view into the lives of others that only the town doctor could beat. And like the doctor, Mr. Kegg never used his intimate knowledge inappropriately. When he disapproved of someone, he still treated them respectfully for post office business, limiting his responses to what transpired over the counter. I trusted him and valued his advice. Still, I was reluctant to involve Mr. Kegg more than he had been in the drama affecting my family.

I shifted in my seat. "I'd like her to stay home and leave us be."

Mr. Kegg lit his pipe.

The easy silence between us acted on my pent-up emotions. I confided what I had learned about my father's other family, and the problems in our house since we got the news about Roy going off with our mother. He listened and nodded, letting me talk through the feelings brought up by looking into the mirror, and my dilemma about taking over my family.

Mr. Kegg leaned forward. "Dan, you are butting up against your history."

"My history?"

"Your pa's line is troubled in these ways."

"What does that mean?"

He shook his head. "Your grandfather. He was a real rascal."

My father's father died before Lillian had me. His wife, Grandma Cora, never spoke of him in front of us, and we were too young when she was alive to know the difference. I could not recall my father or Uncle Charlie talking about him either. A few times when she was angry at my father, my mother put her grievances out to Grandma or Papaw, saying Alonzo was "just like his father." Papaw would shake his head and tell Lillian he could see that.

Mr. Kegg eased back into his chair. "Dan, if you want, I'll tell you what I know of him. The older folks around here knew him. Your papaw knows the story. I would guess it gave him pause when his daughter married Alonzo." He shook his head. "Sorry, that's my opinion, he never told me that."

"Tell me about my grandfather."

"Back in the day, it was easy money letting the logging crews lease land for clear-cutting. Your grandfather Andrew inherited his land from his father and two uncles. He was one of those who took the lease, pulled back on most of the planting and harvesting crops or raising animals. The money from lumber was good for a long time."

"But not long enough for my uncle or my father?"

"This was before their time. The payments allowed Andrew to do as he liked, and what he liked to do was court young women whose fathers had more land."

"My grandmother?"

Mr. Kegg shook his head. "Not at first. Back then, with people off the boats coming in and the town growing so fast, the old farm families split. Some wanted to sell as quick as they could and move into town, get other work. Others wanted to preserve their acres, use the lease money, and they looked for ways to merge with others. Your grandfather saw an opportunity with young women in those kinds of families."

"He got married?"

"I said he liked to court the young women, not marry them. He was courting two girls at once, which might have worked out. If he had been prudent, serious about his intentions, chosen one, and gone to her father. But Andrew moved on, deciding he didn't care for either young woman as a wife." He paused, studying me. "Both girls had a child out of wedlock. Both girls told their folks the child was his. Andrew declared them both liars and would have none of it. One family might have been able to prove him the liar, the other was not so sure, and in the end, to keep things quiet, both let him get away."

We had been sitting there longer than I meant to stay. But I had to hear the rest of the story.

"Where does my grandmother come into the picture?"

"Soon after that, Andrew married a town girl much younger than he was, and before a year was up, she died during the birth of a son, whom he claimed but would not raise, and gave the baby to her folks. Around that time, Cora came to the area with her parents. When they met, he was thirty, she was just twenty years old and smitten with him. He was a good-looking man. Probably didn't know about his past. Or she didn't listen to the stories."

Grandma Cora had Hattie, and a few years later, Charlie. My grandfather was over fifty years old when Alonzo was born.

"Does my father know this story?"

"He must know. Hattie knows, because one of those other children made herself known to the family and Cora quietly acknowledged her. When Alonzo was a baby, his father got hurt out on his land, never healed right, and needed constant tending from your grandma. We'd see Hattie with little Alonzo most of the time."

Mr. Kegg lit the pipe again. "The family moved to a rented house in town to be closer to the doctor. Townspeople knew Andrew's temperament from the way he railed at his wife in public. Hattie never finished school because she was afraid to leave her mother with him at home, and there was Alonzo to take care of."

My grandfather was more than a rascal. Mr. Kegg painted a picture of the tyrant Andrew had been. Charlie left home as soon as he turned fourteen. Tired of his father lashing at him with tongue or belt, eight years older than Alonzo, Charlie worked any job he could for a few years, then got his first step into the office of the gas company. Having gotten Alonzo through most of his schooling, Hattie finally left the family house to marry an older man whose wife had died. She wanted her mother to leave with her, but Cora stayed with her husband.

Charlie had rented rooms from a widow in town and Alonzo moved in with him, finishing his last two years of high school under his brother's watch. When Charlie married, his wife Letitia took over the housekeeping for the two men, in the house that Charlie bought and still lived in. It was to their home that my father took my mother to live when they got married. My grandfather died a few months later.

"Mr. Kegg, you said that I was butting up against my history, but all this happened before my time."

"That's the thing about family history, son." Mr. Kegg leaned in. "It lives on in the blood. You carry it. You see it happen again."

"Are you saying … that we …" I stumbled over the thoughts rushing in my mind. Were we dupes of something as invisible as diphtheria, breathed into us and impossible to fight off?

"I'm saying watch yourself, Dan. Watch yourself."

Walking home, I ticked off a mental ledger of the ways my father was like his father. The other woman and her children, his temper, his disregard for us, the coldness. But did that come from his raising? His meanness had emerged a little at a time, like a slow leak. Were his father's ways implanted in him like seeds that took time to grow and show their poison?

The worst part was wondering about myself, and my brother. If it was blood, like Mr. Kegg said, then we were already ruined. That couldn't be right.

I was late getting back to the house, expecting Jane to be furious with me. Coming up on the porch, Addie's loud crying inside sounded through the windows, and there was something else, a thumping. Jane crouched with Addie on the floor of the front room, trying to cover her ears, holding tight. The other sound came from the cellar, and then George cried out.

Jane's eyes pleaded, tears running, a red blotch on her cheek. "I tried to stop him and he hit me!" she screamed. "He's beating George!"

Sprinting down the cellar steps, George's cries and the whacking pounded with my heart. My father grunted with each thud of his belt. He didn't see me behind him and I lunged atop his back as he raised his arm for another blow. He stumbled sideways, almost fell, and jerked me off of him. My father was twice my size, but I went for his arm a second time, got a grip on the belt.

"Run, George, now!"

Sobbing, George grabbed at his trousers, pulling them up enough to get momentum in his legs. My father lunged toward him and grabbed George with his other arm, yanking the belt from my grasp.

"Get out of here, Dan," he roared, "or you will get the same!"

Wedging myself between George's body and my father's angry face, I used all my height and weight to push my father back, loosening his grip on George's arm. He breathed on me in great gasps, and I heaved myself on him, pinned him to the wall. George got free and stumbled at the bottom step, crying.

The belt in my father's free arm whipped across the back of my legs. Shoving me from his chest, he regained balance and aimed the belt to hit me higher and harder.

Backing away, I saw the baseball gear in the corner and grabbed a bat.

We held our positions six feet apart. Facing him, both my hands gripping on the bat, poised to strike, I watched his face contort with rage. He wound the belt around one palm, leaving the strap ready to swing at me. The cellar closed in like a mine tunnel that got darker as it went deep. The moment seemed to go on forever.

I found my voice. "George is going up the stairs now. Go, George, get up there." He whimpered and crawled up a step, looking back at me. "It's okay, George, go." He stumbled up the stairs and Jane was at the top to grab him.

My father sneered. "Again, Dan? Showing me what a big man you are? I never thought you had it in you. Your mother babied you."

"I am no baby. And you will not hit us."

"I am your father. Head of this house. I will discipline you as I see fit."

"You are not going to hit any of us ever again."

"Says you? Are you going to fight me?"

"I'm not like you." I tightened my grip on the bat. "Or your father."

"My *father*? You didn't know him." He took a step toward me.

I stood my ground. "I know he beat you. And you are not going to do it to us."

"Is that right? This is my house, and you are my children."

"I will make sure the whole town knows what kind of man you are. You have other children, too."

"You listen to gossip."

"You left their pictures here, and I know what you've done at the boardinghouse."

"You don't know anything."

"I know that you have to stay away from this house. You can do what you like about the others."

"You can't turn this house against me. Hattie and Jane won't go along with you."

"You hit Jane. And we don't need Hattie."

"Hattie will do what I say."

"Stay away, or I will take other steps."

"You've got no one to turn to." He sneered. "Unless you think George's farm boys scare me?" He stropped the belt against the wall, one strong smack.

"What people think scares *you*. Lillian and Roy ran off. How much worse do you want the gossip to get?"

His eyes narrowed. "Get out of my sight."

"Leave now, or I swear I will make it worse."

I kept eyes on him as I backed up the stairs. I slammed the kitchen door closed on him.

Leaning against it, shaking, I gripped the bat. Next to me, Jane was backed against the wall, rigid and wide-eyed.

"I heard what you said," she whispered.

I nodded. "Where's George?"

"Upstairs in the bathroom. The welts on his legs are bad."

"The girls?"

"I made the girls take Addie to Marion's."

"Stay with George until I see what happens."

"When did you get so brave?" Jane whispered.

I shook my head. "Everything's different now. We have to be different now. Go." Jane hurried out of the kitchen toward the front stairs.

Rattling sounds from the cellar, then the squeak of the outside hatch to the cellar steps thrown open. My father emerged, his head visible from the window facing the back porch. He slammed the hatch shut and stomped around the porch toward the front of the house. I slid along the walls to position myself at the archway to the front room, where I had a clear view of him standing near the road. He pulled his jacket over his suspendered trousers and checked all his pockets, like he was looking for something. Then a car pulled up. He greeted the driver, got into the front passenger seat, and the car drove away. I breathed out.

When I got to the staircase, Jane was sitting on the top step, feeling the red splotch on her cheek. "He shouldn't have hit me."

"No, he shouldn't."

"I was on his side."

"I know you were."

"What are we going to do?"

"We can figure that out."

"I don't want him here."

"From what I just saw, he planned to leave before I told him to." I started up the stairs toward her. "I'll help George, you go get the girls."

I offered Jane my hand, and she let me pull her up. She threw her arms around my neck for a quick hug and ran down the steps.

Once everyone was together in the front room, I made a show of locking and chaining the doors, including the cellar hatch, and walking around to lock all the first-floor windows. "He can't get back in tonight," I assured them. "The house is locked up, and he forgot to take his keys with him—see, they're here." My father's key ring sat on the table.

"What if he breaks the window?" whined Ruthie.

"He won't."

"What if Hattie wants to come in?" whispered Annie.

"She's not coming back tonight."

"Why did he beat me?" George's voice was a croaky sputter.

I exchanged looks with Jane. She got on her knees in front of George and embraced him above the waist, careful of his soreness. "We will never let him do it again."

Ruthie and Annie added their arms to George's neck, and he sobbed. I took Addie on my knee and hugged her tight. When George pulled back, I gave him my handkerchief to wipe his face.

We sat quiet for a few minutes, then took ourselves into the kitchen to make supper.

Later in our room, I rubbed salve on George's welts and gently settled him under the covers. Addie was already asleep in her crib. I turned off the lamp and hoped for a few hours of rest before Addie might wake up.

In the dark, George said, "Jane's talking to you now."

"Seems like she is."

"'Bout time."

"Yes."

"We're a team."

"Yes, we are a team."

That night everyone slept all the way through for the first time since my mother left.

CHAPTER 12

I woke as the sky lightened, and I woke angry. Feeling it coursing through me, alongside the hunger rumble in my stomach, and my usual alertness to the sounds of the house. I lay on my back, absorbing the sensation, getting cozy with anger's warmth rising from under my skin, the tingly jumpiness in my arms and legs, energy to propel me. My anger was seeking its target. It could be like buckshot, bursting wide, hitting whatever chanced through its path. Or it could be like an arrow, aimed, focusing its force. But my anger split at a fork between my father and my mother. Who should get the larger portion, the first arrow, the brunt?

George and Addie slept on. My baby sister turned on her side and let out a soft gurgle. The movie reel embedded in my head played again: me at that age, my mother holding me, taking my hand, cuddling me. Playing by the stove, learning letters and numbers, singing together. My mother had been different with Addie, often passing her over to one of us or to Grandma. How many times had I walked into the kitchen in the morning or after school and seen Addie strapped into her baby chair, alone, my mother outside or sitting in the other room. What would Addie remember of love and care? We each did little bits for Addie, but what did it add up to? Who was properly raising her, teaching her? My mother left it undone.

And not only Addie, though she was the most obvious one lacking attention. My mother had left three other daughters. Like ducklings, my sisters had trailed behind her, reciting the events of their days, rationalizing their grievances with each other, whining for privileges. My mother sorted out the major issues from the minor and calmed them down. They grabbed onto her instructions like life ropes that pulled them back into the boat. Now they struggled with navigating their world and interpreting things said to them or not said, red-faced shame dredged up from looks and comments made by others. Ruthie strained with schoolwork more than before, failed her tests, had the teachers worried enough to call Hattie. Annie lashed out at any slight and was fiercer in a schoolyard fight than most of the boys.

My sisters fussed over their appearances as though some combination of color and curling would absolve them of the stigma they felt outside the house. Hair and ribbons and hemlines and hats, their clothes and the tilt of their heads as they walked into the schoolyard worn like a silent plea, *Leave us be—our mother did this, not us.*

Jane hid her insecurity with her bossy ways. She pushed herself on the rest of us some days, and other times acted indifferent, eager to get out of the house and see her friends. I observed her at school with those friends, her too-loud voice, the panic in her eyes in the moments when she thought no one would make a place for her at the lunch table, rushing up to the clusters of girls in the schoolyard and foisting herself into their conversations. She tried too hard to act like nothing happened, and the girls milked her for tittle-tattles they could carry home for gossip with their mothers.

While Jane was vying for the attention of the girls she considered highest in the pecking order of our little town, boys were noticing her. Nothing disrespectful had gone on. The boys kept quiet around me, and so far, their attention to Jane was on the edges of the girls' circles. But I could see the future and she was unprepared, for all her brashness, to deal with the nature of boys. Would my mother, who married young before finishing school, have been the best guide? What would our mother have advised Jane? It didn't matter, now. The problem was how to keep her on the right path with no mother.

In my weighting, my mother's unmet obligation to my sisters was greater than hers to George and me, though she wronged us, too. George, eager to please both our parents, to earn their attention, was bereft. He had proudly fulfilled our mother's expectations in his role as Lonnie's big brother, but in her personal attention, he was shuffled back and lost in the middle of the pack. After Lonnie passed, George had become invisible to her.

To please my father, George became the baseball player, and he was much more talented in the game than I could ever be. George discovered that he thrived on the field, and the shared love of the game could have brought him and my father close. Other fathers came out to the games to coach their sons or warm up their arms with a game of catch. Our father paced the side-lines, scowling, collecting nine innings worth of criticism to un-load on the walk home. George developed a shell where he glowered and talked back to hide the hurt. In the quiet moments, in the darkness of our room, if Addie dozed off, he would whisper his questions and fears to me, like a tentative turtle sticking its head out.

My anger fed me the memory of the damp cellar smell, the tension in my grip around the hard baseball bat. Tightening my hold, staring at Alonzo's hands whipping the belt, surging with readiness to hit my father if he hit me first. What had restrained him? That I was his son, or calculating me as a low threat? Did he believe I would have hit him? Did I? And, if I had fought him, where would that leave us? I wanted him to stay away. My anger said I needed insurance he would.

Easing out of bed, padding downstairs to the kitchen, I kept going down to the darkroom. Pulling aside the curtain revealed the workbench had been cleared of printed photographs. The processing trays were dry and stacked. The boxes where my father stored finished prints and negatives were underneath. I clicked on the light box he had clamped to the bench.

His meticulous recording of the photographs in a ledger, numbering the corresponding negatives, made it easy to locate the exact one for a reprint. Knowing what I was there was to find braced me against shock, but still I trembled as I opened the ledger and ran my finger down the records. The most recent were from a burglary crime scene and a Masons' dinner. Not as many shoots in recent weeks as he had normally done before my mother left.

Going back to the start of the year, looking at entry dates and titles, my eye came to a set of four photos listed as "VC." Locating the negatives, I pulled the sleeve holding those four from the box and, keeping my fingers on the edges, hovered them over the light box. There in the grays and murky whites of the negative was the woman with the two children.

Anger steadied me. I had what I needed. I would print the proof.

Cards tacked up on the wall detailed the formulas for the chemical baths. I had observed the process enough times to try it. Still, to be sure I would not wreck the only evidence I had, I practiced on a negative from the Mason's dinner. Getting it into the last bath, the image emerging, I trusted my formula to start on the "VC" negatives. Timing each print in the bath, grabbing it with tongs and sinking it under the chemicals, my father's other family drowned in the trays.

When the prints were hung to dry, I cleaned up the trays and put the workbench in order as it had been. After breakfast I would retrieve the photos. Anger satisfied, I clicked off the lights, closed the curtain, and ran upstairs.

The coffee was ready. Jane, with her head leaning on an arm, nursing a cup, nodded. I poured mine and sat across from her.

"That was some night," she said. "One I never imagined happening to us."

"Things are different now."

"Yeah, you said that before, but what does it mean? Last night we locked our father out of the house, and when he comes back, then what?"

"I think he wants to stay away."

"What makes you think he would stay away?"

"Jane, look, I have wanted to tell you things I've found out. Things he's done … if you are ready to hear them. What I know will upset you more."

She kept a steady gaze. "Let's hear it."

"He's got another family. A woman who runs a boarding house where he stays, and he's the father of her two children. I have proof of it. And I have their photos, in the cellar."

Covering her face with her hands, Jane moaned, shaking her head. "No, no, no. He told me that wasn't true."

"What are you talking about?"

She sniffled, then gulped coffee. "One day, right after you left for the post office, Hattie rode to the market with Aunt Letitia, and the girls went along. George was next door. It was only me and Addie here. A woman got out of a car, and another woman was driving, waiting for her. She came to the door carrying a baby."

Her voice broke. "She asked for Alonzo and I told her my father wasn't home. She said no, that's not right, he can't be your father."

I stared across the table as Jane grimaced with the effort not to cry. I pushed the dishtowel toward her.

"She kept saying he can't be your father, and I was asking for her name, but she didn't answer, just stared at me. Then she looked through the window and saw Addie. Her baby was fussing, she was jiggling it and staring at Addie. The other woman got out of the car, dragging a little boy up to the porch. The other woman called to her, 'Vivian, let's go.' But she didn't move. She shoved the baby up in my face and screeched at me, '*This* is his child,' and pointed at the boy, '*He's* his child.' She was crying, the baby was crying. The other woman pulled her away."

Jane gulped air and blew it out. "From the car, she yelled, 'Tell Alonzo I was here. tell him his children need him.'"

Jane's hands grasped her cup so hard I thought it might break. "I didn't tell Hattie. When Dad came home the next day, I walked with him outside and told him about the woman, and the two children, what she screamed at me. I asked him what she was talking about."

"What did he say?"

"He told me the woman was ill, her mind is not right. She lost her husband in an accident and, at the boarding house, he and the other foremen had to keep a distance from her because she has spells. She works herself into delusions that one of them is her dead husband."

"And you believed him?

"He said he felt sorry for her, and that I should forget about her coming here."

I spoke softly. "She was telling the truth."

Jane sobbed. "I couldn't believe it. I can't believe it. It's too hard."

We sat like that for a few minutes, Jane wiping her face when tears dripped too much.

When her tears let up, I spoke. "I printed the photographs he took of them."

"I can't look at them."

"You don't have to. But I am going to use them to make him stay away."

"How can you make him *do* anything? He's our father, he's supposed to be here with us. No one will help us."

"I have an idea. But it depends on Uncle Charlie."

The sun was fully up and noises from above meant the others were awake. Our brave front at breakfast was faked to calm George and my sisters after the night before, steady them for what would happen.

Around noon, when he would be home from church, I called Uncle Charlie. I gambled making the call, because if my father was there, Charlie might hand the phone over to him. But my uncle sounded surprised to hear from me, leaving me unsure that my father had gone there last night.

Not mentioning the events of the night before, I asked Uncle Charlie if he would come to our house later that day, bring Hattie back, and talk with me.

A long pause, then he said, "Dan, this is an odd invitation. Where is your father?"

"I don't know—I thought you would know." That was true, and a play for time.

"When I left him yesterday, he was on his way home."

"He was here last night for a while, then he left."

"He left? Why?"

"Look, Uncle Charlie, I am asking you to come because there are things to discuss about our situation here, and we need your help."

"Can you explain yourself? What is going on?"

"Please, just come over today."

With a sigh, he agreed to fetch Hattie at her house and bring her before supper, warning me this had better not be a waste of his time.

Jane and I arranged for the girls and Addie to visit at Marion's house while George went to the practice field with Junior. Jane followed my lead, but I could tell it was because she was still in shock from the night before and grappling with the truth of the other family. The red welt on her cheek had faded, but her hand went to the spot from time to time. As Charlie's car pulled up in front of the house, we stood together in the front room and Jane grabbed my arm.

Hattie never knocked anymore, just bustled in, handed off her satchel to me, Uncle Charlie right behind. She and Uncle Charlie scanned our faces and exchanged a look with each other. Hattie asked where everyone was and, satisfied with the roll call, took off her coat. Uncle Charlie removed his hat but kept his coat on, as though he wasn't planning to stay long. Charlie was an imposing, bulky man with the same thick arms and legs as my father. He kept his silver hair slicked back and wore round wire spectacles. He was more often frowning than smiling. Standing, he was a head taller than me.

"Please sit down?" I asked them.

Uncle Charlie lowered his girth into the larger wing chair, Hattie settled on the davenport, and Jane and I sat across from them. Charlie fiddled with his hat, turning it in circles around his knee, impatient or anxious, I wasn't sure, and it didn't matter to me. My anger pricked up, like the ears of a deer out in the open reacting to the hinted sound of a predator. Charlie had to know what my father had been doing. My father must have been involved with the boarding house woman, Vivian, since before Addie was born, while my mother was pregnant, maybe before. Big brother Charlie kept his secrets. Worse than that, Charlie allowed him to do it.

I plunged in. "Uncle Charlie, these are photographs of my father's other two children, with their mother, Vivian, from the boarding house." Jane stiffened next to me, pushed her hands under her thighs, rocked slightly.

I held the photos in my right hand, let them gaze at the first, then moved it behind the others, until they had seen all four images. Hattie fell back and covered her mouth with her hand. Charlie held my gaze as I shuffled the photos. He didn't need to look to know what was there.

"This woman came here—to *our house*—with her children, looking for my father, and by talking to Jane, discovered that he's been lying to her."

Charlie stirred at this. "She came here? When?"

"The day Hattie went shopping with Aunt Letitia. Jane asked him about the woman, and he lied to Jane. He lies to everyone."

"Watch yourself, Dan. I will not tolerate disrespect."

"We are not discussing respect, Uncle Charlie. We are discussing how you will keep my father away from us."

Charlie jumped up. "What the hell are you saying? What is this nonsense? You have a father, and this is his house."

Hattie pulled on Charlie's sleeve. "Sit down, Charlie." He looked at her, she motioned to the chair with her head. He crushed his hat brim harder, grunted, and sat.

Hattie looked me in the eye. "What are you telling us, Dan?" Hattie had lived with us long enough to trust my judgment. I didn't like how she took care of Addie or her deference to my father, but her way of working around the edges was in my favor now.

I described the episode with my father the previous night, his striking Jane, his beating George, including that I had picked up a bat to keep him away from George. The retelling brought streamlets of Jane's tears, running from her eyes to her chin and curving down along her neck and under her collar. She let them run.

Charlie threw his hat spinning across the room. I feared he would be as violent as my father. But he was a man practiced in restraining himself. My father always said that Charlie was good at his job because he was a fixer, never letting situations get so out of hand the higher-ups had to get involved. I was counting on his way of managing problems, that he would see things had gone far enough and he needed to control the damage.

I pressed the moment. "My father cannot live here right now. He frightens my brother and sisters. He might hurt them again, and worse. I am asking you to keep him away."

Hattie looked at Charlie like she wanted to speak but would defer to him. Uncle Charlie sat forward in the chair, rubbing his palms together, scowling. "This is his house. I can't tell him what to do."

"I am asking you to tell him we don't want him here, and he has to stay away."

"You expect your father to take that well?"

"No, but you can put the situation to him in a way he will understand. No one wants more scandal."

"Are you threatening something, Dan?"

Jane threw her arms out toward Hattie. "He hit me, and he beat George! He's supposed to love us!"

Hattie reached for Jane's hands. "Uncle Charlie knows what to do, honey, don't worry. He knows what to do." Hattie glared at Charlie. "Tell them, Charlie, what you will do."

"Dan, what are you proposing?"

This was a turn of things I never could have imagined before. Uncle Charlie's anger zapped in the air and met up with mine, like the unseen vapors in a mine that killed birds and warned the men to stay out. Anger was teaching me it could be manipulated, not only unleashed with bats and belts. It could have a purpose, get a result.

"He has to move out. Hattie can stay with us. No one will think much of it since he is gone most of time, anyway."

"For how long?"

"I don't know."

"What will make him stay away?"

"What he stands to lose."

Charlie knew better than anyone what that meant. His reputation was intertwined with my father's. They rose, or fell, together. They had built relationships, their version of prestige, lives they enjoyed. Neither would risk having to start over. My father differed from my mother in that way. She walked away; he never would give up what he had, and he used every angle to advantage.

The sympathy he was receiving as the jilted father of the six surviving children abandoned by their mother was part of his story now. To preserve it, he would stay away.

"What will you do with the photographs?"

"If he stays away, nothing."

I didn't need to ask Charlie to keep Vivian from coming back to the house. Hattie would take care of that. My father's things were packed and sent off with Charlie. Hattie settled herself in my parents' room, to give the girls more space.

When Jane went to get my sisters from next door, I helped Hattie start the supper. She was quiet. I had more to say.

"Aunt Hattie, we need to do some things differently while you are with us."

She stopped chopping onions and looked at me. "You've surely gotten bold, haven't you?"

"I have to protect my brother and sisters."

"I never hurt a one of you."

"I know."

"And I never asked for this job of living with you. It was just something I had to do when the call came." She met my eyes.

"I'm answering a different call."

"Lord, what is to become of all of you? This is such a mess."

I moved Addie's baby chair away from the table and put a regular chair in its place, with two fat cushions on its seat to raise her up.

"Addie will sit between Ruthie and Annie, and they can help

her if she needs it. You and Jane on the other side, and George near me, on the end."

I felt her eyes on me as I issued my decree. Hattie opened her mouth as if to speak, then closed it. Bringing the casserole over to the table, she motioned with her head. "Bring everyone in, and let's get started."

CHAPTER 13

Anger kept its simmer within me, a stew ready to be dipped into when I needed its fuel. If Hattie questioned me, anger stiffened my spine to stand tall and hold my argument. When Uncle Charlie called asking how we were getting on, anger gave curt replies and strengthened the silence between us until he hung up, leaving what I knew to be his real question unasked. My father was not welcome to return; Uncle Charlie had to deal with his brother's transgressions.

Summer loomed before us as the school year came to an end. I expected to work full days in the post office; Mr. Kegg needed as much help as I could give him. Figuring out how to occupy my brother and sisters over the summer months took Jane and me on walks away from Hattie's ears to come up with a plan. We had few options, and they all circled back to Grandma and Papaw. For different reasons, both Jane and I nursed grievances against our grandparents. To enlist their help, we would have to clear the air with them.

Jane's anger hurled offense at my mother, and at the edges, hit my father, too. Jane argued that if my mother had not left us, we would not have been vulnerable to my father's fury. My mother had violated her duty to protect us. Jane's blaming of my mother bled over onto Papaw and Grandma. Jane understood they had not helped our mother leave, but they were forgiving of her and Jane held a wedge against them for my father's sake, despite his behavior.

My gripe with our grandparents was about their failure to stand up to my father on our behalf. They had essentially left us on our own. Papaw watched us from afar, on the sidelines of the baseball field, on the street across from the schoolyard, walking up and down our hill. Grandma had stayed in the house, unable to cope with the stares and whispers in the store or in church. They had not even deployed Uncle George to help us in some way. In my thinking, Grandma and Papaw bore a measure of responsibility for how we got to the situation, where six children were left to raise themselves. Yet I knew they did not see this coming. They loved us and were also in pain.

If I had to take charge now, I needed them to stand with us openly. We had to have their word that they would. I persuaded Jane to go with me to Papaw and Grandma's house.

At my knock, Papaw answered the door with an expression that said it was ordinary for us to be there, and that broke the ice. Grandma hugged us in turn, not crying, making it easier for us to get through the first minutes. They missed us as much as we missed them.

Sitting in the kitchen with cake and coffee, Jane relaxed into her seat and the tension in my shoulders eased up. Not hurrying us, they waited to hear the reason for our visit. Jane reported on each sibling's current highs and lows, and Grandma made soothing responses.

I caught Papaw staring at me, read his signal.

At the lull in the small talk, I launched in. "My father is not living with us now, and I don't know when he will be able to come back. Uncle Charlie is keeping him away until ... for now."

My grandparents exchanged looks.

"He has not changed his mind about you," I went on, "but we are going our own way without him."

Papaw cleared his throat. "What happened with Alonzo?

"He lost his temper too much, too hard."

Grandma grabbed me. "Did he hurt the children?"

"Yes."

She turned to Papaw. "Oh, Pa, I knew it would get bad with him. I told you we had to do something." Grandma's tears spilled out.

I patted her hand. "It's okay. We are okay. He left, and he can't come back."

Papaw gave Grandma his handkerchief. "What do you mean, he can't come back?"

"We asked Uncle Charlie to keep him away."

Papaw sat back, taking that in. I could tell he felt unsure Uncle Charlie had the means to keep Alonzo away.

"How long will this go on? What about Hattie?"

"I don't know, and Hattie is still with us. What we need is a plan for the summer. I have work in the post office every day."

Jane spoke up. "The girls are at loose ends. George wants to play baseball all summer. Addie needs tending."

"What are you thinking, Dan?" Papaw asked, and Grandma held her breath. The anticipation in their faces told me they hoped for a role to play. But the harder feelings Jane and I carried had to be cleared first.

"Papaw, I know you've been around, watching us, but if you had stood up to my father, maybe things would not have gotten so bad. I had to stand up to him."

Papaw blinked a few times but didn't look away. "I'm sorry for that, son, I am. We kept a distance thinking it was for the best."

"We needed your help."

"But you handled him, eh? You got this far."

We locked eyes again. I did not feel ready brush off my upset. Papaw held back from saying more.

Jane filled the silence. "I was harsh to you both after Mama left. I blame her for our trouble. I know you didn't help her leave us. But it's her fault we have so much hurt."

Grandma's tears flowed. "Your mother is my child, and I grieve for her. I know she did not mean to hurt you."

Jane breathed out. "But she did. She hurt us bad. What did she think would happen to us? She didn't care."

"She cared, she cared. She wasn't strong."

"Grandma, you can't make me forgive her," Jane said.

Grandma sat up at that. She blinked back the tears. "No, I can't make you forgive her. But to help you, I will do whatever I have to. You children are the most important thing in the world to us."

At that, Jane opened up. "Grandma, the way Annie and Ruthie are hurting ... and Addie ... I don't know what to do."

Jane went on telling Grandma about the strife at home and at school. It was like she released the funnel on the flour sifter and turned the handle this way and that, each turn churning the grain and pushing it through the sieve. When she finished, the bulk of our problems had been spilled in a jumble. My grandparents took in the mess, waiting for me to speak.

"I am taking charge," I said. "We need to know you will help us."

Papaw rubbed his palms along his thighs, let out a breath. "What do you want us to do?"

"We're thinking Jane and the girls and Addie could go with Grandma to the farm for the summer. George and I will stay here."

Papaw nodded. Grandma brought her hands to her face and wiped her eyes, then reached across to join her hand with his.

"Grandma, we want you to go with them to the farm. But you have to understand things are different for us now."

I took her other hand. "The girls, especially Addie, have to move on with their growing, get settled with how things are."

"I know," she said.

"If they want to talk about my mother, we do, but we don't get stuck on it. We're trying to find the way to do things on our own. At the farm, I hope they will work out the hurt. When summer's over, we've got to be ready to move on." I squeezed Grandma's hand. "You miss her, too, I know. But they have to grow. Addie has so much to learn."

Papaw spoke. "We've been talking about the same thing, and we were waiting for the right time to get back with you. Dan, I hear you telling me we waited too long. But we are with you now."

Then Papaw wagged a finger at me. "But if we take the children to the farm, Alonzo has to know where his children are. You want him to stay away but he has the right to know where they are. I don't want him sending the sheriff after us."

"Uncle Charlie is the go-between," I said. "I will talk to him and Hattie about our plan for the girls to go to the farm. He'll tell my father."

"Your father has to agree, or there'll be hell to pay when he finds out. If we get on the wrong side of Alonzo, he has his ways in this town. We can't risk it."

I knew what Papaw meant. A vengeful Alonzo could force the authorities to go after Uncle George.

"Uncle Charlie knows Hattie is tired, she wants to go home, and she doesn't know what else to do for us. He will get my father to go along. If we can buy time through the summer, maybe my father will see his way differently."

I didn't really believe my words, saying them more for Jane's benefit. She still clung to my father and the hope of our family being together. Alonzo had taken a fork in the road away from us. That night in the cellar, he had shown his hand. I knew we had no life with him.

The summer plan came together as we talked. Papaw would get a message to Uncle George at the farm the next day. Grandma started a list with Jane of things to pack for the children. Grandma would head to the farm before school ended, to prepare the farmhouse for the summer with Jane and the girls. She was full of ideas about teaching the girls to sew, enlarging the kitchen garden, and occupying their days with the chores of farm life. The talk turned to Addie. There were small children among the farm workers' families and Addie would have playmates and be challenged to practice her words.

Papaw gestured for me to walk outside with him while Jane and Grandma continued to talk. Stepping onto the porch, I spoke quietly. "Can Uncle George keep Jane and the girls away from his business?"

"Yes. The less anyone knows of that, the better." Papaw put

his hand on my shoulder. "Dan, I see a change in you. You are the man of the house now."

I gazed upward, saw flocks of birds making circles over the river, swooping upward where the air cleared out from the smog. "I didn't plan to be."

"That's how it goes for a man—things come your way and you step up to the task. You've done that. I'm proud of you."

I turned my body so his hand fell away. "Proud of me? I wanted to earn your pride another way. We didn't want this."

"That's true for all of us. We didn't know this would happen. But that's how we push through—when things happen, you take what comes and make it go your way. That's what you've got in front of you."

"What is our way? I don't know what I'm doing half the time. The others look at me and I have to say something. But I'm confused, all the time."

"Son," Papaw said, "that confusion is a good portion of a man's life."

"Why did Mama walk away? Why didn't she push through with us?"

His eyes widened. "I believe I knew my daughter as well as anybody could, and I don't know the answer to that."

"Maybe it's like Jane says—she didn't love us."

"Oh, that's not true, son. She loved you all so hard, so much. But Lillian lost the strength she used to have. My girl had ambition to make her way in the world."

"Is that what she's doing now?"

Papaw sighed. "If I found her today, I expect I would see her more worn down."

"I wish I could ask her why she gave us up."

Papaw shook his head. "Like your Grandma said, she's my child, and she's done what she's done. Her children are mine to see after now, and that's what we're going to do."

Later, at our house, I sat down with Hattie to outline the plan we had made with my grandparents. She feigned surprise at learning we had done the forbidden in seeing them. Hattie blustered just enough about how she would miss the girls to mask her relief at having a break from them. But Hattie made the same warning as Papaw.

"Dan, your father will have to agree to the children going to the farm. I cannot go along with this unless Alonzo gives his consent."

"Will you call Uncle Charlie so we can ask him to tell my father?" This request was my bet that both Hattie and Charlie had lost confidence in Alonzo over his violence toward us. Extending the cooling off period would make sense.

Hattie rang Uncle Charlie and introduced the scheme. "Charlie, calm down and give the boy a chance to explain it to you." She handed me the phone with a shake of her head.

Before I finished saying hello, Uncle Charlie lectured. "Dan, do you have any idea what a burden it is on me to manage the situation as it stands? What do you think will happen here? He is your father. I've got him staying away to think things over. He is not going to want to hear that you have involved Lillian's parents."

"It has to be this way for the summer."

I knew Charlie was caught between fearing Alonzo's temper spilling over with us and Aunt Letitia's strong objection to having Alonzo in her house.

Hattie got back on the phone. "Charlie, Alonzo will have to accept their help because we don't have anything better. Now, I can manage to stay here a few days a week to fix meals for George and Dan, but I am worn out. I want to go home."

My aunt and uncle went at it a bit, and when they ran out of steam, I took the phone again.

"Uncle Charlie, are you going to help me or do I have to go to my father on my own?"

"Change your tone with me, Dan, I warn you."

Waiting, not apologizing, I listened to Charlie breathing hard.

"Fine, I will fix things with Alonzo. But understand there is a limitation on this agreement: when the summer ends, you will have to accept your father back in his own house. The current arrangement cannot go on past that."

A gamble, but I had no choice. "Agreed."

A few days later, walking home along the back of the houses, the rise in the yard put me in view of the river. It was funny about that river, how scenic it seemed when you looked over it from afar, framed with the spring green in the surrounding hills. When you got down right to the shore and looked into the depths, the flow was sludge. The stink of it would send you scrambling away, hand over your nose. River Avenue was not far enough above its surface to escape the whiff of stench.

Marion was out in back of the houses hanging washing on the line when I came through the yard. Clothes hung outside gathered the coke dust, grayed with it, but on a very breezy day, the dust would flick off. The dried clothes would smell of the river.

The wind whipped and fought Marion as she tried to attach a bedsheet to the line. I stepped over to grab one end and pin it.

"Whew, Dan, thanks. Getting these clothes pinned today is a chore." The rings around Marion's eyes had darkened and deepened.

"How are your girls doing, Marion?"

She described the same troubles with sleeping and fighting and crying we had cycled through. Nodding my understanding, I helped her finish pinning the wash.

Picking up her empty basket, Marion started back to her house, then turned back to me. "I saw a lawyer in Uniontown. The Feekes want me to keep things the way they are, not take any action against Roy. But I want to move on. I can't move as quick as I want."

"You mean to move away from this house?"

"I don't know about that. The Feekes own this house. But I want to divorce Roy, and I have to wait two years."

"Two years?"

"To divorce him for abandonment. Roy abandoned us, there is proof, but the law says I have to declare the abandonment and wait two years in case he comes back. If he has not come back at all when the two years is up, I can petition for a divorce. If the Feekes will stay out of the way."

"Two years?" Saying it a second time, the meaning clicked.

"It'll be the same for your father to divorce Lillian, and if I know Alonzo, he will get a divorce. He has to wait two years. If your mama comes back, even for one day, the time stops."

"What happens during the two years?"

"Nothing happens. That's just it, isn't it? Nothing but giving them a chance to come back. Why would I want him to come back? There's no coming back, but if he's a coward, if he can't stay away, my children will suffer more."

"Couldn't you get a divorce if he came back?"

"He would have to agree to it. I would have to go through the mess of his petition and my petition, that's the papers saying whose fault it is. It could drag out, the judge could just say, 'He's back, live with him.'"

"What do the Feekes say?"

"Let it be, they'll let us stay in the house and pay me Roy's share, if I don't make a fuss." She set the basket on the stoop. "Where is your father?"

"He's not here. He's staying with Uncle Charlie. I don't know if he wants a divorce."

"Oh, he's thinking about it, all right." She picked up the basket again. "He's been down to the newspaper to publish a notice that declares the date of the abandonment. Alonzo is using the police report from the day he reported her missing as the proof. Lillian has to be missing for two years from that day."

"How do you know this?"

Marion rolled her eyes and shifted the basket on her hip. "Everybody knows what goes on in this town, Dan. Ask Mr. Kegg. He'll tell you I'm right. Besides, the Feekes have a man at the paper who tells them things they need to know, and that man is friendly to me, feels sorry for what Roy did."

With that, she thanked me for helping with the laundry, left me outside.

Marion's report sent me rummaging through the bin of old newspapers kept on the back porch as tinder for starting trash burns in the yard. In the paper from two days earlier, my father's notice appeared in the "Personals" column. He had reported his wife's disappearance to the police on March 24th, there were no leads to her whereabouts, and she had left him with six children. Paper in hand, I went down into the cellar, where Jane was pulling an old kit bag from a shelf, sending the coal dust swirling. Both of us coughed.

"Help me get the hatch open—I need to beat this outside."

Pushing the hatch door open, I grabbed the dirty bag and threw it out ahead of us. Every whack on the canvas from the rug beater swirled dust in the wind. Jane was intent on her lashes, her face grimacing with the effort. Her thwacking the bag made me wince with the memory of the belt hitting George.

"I want to show you something."

Thwack, thwack. "What is it?" Thwack, thwack.

"Dad put a personal ad in the paper. About Mama going missing. Marion told me it's for a divorce."

Thwacking stopped.

Jane grabbed the paper, following my finger to the place. "How does that mean divorce?"

I explained what Marion had told me.

Jane thrust the paper back at me. Thwack. "He has every right." Thwack.

"I just wanted you to know."

Wiping her brow, grabbing the bag's straps, Jane gave me one of her looks. "Now I know."

I understood the discussion would go no further.

With the kit bag and a number of satchels packed and loaded into a farm truck a few days later, Jane with Addie on her lap and our sisters in back, all waved their goodbyes to me and George. He and I relaxed into our routine. In the mornings before work, I walked him over to Marion's porch and they welcomed him in for a second breakfast before he and Junior went off to the fields for their day of baseball. If it rained hard enough to turn the fields muddy, the boys stayed on the porch to shoot marbles, or played rounds of catch in the road. Hattie cooked enough in two days to keep us going for the time without her.

On warm evenings, we ate on the back porch to enjoy the fading light and the breeze.

The anger that had churned through me curdled to melancholy. The post office got only half my attention. Sleepless at night and daydreaming on the job, my thoughts drifted over scenes with my mother, moments I had witnessed between my parents, the children crying, Lonnie dead. Sadness weighed me down like the pounds of brick we used to level the scale for the mailbags. I got up every day because of George, and I went to work for Mr. Kegg, but I had no spirit. I had figured out the summer for my brother and sisters, but I had no view of our future. They looked to me to chart it out, and I had no answers.

One Saturday after we closed the post office, I trudged the five miles to the cemetery and went to Lonnie's grave. Blooming flowers planted there meant Papaw had visited, making good on his promise to Grandma to keep up the grave while she was at the farm.

That talk on the porch with Papaw kept coming back to me. Pondering whether a man is the sum of what comes his way, or does he make his own way and shape what comes? And is it the same for a woman—does she strive to be a certain kind of person?

I had no answers. I stretched out alongside the grassy mound of Lonnie's grave and cried.

CHAPTER 14

The Fourth of July all-league baseball game was the last time I saw my father play ball.

The neighborhood teams anticipated the holiday competition with the swagger and side betting that accompanied the long-time town tradition. Early in the day, short games were played in rounds to eliminate teams and push the winners forward to the championship game that capped the competition. The rosters were open, so the best players from losing squads could play in the big game when the winning teams recruited them on the sidelines.

George and I were warming up at the field with the players on the boys' teams when our father arrived, riding in the back of a truck with a pack of men from the gas company team. They had new uniforms and the bluster of their past victories as they took the field for the first round.

The day was hot and play kept us in the sun for the morning. During a break midway through the rounds, my father walked over to the side of the boys' dugout where I was wiping off with a wet towel. He had lost some weight since the spring game, his belt cinching in his knickers at the waist, the fabric taut around his muscular legs. His arms swung loose. Seeing he carried no bat eased my tension as he approached.

He took off his cap, wiped his head with the back of his arm, and asked, "How are the children getting along?"

Surprised by the power of my anger climbing up on me, I wanted to spit back, "You're asking about the children you beat?" He would never apologize for what happened in the cellar.

I swallowed the anger in a lump down my throat, kept a game face. "I hear they are doing all right."

He nodded, and we stood there. I expected nothing from him. I turned toward the field, meant to leave him standing there, when he spoke again.

"A man will come to the house to pack up the darkroom. I'm moving my set-up closer to the police station."

I nodded. "All right. I will tell Hattie."

My father looked past me into the boy's dugout where George mingled with his team. For a second, I thought he would ask about George, but all he said was, "See to it." There was his order; that's where he wanted to keep us. I walked away.

Part of me was grateful that my father gave me no reason to change our manner with each other. It was easier to keep oriented to his familiar control. No need to argue about the darkroom, simple enough to let that happen. He could tell himself that I had taken the order as I always had. But his removing the darkroom from our house changed something.

Working on photos had been his escape from us when he was home. Dinner was timed to his chemical baths, ready when he wanted to come up to sit at the head of the table and pronounce his orders. My mother tempered his coldness. She emitted silent signals for us to wait out his gruffness, hold on, he would leave soon, either to the cellar or the road. Without her as a buffer, my father thrashed about inside our house, unleashing the worst of his nature with his belt.

The idea that he could return to the house transformed into a caring father was impossible to me. The living arrangement had caused no motivation in him to change as a father that I could see. Jane believed he had better intentions. She held to the notion that once our father had time to put our mother out of his mind, he would be good to us. It had to hurt Jane to read the notice of abandonment he published in the paper, but she defended his reasons.

In public, at work, on the field, he was unchallenged. Walking away from him, I felt a thin thread of understanding between us: he intended to stay away from our house, not because we wanted him to, but because not being with us suited him.

The pressure to figure out our future weighed heavier on me after that. I had mistaken the intensity as generating from my father's impending return into our daily lives, and my having to thwart him. Once I believed he preferred to stay away, the responsibility for my brother and sisters felt like pushing a loaded coal trolley through a narrow mineshaft. If you let go, it would roll back and crush you. I could fix on only one push and step at a time.

One morning in August when I expected to hear Hattie coming in the door, the voice calling hello was Cousin Oscar's. With him was a young woman he introduced as Nedda, his new wife.

Shaking Nedda's hand, I said, "Aunt Hattie didn't say you were getting married."

Oscar grinned. "She didn't know the exact day, but she knew. She just didn't like the idea." Nedda managed a weak smile.

"Where is Aunt Hattie?"

"Here's the thing, Dan. When my mother and Nedda are together in her house all day, it's not working out. And my mother isn't happy with Nedda on her own in the house, while she's here helping you boys. So I worked something out with her, and I hope you'll go along with it."

"What do you mean?"

"Nedda will be your cook and housekeeper. I'll bring her every morning and come back for her after she has made your supper. My mother can stay home, tend the garden, take it easier."

I smiled at Nedda. "Oscar, thanks for thinking of us like this, but we can't pay for a housekeeper. It's something I have been trying to figure out. I know it tires Aunt Hattie looking after us."

"Don't worry, Dan, about the pay. Uncle Charlie's taking care of that."

"What do you mean?"

"I'm driving Uncle Alonzo around the counties, assisting him when he's doing the photography for the surveying. I'm making plenty to cover Nedda being here. It's all worked out, and my mother will stop complaining. You've just got to agree with it."

Nedda spoke up. "Dan, I can cook, clean, do everything you need, and get to know all of you. Hattie's given me all her instructions." Nedda pulled out a composition book like the girls used in school and flipped it open to show me Hattie's writing.

They convinced me. "Looks like this *is* all settled, Oscar. Okay, Nedda, I can show you where things are in the kitchen."

After Oscar left and Nedda and I were looking through the pantry stocks, George came down. Within a few minutes he and Nedda had hit it off. She knew baseball, and that was the key to winning him over—along with blueberry pancakes. As I left them together and began the walk to the post office, some of my worry lifted. Hattie and Charlie and Oscar were looking out for us, something I would never have expected from them before my mother left. Oscar employed as my father's driver translated as Uncle Charlie keeping Alonzo's behavior within bounds. Concentrating on the survey photography would separate him from the old crew, send him into the farther out areas where the gas lines were expanding.

A pang of sympathy for the other woman and her children— our half-siblings—hit me. They would not see my father much, if ever. I had not pitied them before. Maybe he had cut off his ties to her. Her appearance at our house back in the spring might have meant he did. Maybe those children would be better off having their mother and never knowing their father. They didn't get a choice any more than we did. I added them to the total of children forsaken in the wake of Lillian, Roy, and Alonzo.

Nedda proved to be a good ally, rescuing us from the months of make-do living. She was twenty-five, about my height, and muscular. Having grown up on a farm, she was used to household chores. Yet she had modern tastes in her personal habits, her hair bobbed, her dresses shorter than most women in the town wore them. She usually had one of her ladies' magazines open in the kitchen. She liked to keep up with the news and her "stories" as she called them, listening to radio programs while she worked on the mending. Nedda looked into our eyes when we talked with her, had a reassuring way of offering help.

One afternoon, I came home to find Nedda upstairs rearranging the girls' personal things. Nedda bustled me through the bedrooms as she explained.

"Jane and Annie will share the room under the eave." That had been my parents' room. "Ruthie and Addie go together in the girls' room. And of course you and George keep your room, but I've added some comforts."

The walls in each room had been whitewashed, the beds and other furniture reset in different positions, benches near the windows for reading, books lined up on shelves she created in the nooks of the sloped walls. The blankets and bedding all washed and ironed, freshness in the closets from hanging lavender, the waxed wood floors gleaming. The baby crib was put away, Addie's bed now a cot like the others.

"Hattie will come here with me tomorrow to inspect. I think I've done everything the way she said."

"This was Hattie's idea?"

Floating on her excitement, Nedda did not sense my confusion about changing over my parents' room. As beautiful as it was, and as much as it lifted my spirits to think of us making a new start in those rooms, the rearrangement announced that my father had no place upstairs.

Next morning I waited in the front yard for Oscar's car before going to work. When Hattie had given her bundles to Nedda to carry inside, I caught her arm. "Aunt Hattie, the rearrangement upstairs leaves no room for my father."

"You haven't talked to Alonzo, have you?" she asked.

"Not since the league game, when he told me about moving the darkroom."

"He's left Charlie's, took the rooms above the storefront where he located the photography. He's staying there when he's in town."

"Are you saying he's not coming back here?"

"He made this move on his own. I've told Charlie his idea that Alonzo would come home isn't what Alonzo seems to be doing." Again Hattie surprised me with her directness about my father.

"But Uncle Charlie said at the end of the summer ..."

"Charlie will let this be."

The ground had shifted, again. "What should I tell the girls about the bedrooms?"

"Tell them to settle in. Let them get used to Nedda being here."

The next morning, Uncle George sent a trucker to drive Papaw, George, and me to stay at the farm for the ending of August, to spend time with my sisters and Grandma before the start of school. Bumping along in the back, I studied George, grateful for the summer he'd had. Tan and slender from playing so much ball, and having grown an inch over those weeks, he looked older than he was. He threw harder and his swing was stronger, his body leading his mind to a new confidence. Nights, he was asleep as soon as he hit the pillow.

Every week during the summer Papaw had reported on how well the girls were getting along at the farm. When we arrived, the change in my sisters was plain to see. Annie and Ruthie bubbled over with stories of their adventures roaming over the fields, helping with the farm animals, learning to sew, putting up vegetables. They were at the perfect age that summer to enjoy farm life, soak it in, let it soothe their troubles.

Jane still acted the little mother to them, but in a softer way, more protective than pushy. She, too, had enjoyed the rhythm of the farm rituals, getting up early to collect eggs, tending the gardens, working alongside the women and children who planted and harvested the fields. Spending close time with Grandma had furthered the healing of their divide, though Jane held a space within her that none of us would enter. Jane spoke of my father when no one else did. She worked mention of him into conversations, wanted to tell him about this or that, wouldn't he be pleased to see how everyone had grown. I heard these comments as her keeping loyalty to our father, still believing when we got home, he would embrace his family again. I hoped to get her to understand the way things truly were with him before she could be hurt.

The changes in Addie overwhelmed me. When I tried to pick her up, she squirmed, giggling, to run away from me. I caught Grandma's glistening eyes. She had done her best to boost Addie forward. Playing with the other kids who lived at the farm had hurried the transformation. Addie jumped and ran and dug in the dirt, played with bugs and frogs, let the puppies climb on her, and wanted to go outside first thing every morning. She babbled nonstop, in sentences, and when she wanted something, she tried to get it for herself. We had to restrain and contain her energy. It was such a difference I almost didn't want her to go home. I was afraid of losing the Addie who thrived on the farm that summer.

That week at the farm the weather showed its best face: sunny, hot days and mild, starry nights. We planned a picnic day at the pond, about an hour's hike from the house. Early that morning Grandma packed the lunch and snacks to divide among our packs. Papaw was out somewhere with Uncle George, and Grandma was not feeling up to the trek on such a warm day, so we set off on our own.

We had only ever done the hike to the pond with our mother and Uncle George. Jane took the lead, and I brought up the rear with Addie in the wagon. The sun had baked the worn path hard so that pulling her along went easy enough. When we had to get over ruts, George took Addie out of the wagon and guided her steps. We hiked at an easy pace, stopping for water along the way, with no one complaining or dropping back. A peacefulness walked with us.

We made a camp under a stand of trees near the shallowest side of the pond, where the shore was less rocky. Tucked into the wagon around Addie were Grandma's old tablecloths to spread out on the weedy earth, and we set the packs around to hold the cloth down from the wind. In the middle of the spread, we placed the jugs of water and lemonade, the sandwiches and fruit, cake, cookies, and cheese.

Anne, Ruthie, and George immediately peeled off their farm shirts and trousers down to swimming suits and ran into the pond. Jane helped Addie take off her shoes and socks and walked her into shallow water to puddle around. Our old tire swing still hung from a sturdy tree, the rope testing durable enough after the winter to hold my weight. With a running leap and push off, I was in the water.

We swam and ate and swam more. Water games to see who

could bring up the shiniest rock from the bottom, or make fish come to the surface with breadcrumbs got us competing and hollering about who won. We made teams of two for the boat game, which involved creating something that passed for a sailboat from bark and sticks and leaves, launching it on the surface of the water, timing whose boat floated longest.

The warmth and exertion tired us enough to flop onto the cloths and rest. Addie napped. Jane pulled out a newspaper from town to peruse. Annie and Ruthie and George chatted about what other kids they knew had been doing all summer.

Looking at my sisters and brother arrayed around me, my mind raced to what was facing us when we went home. The summer had worked some change for us. I wanted to transfer this peace to home. No one had talked about my mother or my father, not even Jane. None of them had asked me what we were going to do in town. Could we stay as calm as this, in charge of ourselves, not fall back? Would Nedda's alterations in those rooms cause us to live differently? After the bedrooms, her cleaning and decorating powers changed the front room from the mournful place where Lonnie had been laid out to a cozy living room. I pictured us sitting together on the davenport and the cushioned chairs she had slipcovered, games laid out on the rug, the radio playing. The girls' working on their stitches, George sorting his baseball cards, or doing homework at the wide kitchen table. Without parents. Could that be us? Closing my eyes, I willed the picture real.

Rousing ourselves, we loaded our packs and started the walk back to the farmhouse. As I pulled the wagon, a realization came to me. Before taking my sisters and brother back home, Grandma and Papaw and Uncle George needed to understand how I intended for us to live without our parents. I had come to a decision that required their agreement.

The afternoon waned as we straggled back into the yard. Grandma greeted us from the back porch, sending us to the trough at the side of the house to wash off dust and mud. Grandma had the foresight to fix a light supper, and set the table on the wide front porch, letting us eat as soon as we had cleaned up. Addie stayed awake long enough to eat her fill. She was well on her way to a deep sleep by the time I got her into her nightshirt and tucked her in. The others helped Grandma clean up the dishes and then took up spots on the front room floor to hear a radio show. When George's eyes closed, and Annie and Ruthie curled together sidelong, I left them and went to see Grandma and Jane in the kitchen.

"Can the two of you come out to the porch with me? I have something to discuss." Papaw and Uncle George sat on the steps of back porch, Papaw having his evening pipe.

Jane rolled her eyes at me but folded the dishtowel and moved to the screen door. She hated mosquitoes. Grandma ambled outside to a chair behind Papaw, her legs close enough for him to lean back against her, and she stroked his hair. Jane perched on the railing. To have their attention, I moved to stand facing them at the bottom of the steps.

"I want to stop looking for my mother."

Uncle George shifted his legs and leaned on his knees, watching me. Grandma's hand froze in her lap. Papaw leaned away from her and blew out pipe smoke. Jane folded her arms and studied me.

Grandma spoke first. "Why, what do you mean, Dan? Of course, we'll keep looking for her."

"I want end the search. I don't think she should come back."

Papaw set the pipe down. "Dan, you know we want to find her for you children, to get you back with her, settle things with Alonzo."

"Papaw, if you've been looking all summer, what do you know about her?"

Uncle George answered. "We lost her trail in Ohio a few weeks back. But I still have men keeping their eyes open. I can put notices in more papers."

"We don't need her to come back."

Grandma sucked in too much air and coughed, couldn't catch her breath. Jane went inside for water and, coming out with it, shot me a look I couldn't quite read. She helped Grandma to sip the water, then asked, "Why are you saying this now? You wanted her back."

"I did. At the beginning, even after we found out about

Roy. But now, her coming back will hurt us more." I set my gaze on Papaw and silently pleaded for his understanding. But I knew he wanted his daughter back, yearned to ease Grandma's heartache.

Papaw tamped more tobacco into his pipe, kept his voice steady "What are you saying to us, Dan?"

"Papaw, you tell me sometimes a line has been crossed, and there's no going back. We've crossed a line this summer, I see that in all of us. We can find a way to go on without her. We can't go back with her."

Grandma wept and wiped her eyes on her apron.

"Grandma, I don't mean to hurt you. You love us, I know. When you brought the girls here, I told you, we all have to grow. They did. We all did. Grandma, you helped so much. If my mother came back now, she wouldn't know us."

Jane pushed her way around Uncle George and Papaw to come down the steps. "Oh, Dan, I don't want her to come back, either. I was afraid to say. I don't ever want to see her again."

I put my arms around my sister. "You can't stay mad at her forever, Jane. But she shouldn't come back."

There was a long silence. I knew my mother's family well enough to wait out the leap they would have to make in their feelings. Uncle George hung his head, Papaw let the pipe go without lighting, Grandma wiped her cheeks. Jane wiggled free of my arms but stayed next to me, waiting.

Papaw turned and grasped Grandma's hand. "Ma, you know

he's right. Even if we find Lily, she probably won't be fit to care for these children."

Grandma sobbed. Uncle George ran his hands through his hair and looked at Papaw for the decision.

"All right, Dan," Papaw said, "the search is ended. But this doesn't make the road you're taking any smoother."

CHAPTER 15

After the talk with my grandparents and Uncle George, Jane and I agreed there was no need to tell our brother and sisters about the decision to stop the search. Their questions about my mother returning had tapered to few. We continued the practice of not pushing away any mention of our mother, but not opening the subject of finding her. Jane relaxed around me. I was grateful we had reached a working truce to navigate our different feelings toward both our parents.

As our days at the farm wound down, one of George's men delivered a letter from Uncle Charlie. My father had taken the rooms over the photography studio and was staying there indefinitely. Uncle Charlie may have known Hattie had already told me, but with the letter he intended to make a point: he was firm he would no longer be the middleman. Whatever the "arrangement" was to be, I would have to work that out with my father myself. He had announced the same to Alonzo.

On our last day at the farm, I worked threads about the differences in our living situation back at home into the breakfast chatter among my brother and sisters. When the girls heard about Nedda caring for us, George had so many good things to say about her that I needed only add my agreement. Jane perked up at having a young woman in our house. Nedda had warmed her way into George's heart and his regard for our cousin's wife pulled the others into her embrace from afar. George's enthusiastic comments opened a path for me to hint about the redecorating to give us more space, leaving the actual bedroom arrangement to be their surprise.

George came out with the question. "Will he be there when we get home?"

The chatter around the table quieted. Ruthie and Annie stopped eating, waiting.

"Uncle Charlie says Dad is so busy with the photography, he opened a studio in a storefront in town. He has taken the rooms over the studio. It's saves traveling time for him, and there is space for people to have their sittings there."

An exchange of glances around the table. George shrugged. I fooled no one except Addie, too young to understand. The tension would not ease until they were home and felt safe.

Jane huffed her concern. "I will go to see him, make sure he is comfortable there, see what things he needs from home."

Her continued worry for his welfare confused me. But I let it be, needing Jane on my side at home. No one else voiced a desire to visit our father.

Early the next morning, as we were packing the truck to leave the farm, Uncle George took me aside. Although we had been friendly with each other since the talk about not looking for my mother, I sensed his doubt about stopping the search even though he had said no more about it. As he pulled me away from loading the truck, I had an idea what was coming.

"Dan, I've been thinking over the whole situation since the talk the other night, and I see your point. I really do, but I am worried for my mother."

"Worried about … what? Did Grandma say something more to you?"

"No, not directly, but sitting with her, watching her these last few days, I see the sadness in her. She wants to see her daughter again." He leaned against the wide trunk of an old tree that shaded the house. "Hell, truth is, I want to see Lillian again, too."

"What are you saying?"

"I'm saying we agreed to stop searching, Papaw made me agree, but your Grandma is aching on this, and I'm worried she'll go on poorly."

I threw up my hands. "We're all going on poorly. That's how it is now, isn't it?"

He stood straighter. "Whoa, Dan, settle down. I have to take care of my mother. You can understand that, can't you?"

I folded my arms. "I care about Grandma, but you're troubling me when I have to take my brother and sisters home and hold us together. You've got no call to put this worry on me." The next words flew out before I caught them. "It's *your* fault *my* mother left this farm. You should have known to watch her and keep her here."

Uncle George hooked his thumbs in his jeans and moved in toward me. "Look here, Dan, I told you, your mother knew her own mind. There was nothing I could do. Lillian did what she wanted. Always did."

"But if you had kept her here until her mind settled, we wouldn't be in this mess."

"You'd be in a different mess, but a mess all the same. Blaming me is no use. Don't work against me."

"What does that mean?"

"It means I need to find Lillian for Grandma's sake, but that doesn't mean bring her back. Just for my folks to know where she is, how she's doing."

"If you intend to do that, why tell me?"

"If I find her, you might want to know."

"I won't."

The complication of seeing my mother again was beyond me. She had made everything too hard for us, the wreckage piled over us like a cave-in that could not be dug through. She was not alone in that; my father had done damage, too. But seeing her again would tear the scabs off the wounds, and the healing might never come.

Uncle George frowned at me with a shake of his head. "I can't believe that."

"Believe me. I want none of it."

I walked away from him back to the truck. My anger climbed me again, reddened my face, clenched my jaw. It had slumbered and let me be during the lazy days at the farm. If Uncle George was not ready to let my mother go, he needed to respect that I was. He had sworn to Papaw he would stop searching; now, he was not going to honor that. More lying. I was so tired of pretense.

Then Papaw took me aside. He was worried about Grandma, too. "Will your father object to our seeing the children in town? Your Grandma can't go without seeing them."

My father was no more likely to welcome us having contact with our grandparents than before, but he could not stop us when he lived separately. I was banking on his taking the rooms over the studio as evidence he did not intend to control our daily lives, although I could not prevent him from entering our house. If we were to have peace at home, I would have to renew the fragile truce with him on terms I could live with. My knowledge of what he'd done was my leverage.

"Papaw, I intend to tell him the truth. If I am going to draw my father's anger, I will do it straight." Papaw clapped me on the back.

Nedda and Oscar welcomed us at the end of the long drive home. The girls took to Nedda in the first ten minutes. Her enthusiasm smoothed the settling into the rearranged bedrooms, even for Addie, who jumped up and down on her new cot. Starting the new school year, me getting back to the post office, Nedda with us, it all fell into place, as if the peace of the farm was un-packed with the sun-dried clothes and fresh vegetables. I let my-self ease into that first week at home, keeping the churning thoughts about going to see my father at the back of my mind.

Jane took the initiative. "I've got some things to take to Dad. Let's go there together."

We had different motivations for visiting the photography studio. My confronting him would be uncomfortable for her to witness, but I judged it better for her to realize first-hand the terms I required from him. If she decided to maintain her rela-tionship with him, she would have to separate that from our liv-ing arrangement.

"Meet me at the post office Saturday at closing and we'll walk over."

In our town, many of the old company stores built in the boom days of mining were in half-use or shuttered with the clos-ing of the larger mines and the continuing exodus of miners and their families from the neighborhoods. My father rented a two-story wooden structure with rickety outside stairs leading to the living quarters above the storefront facing the street. When we stepped from the road onto the shallow wood porch, our father opened the double glass doors. He stood looking down at us from his height like we were beggars at his door. Anger crawled up my spine like spiders.

Throwing my shoulders back, I held steady. "Dad, we've come to talk to you."

He nodded and stepped aside to let us in, his eyes surveying the street before he closed the door behind us.

Inside, wood plank floors under the high ceiling were indented with marks where shelves had once stood, but now the room was a deep open space. An oak counter that must have held the cash register remained near the door. Floor-to-ceiling windows on either side of the door spread light around the entrance but left the larger space dim. My father had organized the picture studio into areas with different backdrops separated by panels of canvas over wooden frames. In the studio, he made the portraits of town leaders, prominent families, and civic groups by private arrangement. At the back was the door to the darkroom. Most of his equipment sat packed near the door, for traveling to the gas line sites.

Jane scraped a toe along the dusty floor. "I hope it's cleaner upstairs."

With a wry half-smile, my father said, "As clean as my own home? No."

Jane looked away. My father stood with his arms crossed, his eyes on me.

I launched straight in. "You know that Nedda is housekeeping for us. Uncle Charlie told me he will not bring money by the house anymore. I want to arrange that with you."

"Arrange it?"

His sarcastic tone felt precarious, like ginger-stepping from slippery stone to stone across a rushing stream, the fear of falling high. Anger accelerated my heartbeat.

"Yes, the weekly house money."

He snorted. "Money for my own children who you have turned against me."

"You made them afraid."

Jane spoke up. "Dad, I know you didn't mean to hit us."

I gave her a look meant to quiet her. He took a step toward me, leaned in, voice low.

"I will have order in my house. All these years I have worked to build a position, and I am known with respect in this town. Your mother had the benefit of everything I built. The money I made got us away from the hard life. I will not let what she's done ruin what I've worked for, the standing I have in this town."

Jane drew herself up, reached out to touch his arm. "You didn't mean to hurt us, I know. You didn't lie about the other family, the woman who came to our house." She glanced at me and I shook my head to warn her off. "Dan says it's true."

My father looked as though he wanted to spit. "Jane, people lie all the time. The sooner you learn that the better."

She went white, winced, stepped back. He might as well have hit her again. Anger churned in my stomach, my hands remembering the feel of clenching the baseball bat, ready to strike. Swallowing it down, I pushed to the nub.

"You know I have the photographs. And you want to avoid a scandal."

"You are threatening me again?"

"I am proposing an arrangement. You can bring the money to the post office, or I could come here."

Silence as we stared at each other.

"I am not walking into the post office to hand my son money while the town looks on." The awkwardness of that would be difficult for both of us. "And I don't want you to come here."

He reached behind the counter to pull out a cloth money bag like the ones we used in the post office to bundle the receipts. "A man will come to the house on Fridays with a bag like this and give it to Nedda."

He would stay on the edge of our lives. At least for now.

"I will tell Nedda to expect him."

Shoving the bag at me, he sneered, "You take the money, Dan. And see that you keep order in my house. I will be coming back."

With the bag in my hands, I took the second leap. "I plan for the children to see Papaw and Grandma. We need their help."

"Don't ask for that permission. You know my orders."

"I'm not asking."

"My orders about your grandparents will not change." His voice was low and tight like a growl.

"I am going to do what is best for the care of my brother and sisters."

I half-expected him to shout or put his hands on me, but he didn't. I pulled Jane by the arm toward the door, the money bag in my other hand.

As I held open the door and maneuvered us through, Jane shook me off, having one last thing to say to my father. "I know you didn't mean it."

The door slammed behind us.

On the street, I confronted my sister. "What were you doing in there? Why did you say that when you know he lied?"

She walked fast and her words came out harsh. "I keep telling you—he wouldn't be like this if Mama hadn't left."

"It was because she knew his lies that she left!"

"That's *not* a good reason," she yelled, whirling around so that I ran into her. She pounded her balled fists against my chest. "That's not a reason to leave *us*."

"No, it's not a reason, Jane, it's just what happened." I linked her arm over mine, the money bag wedged between us. "Let's go home."

We made our way back to River Avenue in silence.

The monetary arrangement with my father held. We took each week as it came. If Oscar had a day off from driving my father, he would get to our house before supper so he and Nedda could eat with us. Sometimes on Saturdays they would take George and the girls to a picture show, or just hang around for games and listening to radio programs. Nedda and Jane had similar fashion tastes, spending hours together over patterns to sew new dresses for themselves and the girls.

Oscar and Nedda were affectionate with each other and with us. Nedda naturally hugged and kissed George and the girls each day on the way out the door for school. Oscar threw an arm around me or George when greeting us or talking about something personal. Listening to our day-to-day highs and lows, they had ideas for solving problems. They added back the caring to our daily lives that my mother's grief had snuffed. When they were in the house, relief squeezed out my anger, diminished the burden in my head.

My father made a public show of pretending he was our full-time father. His residence above the photography studio when he was in town was not obvious, as he was away so often. His family, Jane, and I colluded in the charade. Our holding his secret allowed my father to protect his public position. Having bartered for the arrangement, I kept it quiet from everyone except Mr. Kegg. I no longer argued with myself about truth.

My father's family had also settled into an arrangement that kept the peace. We endured the charade of dinner with our father at Uncle Charlie's for Christmas. With perfunctory handshakes, pats on the head, and comments on our growth, my father acted like another uncle, observing us from his distance. My brother and sisters followed my lead in playing along, politely answering his few questions, quietly acquiescing to my aunts' fussing at us. Hattie telegraphed her unease with Alonzo but did not interfere. Only Jane attempted to get more from my father, moving to sit by him when she could, asking him to come to school for the events when parents were invited for recitals of student work. He avoided commitments. Seeing us off with Oscar and Nedda at the end of the evening, he barely waved goodbye. Silence rode with us in the car on the way home.

Around town my father's public guise never faltered. He continued to use our house mailbox in the post office; when he came in to check for his letters, he greeted me and Mr. Kegg, acted as if he would see me later at home. Mr. Kegg, watching my father leave, would shake his head. Sitting over casseroles by the stove, Mr. Kegg never asked me for more than I volunteered.

I became accustomed to the calm of the pretense. I should have known better than to let down my guard.

CHAPTER 16

Spring, 1932

The two-year mark of Lillian's departure from our lives passed as a normal day. Normal in the way that six siblings abandoned by both parents had learned to carry on, with aid from Nedda, Oscar, and our grandparents. As the months passed, new habits had taken hold, and the troubling tantrums and crying episodes had abated. Nedda and Oscar upheld my father's decree against seeing our grandparents, and protected their livelihood, by looking the other way when we wandered up the road. Papaw and Grandma repaid the favor by never coming to our house.

Shortly after the anniversary of my mother's departure, Marion shook my complacency. Marion had waited out the two years, not wavering from her resolve to divorce Roy despite the cautions from the Feeke family. Having received no word from or physical sign of Roy, she intended to legally divorce him. Marion alerted me that the two years of my mother's and Roy's

255

abandonment were officially recorded in the court. The divorces could proceed. My father, too, intended to pursue his case.

"The same judge will hear both cases in June, but not on the same day," Marion informed me one morning when we met in the yard. "The judge first scheduled my petition and your father's to be heard together to save everybody time. I told the judge that Alonzo was half responsible for my divorce, and I wanted him to answer for that in the hearing."

"My father would never do that."

Marion folded her arms, red in the face. "No. His lawyer convinced the judge that separating the cases would spare the court having to hear what he called 'emotional outbursts from Mrs. Feeke.'" Marion stomped her foot. "Damn him."

My father's lawyer made sure his case was scheduled first, preventing Marion having any opportunity to say something in front of the judge that might tinge his decision about my father's petition. Alonzo would appear in court the day before Marion.

Marion sighed. "My lawyer says separate cases is the easiest path to getting the whole thing over with. And I want it to be over with."

"What will Mr. Feeke do when you divorce Roy?"

"They say they will support Roy's children. I guess I will find out if they mean that." She turned the question back to me. "And what will you do when your father is granted a divorce?"

"I don't know."

The impending court date meant my father's next move had

to come with the divorce. We had not seen my father in town, at the ball field, or even at Uncle Charlie's house for Easter dinner. Hattie and Charlie had stopped making excuses for him. I suspected that Jane had visited the studio but did not ask her.

The date for the end-of-year class photographs had been announced at school, with my father as the photographer, making it certain I would see him. My edge against him had dulled, would need to be sharper for what he might do.

On picture day, the weather cooperated for the planned assembly of the grades in the garden next to the schoolhouse. When I spotted my father, he was chatting with the teachers. He waved to the girls as though they had just seen him at breakfast. Jane took up the act with ease, laughing and posing with her classmates, calling to my father to take an extra shot of her with her best friends. When my senior class lined up and clustered together, I could not meet my father's eye. I stared into the camera lens with tight lips. He stayed away from me.

The school printed the photographs in the remembrance book handed out on graduation day. Before the ceremony, my father roamed the yard taking candid pictures. Papaw and Grandma took seats in the midst of the crowd, away from potential contact with him. My brother sat between them; George still trembled when my father closed in. On the front platform, Ruthie and Annie were out of his reach among the chorus. Jane sought him out, staying by his side while he did the photos, chatting with family members of her friends as he set and reset their poses. Sitting amid my classmates, I focused on the speeches, and accepted my diploma with the principal's handshake without waiting to hold the pose while my father aimed and clicked his camera. He gave no sign of missing my shot.

Neither did he approach me with congratulations, relieving me of having to decide whether to accept. If the moment had come, his clap on my back or a handshake would have deepened the pit of lies. I colluded in the act we carried on. It was also in my interest, not that my father thought to make things easier for us, because he was always acting for himself. But the script we followed, as though we were characters in a radio play, had benefitted my family. By cooperating, calm had prevailed. The gas company man showed up every Friday with the house money, chatty with Nedda, saying how "Mr. Alonzo" wanted to make sure she had what she needed for the shopping.

Two years of calm traded for lies. But wasn't that what I had demanded from him?

A beaming Mr. Kegg grabbed me after the ceremony to double the handshake and hearty clap on the back I received from Papaw. The week after, Mr. Kegg took me on full-time permanent at the post office. Small town operations like ours survived on efficiency, and Mr. Kegg's experience in organizing how we worked had turned fortunate when the Depression hit the postal service. We were not affected as much as other laborers, but we lost some wages. He got me on the roster before the worst hit. But Mr. Kegg's grand plan to start delivering mail house-to-house in town, like a city service, had been shelved with hope for better times.

The daily parade of townsfolk through the lobby brought story after story of hardship. People we had known for years were suddenly desperate. Some came in to forward their mail to a city where the talk said there were jobs. If word spread that one man found work in Detroit or Cleveland or Chicago, five others would follow, leaving their wives and children behind to wait on cash in the mail. Many a day we had ladies crying in the lobby over an empty box.

Floating above those who suffered were the prominent people in town, my father's regular cronies, whose lives seemed unaffected. A veneer of normalcy spread across my father's dealings with the men who still made money. Between the photography and the gas company, he had no apparent financial worries and his public status grew. Reading in the newspaper personals column about him attending house parties or photographing community functions, Jane puffed with excitement about our father's connections.

Jane was caught in the pretense as much as I was but displayed no reservations about it. She relished the social easiness that my father's public efforts provided; her friends were the daughters and sons of the businesspeople he collected in his orbit. Jane enjoyed going out with those friends, and the chief benefit of the separated living arrangement was that it prevented my father from restricting her activities. Two years gone from my mother's watchful eye, sixteen and full of herself, she assumed her privilege to go out as she pleased.

Nedda and I allied in trying to rein in Jane's social life. Sparring about coming home late strained her closeness to Nedda. The three of us juggled the hours of responsibility for the younger children, hard enough with Nedda having a little one of her own by then, and my working full time. Jane shrugged off duties around the house, complaining that having to hang around to take care of Addie or make supper was work enough, refusing to add cleaning or laundry to her chores.

Jane shortened her skirts and altered the dress patterns to follow the curves of her bustline and hips. She gave her hair the wavy look of movie stars and used the reddest lipstick available from the drugstore. Grandma didn't see her often enough to comment on her looks, but Marion did. Hanging wash in the yard, Marion asked Nedda, "Do you think Jane is looking too racy?" Afterward, Nedda came to me, saying one of us needed to talk with Jane about her clothes.

"What about them?"

"You're her older brother, you see how she looks."

"What am I supposed to tell her about how she looks?"

Nedda rolled her eyes. "Daniel, you know how boys look at girls. Your sister is getting over the line."

Marion and Nedda were reading signals I had been blind to. While I had noticed the changes in Jane, I was not operating in the same circles, wasn't aware of the attention she attracted, or wanted to attract. Before, it had not occurred to me to question where Jane went and who she was with. She would tell Nedda she was going to a friend's house or meeting girls at the movie theater, or to a dance at the church hall. But I had no language for talking to Jane about the risks Nedda implied.

Soon after the conversation with Nedda, I was sitting on our front porch on a warm evening when the son of the neighbors on the road behind us drove by. He and I had gone through school together, and we had been friendly enough as classmates. He tooted the horn when he saw me, stopping to stick his head out the car window.

"Hey, Dan, how are you?"

I walked over to the gate. "Fine, fine. What are you doing with yourself?"

"Oh, you know, I got in at the mine. They're only giving three days a week, but what else am I gonna do?" He shrugged. "You're sure lucky to be in at the post office."

"I am at that."

"The boys must be looking for your sister these days."

This was a surprise. "Jane? She's young for that."

"I see her around town, and she seems old enough."

"What's that mean?"

He heard the friction in my voice and came back quick. "Not a thing, nothing at all. Just asking after her. Gotta go now—you take care." He shifted into gear and drove off.

My skin crawled. Inside, Ruthie and Annie lay on the rug in

the front room listening to a radio show. Addie was sleeping upstairs, and George had a batch of baseball cards spread out on the kitchen table. I told Annie I had to walk downtown for something and would be back shortly, and she was in charge. She nodded, keeping her eyes on the radio. Ruthie waved her arm to make me stop talking.

There were few places to go in our town for amusement. From the ice cream parlor, I walked to the movie theater, where I asked the ticket seller if Jane had been there that evening. No luck, and she was not in the park at the center of town where couples strolled in the warm air. There were no dances that I knew of that night. She could be at a friend's home, but I could hardly go knocking on doors asking for her.

Turning back toward River Avenue, racking my brain to recall if she said where she would be, I told myself it was crazy to rush from not thinking about where she went in the evenings to being scared to find her. Jane was too smart to get into any trouble. Her friends were the children of the best people in town. I convinced myself I was worrying for nothing.

Back on our porch I sat thinking and waiting. Part of me envied Jane's easy way with other people. I had not gone to a dance or any of the social events during my high school years. Even before Lonnie got sick, my mother's days veered toward unsettled often enough that I went from home to school to work, and back again. Working in the post office, I talked to a lot of people, but it was outward contact.

Now, no friends were calling me or waiting to meet me in town on a fine evening like this. Papaw, Nedda, Oscar all referred to me as "man of the house." And I was always home, keeping my self-imposed limits. I could have been like Jane and demanded time for myself, but I hadn't. She wanted to do things and see places outside our house, our town. It jolted me to realize that she wanted her life, an adult life. Although she and I had not reconciled our different views of our parents, I operated on the assumption that we were united in staying together. Me finishing school and starting full-time work hadn't changed that for me. It dawned on me that Jane planned to make a different choice.

What did I want? I had no answer.

Eleven o'clock chimed on the hall clock. The street was dark, the only light coming from the lamp behind the filmy curtains in the front room. Sitting in shadows on the porch, my mind's eye flashed to the moon glow on the icy street the night I had spent waiting for my mother. No longer waiting for her, what was I hoping for?

The sound of a car engine and tires crunching gravel coming up the hill, then headlights, tugged my attention back to the street.

Pulling in front of the gate was Uncle Charlie's sedan. My father was behind the wheel, a woman next to him in the front seat, her face obscured in the dark. The car had barely stopped when the rear door opened. Jane jumped out, slammed the door closed. That got my father out of the car quick.

He grabbed Jane's arm before she got through the gate. "What do you think you're doing, slamming that door?"

"Let go of my arm. I'm going inside."

"I am not finished talking to you."

She jerked her arm away from his grasp, rubbed it with the other hand, stood up straight and looked him in the eye. "I'm done talking to you."

The slap was swift, and she took it with a howl. I jumped forward and the woman in the front seat dragged herself to the driver's side window, reaching out for my father.

"Alonzo, stop!"

His hand ready to strike again, my father saw me.

"Ask your sister where I found her tonight, Dan. Ask her where she was. You ask her—because you don't know where she was, running around, and I'm telling you, this is going to stop."

Jane hissed, "He's not in charge of me. I'm almost seventeen, I can manage myself."

"One was not enough for you? Should I give you some more?' my father growled, with a raised hand. "You think you're doing a good job here, Daniel? Your sister running around in the next town?"

That did sound bad if it was true. "She won't do it again."

"Damn right she won't! She's as shameless as her mother!"

"I am not like my mother!"

Again, the voice from the car. "Alonzo, please, let's go."

Jane had the sense to come inside the gate, putting it between them, and I stepped in front of her. "Whatever happened, you can go. We're going inside."

"Whatever happened?" he repeated. "If I hadn't taken her out of there, who knows what would have happened!"

Jane was defiant in a way I had not seen her before with my father. "I didn't do anything wrong! I was only dancing."

A window sash creaked open. Marion's voice came from the darkness. "What is going on out there? Dan, is that you?"

"No, *Mrs. Feeke*, it's me, talking to *my* children in *my* yard, and I'll thank you to close the window and mind your own business!"

Marion was having none of that. "Alonzo, get out of here or I'll call the police."

"The police? At my own house? That's a laugh!"

"I'll call them, I will, if you don't go!"

Pushing Jane toward the porch, I called to Marion. "We're going in, it's okay. No need to call anyone."

Silence from Marion, no sound of the window closing, sensing her waiting. Dogs began barking at the next house down.

My father waved his arm toward the porch. "Both of you, get inside before you have the whole street awake."

Jane stood glaring at him from the porch, and I waited at the gate. He yanked open the car door and the woman jumped back to her side. Slamming the door shut, my father leaned out the window, pointing a finger at me.

"You keep your sister at home, you hear me? So help me, she

is not going to turn out like her mother!" Gears crunching with the shift, the car pulled away fast.

I heard Marion mutter, "Son of a bitch," before she shut her window.

Inside, Jane stood at the kitchen sink holding a wet cloth on her cheek. She turned her face into the light and asked, "Is there a mark?"

"It will fade by morning."

I hadn't seen her before she left that evening, and now I took in her slender arms coming out of the wrinkled dress, the cinch of it around her waist, the waved bob, lipstick smeared. She had dressed to impress someone, in the bedroom with my mother's mirror. My perception shifted, seeing Jane with the eyes of boys like the one that asked about her earlier. What did she know of boys' minds?

"Are you going to tell me what happened?"

"So you can yell at me, too?"

"So I can understand why he brought you home."

Jane plopped into a kitchen chair. "We went to a dance at a new hall we heard about. Jimmy Taylor drove six of us." She fidgeted with the belt on her dress. "We planned to leave for home by ten, but everyone was having such fun, the music was good. There were lots of people to dance with."

She touched her cheek, her eyes tearing up. "It was after ten and I knew we should go. I went around collecting everyone, trying to get Jimmy to go to the car, and then I saw Dad. With that woman."

"The woman in the car?"

"I don't know how long he was there before I saw him—it was crowded. He had his arm around her and when he saw me staring, he jumped up and grabbed me. He yelled, 'Who are you with?' It was so humiliating!"

Tears ran down her face. "*She* convinced him to go outside. He dragged me out. In the parking lot, he shook me and kept asking who I was with, and I wouldn't answer, and he got madder and madder."

"And he drove you home."

"Shoved me into the backseat, drove fast the whole way, shouting that he was not going to stand by while I acted like my mother, running around loose. That's what he kept saying, 'loose.'"

Jane sobbed. "No matter what I said, he kept saying I was like her. I hate her, I told him I hate her, and he just said, 'You are no different.'" Sniffling, she whispered, "You heard him."

Cracking a wedge of ice from the block in the icebox, I wrapped it up and handed it to her. Our eyes met and she said, "I don't need to hear what you're thinking."

After Jane went upstairs, I lay down on the glider on the porch. The night air was warm, humid, more bearable than during the smoky days. My father would not let this go, that I was sure of. I wondered who the woman with him in the car could be.

Next thing, I was waking up in the same spot, to the sound of the rooster at the house on the road down below. Sitting up, I heard Marion call my name. She walked over to our porch.

"Jane made a big mistake last night."

"I know."

"The divorces are coming up. He's going to be a free man."

"What's that got to do with Jane?"

"He will get custody of his children. Not you, you're over age now, but he'll get the rest, and he'll come back."

"He had us all along."

"Yes, but when the court makes it official that he is the sole parent, he's going to take that as license to come back here. You'd better be ready."

A week later, Marion's divorce was granted without a public hearing, the Feeke family having a good amount of pull in the town to avoid publicity. Roy's brothers had been against Marion going through with the divorce but could not stop her. After she received the decree, they informed her they were taking back her house, that if she wanted to stay, she would have to buy it from them. Marion had saved some money, but after paying the court fees there was not enough to buy the house. She decided to move her children to Cleveland where she had kin. The Feeke brothers gave her money for the children and a week to pack up.

On the day my father's case was scheduled, I hitched a ride to the county courthouse in Uniontown on one of the mail trucks. I entered the courtroom a few minutes before the start of the hearing. My father wasn't expecting me there and didn't notice me slip onto one of the hard benches near the door. In front of me were five rows of seats, then a wooden barrier with a gate that swung open. Beyond the gate, my father and his lawyer sat at an oversized wood table that reminded me of the reading room in the library. At the front of the courtroom, butt up against the judge's bench, was the stenographer's desk. A young man smoking a pipe approached the desk and set out pads and pens, then arranged himself in the chair, tapping his pipe out in a glass ashtray. On a side wall an ornate clock with Roman numerals that looked to be gilded in gold leaf around the edges ticked over the hour.

A door inset in the wall at behind the judge's bench opened and the clerk called out, "All rise," and we did.

The judge bustled through, letting the door slam behind him. He glared out over the courtroom as he swept aside the black robe and settled into his leather chair with a grunt. Just then, Uncle Charlie entered through the public door, saw me on the left side, and took a seat on the right as we all sat down again.

While the formalities of reading out the docket number and such went on, I studied my father's faultless game face, the practiced facade that gave nothing away when he stared down a pitcher, smirked at fast balls that grazed him speeding by, and then leaned back in for the next pitch. Keeping control, his strategy set, never letting anyone believe otherwise. It worked for him in the courtroom, in the way he deferred to the judge, answered in a clear strong voice, saying with his full-height, toned figure in a business suit that he was up to the obligations of a divorced head of household, having been deserted by the afore-named defendant.

The lawyer called Uncle Charlie as a witness to my father's employment, character, and position in the community, all of which the judge listened to with no comment. Then his attorney read out the summary of Lillian's desertion, omitting the detail of Lillian's connection to Roy, careful not to remind the judge of the direct linkage to the Feeke case. Alonzo's pleading for divorce was strong without it, given that she had abandoned her husband and children more than two years prior, as attested by the police and news reports.

All seemed to proceed without a hitch to the point when my father and his lawyer waited patiently while the judge scanned the papers put before him by his clerk. It was expected that a verbal decision would be announced and recorded, and my father's attorney would then retrieve the legal paperwork in about two weeks.

The judge finished his review. Peering over the spectacles that had made their way down the bridge of his nose, he asked my father to stand. He and the lawyer did so. "You are caring for these six children on your own, sir?"

"My client has the assistance of relatives, your honor," said the attorney.

"My question is to your client, if you please."

My father cleared his throat. "My sister and my niece have stepped in to help, your honor."

"Stepped in, as in living with these children?"

"Yes, your honor, for the most part."

"For the most part, sir? You have six children to care for. If I read this correctly, only one is old enough to be emancipated. The court has an interest in the arrangements for their care."

"Yes, your honor, I have seen to their care."

"The court reminds you, sir, of your obligation to these children. With one parent gone, if you do not live up to that obligation, the court will seek other arrangements for these children."

Panic rose in me. On the other side of the aisle, Uncle Charlie leaned forward on the bench and twisted his hat around with both hands, intent on the judge's words. The lawyer intervened.

"Your honor, as our papers indicate, my client has good standing in his community. He is employed and intends to remain in the community where the children are being raised. There will be no problems with their care."

"Understood, but the court sees too many cases these days where the abandonment by one spouse results in the remaining party being unable or unwilling to care for the affected children."

"Your honor, if I may." My father clasped his hands before him, drew himself up, focused on the judge, who waved at him to speak.

"I intend to remarry and will announce the engagement when the divorce is granted. If your honor finds in favor of my petition, I will have a wife to help me give my children the home they deserve."

Uncle Charlie and I mirrored looks of surprise to each other across the aisle. He had not seen that coming either. My father had all kinds of ways to get on base.

The judge was silent as he gazed from my father to the papers and back. His hand on the gavel, he raised it, said, "Petition granted," and pounded the next phase of our lives into being.

CHAPTER 17

As the judge gaveled the hearing closed I slipped out of the courtroom, waited out of sight under the building's side portico. My father walking out with his lawyer gloated over the outcome, his sly grin arousing my suspicion. Did he lie about his intention to remarry, to get the judge to sign the decree? Uncle Charlie caught up to them, speaking too low for me to hear, punctuating his words with taps of his hat against my father's chest. Alonzo listened with a smirk, then shrugged and strode away.

At home, after I reported to Jane what our father had told the judge, she folded her arms and said, "That woman he was with that night."

Two weeks later, the six of us were summoned to Sunday dinner at Uncle Charlie's house.

All our bodies piled together in Oscar's car on the sticky day, along with Nedda and their boy, Ollie, made for an uncomfortable ride. By the time Oscar parked in front of Charlie's house, even Nedda was at the end of her patience. Ruthie and Annie had pulled the ribbons from each other's hair, Jane fussed in dread of Aunt Letitia's critique of her wrinkled dress, Ollie whined for lunch, and Addie kicked the seat, refusing to get out of the car. George and I, underneath the girls on our laps in the back seat, had to foist them off to get out and fan our damp shirts away from our sweaty fronts. The back-and-forth arguing and moaning continued until Hattie came outside to hustle us in.

"What's all the fuss out here? We have a guest inside, so gather yourselves, c'mon, go in. Enough, girls," shooting one of her looks at my sisters. "Don't make me say it again."

Jane muttered in my ear, "Guest? What is going on?"

I shook my head, and turned to Nedda, who also shook her head. "They told us to bring you, that's all."

In the front hall, Uncle Charlie and Aunt Letitia greeted us with beaming smiles we didn't recognize. Before our huddle could disperse, they ushered us into the parlor. My father sat on the settee close to the woman who had been in the car the night he brought Jane home.

Jane and I exchanged a knowing look.

My father gathered the woman's arm under his and pulled her up with him as he stood. Hattie waved us forward with hand gestures, then took Ollie by the hand and walked him to the kitchen. Nedda and Oscar caught her look to follow. Silence as the six of us, stranded in the middle of the floral carpet, waited for what would come next.

"Hello, hello," my father greeted us. He let go of the woman, stretching his hands to pat the girls on the head and thump George on the back. Hardened against him since the night at the dance hall, Jane drew back. He deftly made his gesture toward her seem intended for Addie, stooping down to kiss her on the cheek. Jane rolled her eyes. As he stood, my father nodded to me.

Circling his arm around the woman's waist, he said, "I want you all to meet Miss Della Carson. Della, these are my children. I think you can tell who's who. Dan and Jane the two oldest, then Georgie here, he's the baseball player, Annie and Ruthie, and Addie, the baby, not so much of a baby anymore." The words rushed out of him like a rehearsed speech he needed to say before he forgot his lines.

Della looked well-looked-after, mature but still youthful, not as old as my father, with wide, lively eyes and short curly hair. Her smart dress and heels distinguished her from the women in our town who made their clothes at home. Hers was a polished, modern, money-in-the-bank style. After a moment, I recognized her as the woman in the photograph in the window of the Chevrolet storefront owned by the Feekes—she had been their first female customer. Mr. Feeke had my father take the picture when she picked up her car, and so they had met. My father lost a wife to a Feeke and found another while in their employ.

"I am so happy to meet all of you," Della said, "and I hope to get to know you before the wedding."

Jane gasped and stiffened next to me. Ruthie's and Annie's

panicked eyes asked me, *Did you know?* Addie, tired of standing still, pulled away from Jane and ran into the kitchen. George made a beeline after her to get himself out of there. I stared at my father and waited for how he would explain his way through. Or lie, more likely.

"That's our surprise," he said with a grin. "Della and I wanted to surprise you with the news we are engaged to be married." He winked at me like he was acknowledging a conspirator.

Jane saw the wink and took it that way. "You knew this?" she spat at me.

It was so like my father to point things away from his own misstep. "No, I did not know this," I emphasized, staring at my father. "We are all hearing this for the first time."

Now Della understood that we were more than surprised. "Alonzo, I thought you talked with your children, at least the older ones."

"I decided a surprise would be more fun." He turned to me. "Where are your manners, Daniel? What do you say to Della?"

About the same height as me, Della, a flush creeping up her neck, ran a hand under her brown hair frizzing in the humidity. Her lips formed a weak smile and her eyes crinkled with concern. The disturbance in that moment—perceiving how my father had hoodwinked her, her understanding that in accepting his proposal she was inheriting not six imaginary children but the complications of the six beings gathered before her—rippled on her face. She was new to his game, and he was not playing fair with her.

"How do you do, Miss Carson," I said offering my hand. As she took it, I went on, "My sisters and brother are pleased to meet you, too." Jane, keeping her arms folded, grimaced a half-smile. Ruthie and Annie mumbled pleased-to-meet-you. George towed Addie back into the room, gave Della a shy smile. Addie glowered at Della's question asking how old she was. My father took all this in with hands behind his back, smirking at me.

Hattie broke the awkwardness by announcing lunch. Through the archway beyond, the dining room table was set with fresh flowers and the good dishes. We chose chairs at the table, waiting for Aunt Letitia to approve before we sat. We were arrayed along the length of the table opposite Della and my father. Acting as though our reticence was unusual, Aunts Letitia and Hattie proclaimed their surprise we were not chattering, and assured Della our restraint was evidence of our impeccable manners. Jane snorted at that, her hand clenching the side of the chair next to me. Della matched our quietness, taking discreet peeks at us as she ate. I could feel her mind churning with reactions to my father's "surprise."

Nedda played translator, reading our silent questions, making polite inquiries to elicit some information from Della. We learned she worked in a steady position in an insurance company in Uniontown.

Jane hissed under her breath, "What does an independent working woman want with a man with six children?" Aunt Letitia glared us into silence.

The car from Feeke's was indeed hers, all paid for. Her parents lived on a farm in another county, and her large family was spread throughout the area. Most of them would attend the wedding.

Della managed the panic I had seen cross her face so that when my father spoke to her she smiled, but the shadow was still there. If my father had let her believe he had told us about the engagement, what else had he failed to tell her? I decided to test what she knew.

"Della, will you be moving into my father's apartment over the photography studio?"

Hattie and Letitia sucked in their breath. Oscar let a little smile glint across his face and Nedda elbowed him.

"His apartment over the studio?" Confused, Della touched my father's arm.

Jane turned her nose up at my father and joined in. "Where he lives."

My father stone-faced his disgust at us, then fast-composed a smile for Della, squeezed her arm. "There has been an arrangement, with Nedda looking after them and housekeeping. After the wedding, we will go back to our normal family life."

Too much for Jane, she stood and threw her napkin on the table. "Go back to normal? We do not have a normal family. My mother left us. You lied, you hit us, and you embarrassed me, accused me of things I did not do. Now you tell us you are getting married and *she* will make things normal? No!" She stomped out of the room and slammed out the front door.

Della grimaced to hold back tears. "I was afraid of this, Alonzo. I told you, I was afraid of this."

My father, torn between anger at Jane and needing to reassure Della, stayed with his fiancée. "I can manage my children, Della, don't worry."

Silence around the table. Uncle Charlie signaled to Letitia and Hattie, who coaxed Della up from her seat and led her upstairs, soothing her. Nedda began clearing plates, asking Oscar to help. Ruthie and Annie asked me to be excused. I gave them permission before my father could refuse it, and he seethed at the understanding of his lost control. With the promise of cookies, George bribed Addie and Ollie out from under the table, where they had gone to escape the tension. They followed him outside.

My father, Uncle Charlie, and I remained at the table.

No longer the son who waited on the defensive for my father to start our skirmishes, I went straight at him. "You didn't tell Della the truth, did you?"

He would not take that from me. Launching out of his chair and reaching across the table, he grabbed my shirt. "I am your father. When I bring her to *my* house, *I* will be in charge. Things will be the way they should be."

Uncle Charlie rapped the table, motioned my father to let go. "Dan, you need to get your brother and sisters ready for the change. Della will come home as your father's bride in less than three weeks. Hattie's instructing Nedda about getting the house ready."

My father swirled iced tea in his glass and drank it in one gulp, making me wonder if Uncle Charlie had strengthened it from a flask. My father spat words at me. "The so-called living arrangement was never meant to be permanent."

"I have to keep you from hurting the children."

He looked at me with scorn. "I am not going to hurt my children."

"No. You won't."

"*You* have no standing. My household will be proper again, with my wife there to see to it."

"Is that the order you've given to Della?"

Glowering, my father issued a command. "I expect all of you to attend the ceremony at her parents' farm."

My face burning, I pushed away from the table. "Uncle Charlie, thank you for lunch. We are leaving now." Anger churned up stronger, anger with them, anger with myself, but unsure of my play at that point.

Della remained upstairs, and Aunt Letitia had nothing to say to me. George and the girls huddled on the porch and when they saw me, ran to the car. Sullen Jane was already in it and took Addie on her lap. Hattie came outside to see us off. Oscar loaded Nedda's food baskets into the back and the rest of us piled in. The humid breeze from the open windows lulled us. We rode in silence except for Ollie's blabbering to himself.

The next morning Jane and I stewed over coffee, hot air moving from one side of us to the other with the rotations of the fan sitting on the sill. Nedda bustled in the back door. She plopped into a chair with a groan.

"Well, it's a pickle we have now, isn't it? I'm worried."

We made no reply, continuing to sip, Jane leaning on one elbow, me shirtless in the heat.

"I'm supposed to rearrange the bedrooms so your father and … his wife can settle in. It pains me to do this to all of you."

Jane huffed. "Let *her* do it."

"What?"

"If she's going to be the *lady* of the house, tell her to do it herself."

Nedda knew better than to engage with Jane when she was in a mood. "I'll see to it, never mind. Can you start on the mending, please?" With that, Nedda swept out of the kitchen to get the others up for the day.

Jane sighed and dragged herself out of the chair with a parting barb for me. "All your fussing with him did us no good. He's angry and intends to get his way. No wife will change that."

Walking to work at the post office, I could not conjure any scenario in which we could get along with my father back in the house. Jane was right about him not forgetting all that had passed between us; it was not my father's style to forget, let alone forgive. His demeanor at the Sunday meal had shown his true colors, and

I suspected Della did not know how to read him the way we did. She had accepted the man he let her see, the man who had his world under control. She had no idea how he maintained that control.

Della in the house would give him an ally. There were six of us against her—was she strong enough to enforce his commands if we opposed her? Or would she leave it to him, reporting on us and letting him dole out the penalties? That was more likely. I felt like we were in a vise with the clamps forcing us rigid.

At the corner near the post office Uncle George was sitting in the cab of his truck. He saw me coming in the side mirror and with an arm motioned me around to the passenger side. Getting in, I blurted out, "What are you doing here?"

"That's how it is, now, we don't say hello?"

"Okay, hello, and what are you doing here?" The passing of time had not changed my anxiety around Uncle George. Seeing him provoked an undercurrent of my mother's hurtfulness melded with the blame I laid on him.

"Well, Dan, I heard about your father's engagement, and I have something for you."

"How did you know?"

"I have customers in several counties and when people plan big parties, they order extra product."

The upcoming farm wedding and reception, the talk of Della's large family, came to mind.

"With your father marrying, I figure it's time to give you

this." He handed me a muslin bag.

Opening the drawstring tie revealed rubber-banded bundles of cash. "What…?"

"It's your mother's share. I've been keeping it for you all. If she had been here all this time, that's what she would have earned. You can use it how you want, but I'm thinking you'll need it to get out."

"Get out…?"

"Think about it. Alonzo's getting married and his new wife is coming home to six children—not her own. The young ones, okay, she accepts raising them. But a grown man? She doesn't want you crowding up her house."

His words cut through the fog in my brain. Uncle George was right. Della could find a way to mother the younger children. But she could also make demands to lighten the burden. My father would kick me out with glee. With me gone, he could manipulate Jane and punish the others into submitting to him. Maybe he was saving that to spring on me, for the pleasure of watching me leave.

"I can't leave my sisters and brother with him."

"You might not have a choice. You need this money to move on."

"I'm not leaving them."

Uncle George leveled his eyes with mine. "I'm giving you this money and you can decide what to do with it." He started the engine. "But think about what I said."

"I am grateful. I need to think."

"All right, then. Let me know if you need my help." He waited for me to get out and pulled away with a wave.

I tucked the bag away until the end of the day when I had a chance alone to examine it. The amount startled me into realizing how good the business had been for Uncle George over the last few years. My conflict about the bootlegging had disappeared, replaced by my desperation. What the money could buy made my head swim.

I could walk away, like Lillian did. For the first time I had an inkling of how she might have done it.

Indignation shoved that away. She was our mother, an adult, and she walked away from what she was supposed to do. Now I was an adult, a young one, but old enough to know the right thing to do. What kind of man left his brother and sisters behind with a tyrant father, to go off and pretend he could have his own life? I would not leave them; I knew that about myself. But Uncle George's logic about Della rang in my head.

When I got home that afternoon, commotion upstairs and the tone of Nedda's voice giving direction to George told me she had undertaken the moving of beds and clothing. Girls' room, boys' room, parents' room. I wandered into the kitchen, too depressed to act on the list of chores Nedda had left on the table for me.

I needed to hide the money while I figured out what to do.

In the pantry, my mother's cookbook library had been piled into a niche at the back of the lowest shelf, behind jars of pickles

Grandma had put up that no one liked to eat. Nedda and Jane going into the pantry to grab dishes and flour overlooked the hidden books. Acting fast, I pulled out the jars and, sticking my hand behind the books, felt open space. Removing books, I shoved the sack of bills in, replaced the cookbooks, and lined up the pickle jars in front. No one would touch those pickles.

The next day, I sweated up the hill after work and saw Della's car parked in the road at our house. Nedda, Jane, and Della stood together on the porch, Jane and Nedda in housedresses with kerchiefs over their hair, Della in a business suit, hat, and gloves. No trace of discomfort about her in those clothes, as though she existed within a bubble that kept the humidity from touching her.

Jane scrambled down the steps to mutter, "She's here to see the house. Unannounced."

Nedda was apologizing—they were in the middle of cleaning, could Della please overlook the mess, as the house was normally not in such disarray. Della in turn apologized for the unexpected visit, saying it was the only time she had to get away from her office. It was all cordial from the outside.

Nedda directed Della upstairs to begin the tour. Going to the kitchen to make cold drinks, Jane fumed. "Why is she taking her upstairs first? That's the worst mess."

Shrugging, I cleared the table. "She's going to see it all."

Thankful the others were at Grandma's house, we waited at the kitchen table with lemonade and the few cookies left to offer as Nedda steered Della through the front room, the pantry, into the kitchen, a review of the back yard, a peek down the cellar stairs, a discussion of how the wash was done. Jane sat legs and arms crossed, swinging one foot, rolling her eyes at Della's questions. It was obvious she had never managed a house before, never mind a household of eight.

Tour finished, Nedda invited Della to sit with us for lemonade. Della perched herself on the edge of the chair I pulled out for her, looking over her shoulder as though she half-expected me to pull it away before she could land.

Jane kept her tight pose, said, "Cookie?" like throwing down a challenge to a duel.

Nedda gave her an exasperated look and offered the cookie plate to Della with a smile. "You must have more questions we can answer about the housekeeping and such."

"I don't know, I don't really know."

Della shook her head at the offered cookie plate, twisted the strap of her handbag, looked from me to Jane to Nedda. "It's a lot to get used to, being a wife and a mother, right off. I want to have things perfect for your father."

Jane came back at that. "Things have never been perfect here."

"Well, I would like to try." Della looked around the kitchen. She turned to Nedda. "You'll have the kitchen cleaned out, and our bedroom upstairs, too?"

"Cleaned out?"

"Yes, for the new things that will be delivered here after the wedding."

"New things?"

"Alonzo and I have chosen some new furniture, and my family is giving us everything new for the kitchen, new dishes, everything. He will be away for a few days after the honeymoon trip and that will give me time to organize before he comes home."

Jane picked up half of a cookie and crushed it in her fist, letting the crumbs fall between her fingers. Della watched with pursed lips, seeming to struggle with the impulse to grab Jane's hand. Placing my hand on Jane's arm, I said to Della, "We have our routine. We can tell you how the days go here."

"Shouldn't I be deciding how we'll do things? I mean, once I marry your father, that's my job."

"We're not a job!" Jane shoved away from the table. "This is not your office!"

Della, flustered, persisted. "You will be my responsibility. And your father is expecting your behavior to change."

"My behavior? What about his behavior? You know, he lies about what he does. Has he told you his lies?"

Nedda was on her feet. "Jane, leave the kitchen. Now." She pointed at the back door. "Wait for me outside." With a glare at Della, Jane stomped out.

Della asked Nedda, "Is she always like this?"

"Not with me."

Della sniffed. "I see. Well, if we are to get along, everyone will have to follow the rules."

Nedda held her hands out. "Della, if I may say, there are six of them and one of you. Maybe it would be easier to get to know them and see how they manage before you make rules."

"Alonzo will not be happy with that."

I piped up. "He won't be here, most of the time. You'll be alone with us. Think about what Nedda says." She had to realize he was going to continue spending days at a time on the road.

Della turned up her chin, still twisting the handle on her bag. "He tells me he's not gone that much."

Nedda tried again. "You will be alone here with six children most of the time. And then you'll have your own babies."

"Yes. Soon, actually," Della whispered. Gathering herself, she stood. "I must be on my way. Thank you for showing me the house."

Nodding to us, she strode out of the kitchen and let herself out the front door. We heard the car leaving.

"Well, I imagine we will hear from your father about this." Nedda sighed. "And I have to figure out how to clear their bedroom for her furniture. She was upset about how small the room is. Not enough space for her clothes. And she worried how to make do with only one parlor, no dining room."

Nedda leaned in closer. "She asked me if there was a cradle."

"I don't know what to do, Nedda. I can't figure a way out."

"If this is the way it's to be, you need to come to an understanding with your father. Time to end the war." With that she went out the back door to find Jane.

From my place at the table, I had a direct view into the pantry. Nedda's words echoed in my head. End the war. I pulled myself out of the chair and knelt on the floor in front of the pickle jars. Pushed my hand past the books of recipes, fingered the bundles of bills through the muslin bag. The money from Uncle George was more than most families in town could hope to earn, more than I would make at the post office for many years ahead. My mother had walked away but leaving her share of the profits behind was a gift to us. Men like my father respected money's power. Maybe I could buy our way out. If I took a gamble.

I telephoned Uncle Charlie. With all the force of voice I could muster, I asked him to arrange for me to meet my father the next day, at his office. After a long silence but not questioning me, he agreed.

The next afternoon, the brothers both opened their pocket watches for a look at the time when I entered Uncle Charlie's office. My father was settled into the oversized leather armchair to the side of the desk, and Uncle Charlie swiveled behind it in his matching rolling armchair. They reminded me of a photo my father used to have tacked up in the darkroom, showing Andrew Carnegie and Henry Clay Frick hunched over some business documents back in the days of their young partnership. I silently prayed for the spirit of Carnegie to help me make this deal.

Uncle Charlie waved me to the straight-backed chair in front of the desk. "Let's get to it. Dan, what's this about?"

"I have a business proposition."

My father raised his eyebrows, pulled back the smirk. I imagined myself as a pitcher about to blow my curveball by him.

"I want to buy our house."

Uncle Charlie's eyes widened behind his rimless glasses. My father laughed. "You have come here to waste our time, and I don't appreciate that. If you're not happy in the house, leave."

"I am happy there. That's why I want to buy it. Hear me out."

Uncle Charlie, the fixer, was intrigued. "Go on, then."

"Della will not be happy in our house. She finds it too small, with too many children to take care of. And when she has her own children," I paused for the effect of that fact, "she'll be wanting a new house. Why not give it to her now? I will buy ours and continue to take care of George and the girls, and you buy Della a house of her own."

"You have no way to buy a house."

"I have the money. If you agree to a fair price."

"Where would you get that kind of money?"

"I earned it."

My father snorted. "There's only one way for you to get that much money. George got you involved in his *trade*."

Keeping my voice steady, I held my head high. "May I have your answer?"

Uncle Charlie had taken all this in. "Alonzo, think about this. You want a clean start with Della. She is *not* happy with the house, that's clear. You'll hear it every day." He waved his hand at me. "Dan, if you will leave us for a moment."

My father protested. "I have not said I would do this."

Uncle Charlie motioned me to the door, and I stepped into the anteroom to wait.

Sweat tricked down my back. Sadness overwhelmed me. My father had not mentioned any concern for the future of my brother and sisters. Although I had gambled on his willingness to engage in a business transaction that would satisfy his self-interest, I had held onto a thin wish that he would love us enough to protest. To promise to care for his children as a real father. To declare a new start, with Della, as a real family. If he had done that, if I had felt sure of their safety with him, and the children were happy, I would have taken that chance.

Frustrated with my sappiness, telling myself I should have learned better about him by now, I squirted a cup of water from the cooler, splashed some on my neck.

The office door opened.

An hour later, I walked out of Uncle Charlie's office with a contract for purchase of the house on River Avenue.

CHAPTER 18

"Do you, Alonzo, take Della to be your lawfully wedded wife?"

"I do."

Exchange of rings, the kiss, and we broke free. As soon as we were out of sight of my father parading Della down the path, I motioned for my brother and sisters to follow me. No way were we walking behind them into the throng of relatives. The side path out of the garden where the wedding had taken place put us near one of the hay barns. We ducked inside the open door for relief from the sultry midday heat.

"Aunt Letitia saw us leave," Ruthie reported. I shrugged, mopped my neck. Jane shook out the folds of her dress, instructed Annie to retie her sash. Addie kicked stones with the polished toes of her good shoes. George pulled at his tie, loosened it as far as it could and still hold the knot. Winking at him, I pulled the knot out of mine and whipped it off. Grinning, he did the same and stuffed his into his pocket.

Jane clucked her disapproval. "Isn't it bad enough we have to endure this without you two getting us yelled at?"

I put my arm around her. "Let's find the lemonade and see what there is to eat."

A country wedding reception started with lunch, paused for an afternoon period of rest, then resumed in high gear around five o'clock for dinner and the evening party. On a platform built of barnwood planks, a band of country musicians had already begun serenading the guests, a prelude to the dancing later.

Aunt Hattie had taken over one of the trestle tables set under the canopy of trees near the large farmhouse. The farmhands' children, young boys and girls pressed into service for the event, brought around pitchers of lemonade, iced tea, and water. Nedda settled on one side of the table with Ollie and motioned for Addie to sit. Aunt Hattie made room for the girls on her side as Jane filled glasses. On the way to the table, George had detoured with some boys off to the side of the festivities for a game of catch. Aunt Letitia bustled toward us, and I stepped away before I could hear about my tie.

Della and my father stood under an open tent with the line of guests waiting to congratulate them snaking off to the side. My father seemed baked into his suit, his neck and face flushed. He kept his hand on Della's back as she hugged and kissed family and friends. She ignored the drizzle of sweat making its way from her temple down her cheek and under the folds of lace at her neckline. Behind them were two large tables covered in white cloths, the gifts piled on one and on the other a wedding cake of six tiers, wildflowers decorating its top and cascading down the sides.

The Carson farmhouse towered four stories, mostly brick, unusual outside town, with expansive windows and wrap-around porches on every floor. My father had married a woman with family money. Knowing him, I supposed it had increased his attraction to Della.

Earlier that morning, Della's mother and father had greeted us with stiff smiles when we popped out of the three sedans Uncle Charlie organized to drive Alonzo's kin to their farm. Handshakes all around, and the six of us diverted to the parlor where my father paced, jaw clenched, brow furrowed, a forced glance of a smile when we came in. Aunts Letitia and Hattie arranged us on two settees, with the warning not to move until called for the ceremony. Best man Uncle Charlie walked my father outside to mingle with the arriving guests.

Assured by her mother that Alonzo was outside, Della had come downstairs in her wedding gown, with her sister lifting the trailing veil to keep it from dragging behind. When I saw Della, I flashed on a day in school, some book we were reading, our English teacher writing *resplendent* on the board and making us look up the definition. Bride Della dazzled in white lace and tulle, her face glowing, carrying a bouquet of country wildflowers. It was the moment I understood how much she must have loved him to commit to my father despite the turmoil he brought with him, enough to willingly entwine her life with ours.

Hugging and kissing her parents, she caught sight of us in the parlor. She waved her bouquet. "Hello, I am so happy you are here."

For once, the girls were mute. Addie ran toward Della with a hand outstretched to touch the dress and Jane got there to grab her back.

Della asked, "How do I look?" Jane had no words, tried to smile. Della heard her mother calling and cooed "See you later," swept her dress around and left us.

I sensed Jane stumbling over the moment that had just transpired. She caught me looking at her. "How did we get here?"

One of Della's cousins introduced himself as our escort. We marched to the garden that had been transformed into an outdoor chapel for the ceremony. Some two hundred people milled about finding their seats. Other than our few family members, there was no one we knew. But the guests recognized us as we made our way to the chairs. Taking the girls' hands, I strolled up the aisle aware of the glances and whispers about Alonzo's children. None of it mattered.

I admit to feeling smug after my takeover of the house. It was a feeling like laying a winning poker hand out card by card and taking the pot. I was a recent convert to poker. Since I became a full-time working man, Mr. Kegg included me in the friendly circle of players he hosted for occasional evening games at his home. I figured Uncle Charlie for a poker player. Not my father though. Not patient enough.

Waiting for the violins that cued the start of the wedding march, my mind was at ease. Let my father vow to be true to Della, let his new relatives talk behind gloved fingers about us, let Della take on his moods, his orders, the anxiety. His clothes gone from the house, his keys on my ring, his mail forwarded to a different town. At my father's wedding, I was a contented guest.

Having worked their way through the well-wishers, Della and my father took their seats at the bridal table. A line of servers paraded from the kitchen hauling platters of smoked ham, fried chicken, grilled corn, and summer fruits and vegetables to the hungry horde at the tables. The abundance on display heartened my good mood. I walked the perimeter of the clustered tables to step up onto the side porch of the house and take in the view of the fields beyond.

Della's family farm was a larger spread than Uncle George's, dotted with barns and small workers' cabins. Her family was large, too, with numerous aunts, uncles, and cousins on both sides. The men had congregated in the rear yard, in front of what looked like an icehouse. Figuring that to be where the beer was, I ambled into the group. Two of Uncle George's drivers filled mugs lined up in a trough. The thirsty men grabbed for them, guzzled the beer, and reached for more. Behind the trough, Uncle George, at the doorway of the icehouse, directed two other men to ready more bottles for pouring. I waited at the side for him to see me. When he caught my eye, a big grin spread across his face, and he raised a bottle. "Get over here, Daniel, and try our brew."

I had never had a drink of alcohol. Prohibition was on its last legs, the common-held belief that repeal would come within a year. The men drinking around me had no qualms about legality. And the business of supplying beer had been lucrative for my family and me. My old hesitations had evaporated.

The coolness of the icehouse enveloped me. Uncle George motioned me back into the shadows, away from the door, to sit on an overturned crate. He grabbed two bottles swimming with others in a tub of icy water. Popping them open, he handed me one. "The old country guys like theirs warm but most of us fellas like 'em as cold as we can get 'em. Here's to you." He took a guzzle, his eyes on me for my reaction.

I tipped the cold bottle to my lips and let the bitter liquid drip down my throat. He nodded at me to go again. I gulped more. I had no taste for beer yet, but I enjoyed the cold rush. Uncle George laughed. "Keep drinking, you'll get to like it fine," he said. I gulped again. A few gulps were enough to enhance my giddy feeling.

"Papaw told me you bought the house."

I nodded. "Thanks for the money."

"Don't have to thank me. It was rightfully yours."

I took another gulp of beer. "I couldn't leave."

He put his hand on my shoulder. "Staying takes guts." Uncle George swigged the last of his beer and stood up. "I have to keep an eye on things here. You enjoy the party."

When I returned to our table, the family had eaten pretty

well but there was enough remaining on the platters for me to have hefty servings. I was hungrier than I had been in months. The beer made me light-headed—not tipsy, as Hattie would have called it, but agreeable with the celebrating going on around me. It had been so long since I had felt carefree.

The band played listening tunes, lulling people into afternoon napping or quiet conversation. Hattie instructed the girls and George in clearing the platters and pitchers, returning them to the trolleys lined up at the perimeter of the dining tables. Nedda coaxed Addie and Ollie onto blankets she had spread out and settled them in to read and rest. A cousin of Della's had drawn Jane into a group of the younger women fanning themselves in chairs under a stand of shade trees.

Content that everyone would see to themselves for the afternoon, I thought about finding a cool spot to rest when a commotion on the formal front porch of the house drew my attention. Oscar and Uncle Charlie were mingling among the group of laughing bridesmaids trying to arrange themselves for photographs. My father was instructing the young man with the camera about angles and poses. Della whispered to him and he smiled, guided her up the few steps. The photographer motioned to the bridesmaids and groomsmen to cluster around Della and my father. After a series of group shots, he asked for Della and Alonzo to pose. Della beamed at my father and he drank in her adoration.

I couldn't figure out her motivation for wanting him and caring for him so much. Yet everything about her demeanor stated her love. How much could he return to her? And was she curious about his marriage with my mother, how it had gone wrong? Or did his blaming Lillian satisfy Della's need to know what had happened? I had stumbled into the secrets my parents kept from each other, but I had no understanding of the marriage between them.

Watching Della and my father pose and repose for their wedding pictures, the photograph in Lillian's trunk of my parents on their wedding day floated in my mind's eye. If they had marked or celebrated their wedding anniversary each year, it was only between them. I recognized a hesitation in the marriage between Lillian and Alonzo that was not present in the relationship between Nedda and Oscar or, if today was evidence, between Della and my father. Or at least Della was all in. Did she know Alonzo's father had stranded women when he finished with them and his son had done the same? Was she taking the chance on him in this marriage by believing his past was behind him, or did she have only the selective history he had given her? It was disheartening to hear Della laughing, see her serene face as she leaned back against him, watch her lift her hand confident he would grasp it, and wonder if he had been like this with Lillian and she returned his feelings, or if she had craved affections he withheld from her. My father was husband to Della now. I prayed she would not be another woman miserable in her life with my father, not have another set of children wounded in the crossfire.

The photos finished, my father and Della disappeared into

the house. Oscar saw me and ambled over. "Think they took enough pictures of themselves?"

"Think there's a chance they'll be happy together?"

Oscar sighed. "Can't tell you that, Dan. On the wedding day, there is a lot of hope. But you don't live on the hope."

"You and Nedda seem happy together."

Oscar grinned. "Our combination works pretty well. Nedda's a special woman." He shoulder-bumped me. "What about you? Looking for a special woman?"

"Not me."

Oscar put his arm around me. "You will, someday." He let go, took off his jacket. "My official duties are over. Where is everybody?"

We headed to the blankets where our family rested in the shade, except for Jane. I asked Nedda if she knew where Jane was, and she looked around. "She was sitting with that group of young ladies under the trees for a long time. Now, I don't know. She didn't come back here." I shrugged and took a spot on the blanket and reached for the lemonade pitcher.

When the afternoon sun shifted and the shadows lengthened across the lawn, people stirred from the blankets to ready themselves for the evening celebration. The boys and girls who had served lunch now brought around warm moist towels to clean hands and faces. George and I shook out the blankets and took them to stow in the cars parked a short way from the house. On the walk back, seeing the cluster of men formed again around the icehouse, I smiled to myself. Another beer during the evening would suit me.

The band took their positions on the stage and tuned their instruments. The lights strung around the dance platform glowed brighter as the sun receded. The kitchen hands lined tables end-to-end on one side of the dance area and covered them with cloths for the serve-yourself dinner. We reclaimed our trestle table, Hattie surveying the girls and George for clean hands.

Coming towards us were my father and Della, holding hands. They had changed into dancing clothes, a shorter, flouncier white dress for Della and a shirt and a vest with a bow tie on my father. He looked as satisfied as he did after hitting a home run to win the game in the ninth.

Della threw her arms around Annie and Ruthie. "It's so good to see you here. Addie, are you ready to dance?" Addie, who loved to dance, bobbed her head up and down.

My father took Della's hand again. To us, he said, "Did you have a good afternoon?"

Ruthie and Annie were mute under Della's spell, George leery of what might come next from my father. I spoke for all of us. "We're having a fine time."

Della prompted him with a squeeze on his arm. "Good," he said. "Della and I will be pleased if you enjoy the dinner, and then join in the dancing with us."

Della beamed at us again. "Oh, yes, we want you all to come

dance with us this evening," She blew us a kiss as my father led her away.

Hattie said to me, "There, you see, she's a good influence on Alonzo."

Jane had missed the encounter. Strolling among people congregating around the dance floor, I spotted her sitting on a bench to the side of the house, talking with a young man. Jane's face was flushed and her gestures animated; he leaned in close to her. When she saw me approach, Jane stood, saying, "Dan, meet Glen Elliott. He's one of Della's cousins. Glen, this is my brother Dan."

Glen said, "Distant cousin, but the family invites everyone to weddings. Hello, Dan." We shook hands. Glen looked to be Oscar's age, and an alarm went off in my gut.

"Jane, the family is missing you. We're having supper before the dancing begins."

Glen took the cue. "Nice talking with you, Jane. Perhaps you will have a dance with me later?" Nodding to me, he strolled away with a wave to Jane.

Walking with me, Jane said, "Don't say a word. He's a nice man, and we were only talking. It's nothing to get excited about." Yet her blush said Glen intrigued her.

"Okay, we're at a party, we can enjoy it. But he's a lot older than you. Stay where I can see you."

"You sound like Nedda and Hattie."

"I'm looking out for you."

"Keeping me in line, you mean. Oh, never mind—let's have

fun tonight, okay? We had to come here, and I'm making the best of it." Her attitude about the day had changed since meeting Glen.

The band played slow melodies until most people finished eating. Two servers rolled the wedding cake to the middle of the dance floor on a wagon covered in white lace and flowers. My father and Della stood behind it. Uncle Charlie, master of ceremonies, called for the crowd's attention and made a toast to the couple. The guests cheered and toasted to their lifelong happiness. The band played a jaunty tune while Della and my father cut the cake, with their two hands joined around the knife. More cheering and servers rolled the cake to the side, where it was sliced onto plates for the guests.

My father twirled Della into the middle of the dance floor and took her into his arms. Murmuring from the crowd and applause as he guided her through their first dance to a love song popular on the radio programs. Jane was entranced by the spectacle. The romance may have been lost on my younger sisters and George but their eyes were fixed on my father and Della, too. I wondered if my mother had ever danced with him like this.

Hattie breathed out a long sigh next to me. "Things might be better, you know," she whispered.

"I have already made things better."

"You'll need Della on your side."

"Why?"

"Because Alonzo must continue to care for his children. Yes, you can live in two houses, that's decided. But she is the mediator when you need something from him."

The dance ended to the guests' cheering, and the bridal party joining the couple on the dance floor as the music continued. Oscar took a few turns with his bridesmaid partner, then escorted her to her husband and strode over to grab Nedda's hand to finish the dance. Uncle Charlie came for Aunt Letitia. Aunt Hattie accepted my request for a dance. The band blended one tune into the next and the dance music attracted all kinds of pairings—old ladies together, children with cousins and siblings, and the younger unmarried people who found each other. Della and my father separated to mingle among the dancers. New partners took turns dancing with Della. My father danced one after another with Della's female relatives.

After Hattie, I danced with Jane until a young man cut in and swirled her away. Ruthie and Annie asked me to help them practice their steps, and we got George to join. We danced over to Nedda and Oscar and I cut in to take Nedda's hand, Oscar taking Annie. After several vigorous numbers, the band slowed the tempo to a languid melody and Nedda drifted back to Oscar. I turned and came face to face with Della. She held out her hand, and I embraced her for the dance.

"I see you're a good dancer," she said, as we moved in pace with the other couples.

"My mother taught me." I smiled at Della, thinking of Hattie's words. "But I haven't had much chance to practice, so excuse my feet."

"No need to apologize, you dance beautifully." She looked into my eyes. "We can be friends, I hope."

"What does my father want us to be?"

"I think he wants peace in the family. And so do I."

"We can try, but it depends on him."

"Dan, it depends on us making things work."

Oscar's words about hope echoed in my head. "You're optimistic."

"I have to be. We'll have a baby to think of, and all of you."

"What do you mean, make things work?"

Della smiled and squeezed my arm. "If we cooperate. Let him see things can go smoothly without him having to manage everything."

"I can cooperate, depending on what you have in mind."

"Just to help each other. I've made sure he will continue to send the money every week."

"He's supposed to do that."

"And he will. Can you do something for me?" I waited with my eyes on hers. "Can you give me the recipes for some of his favorite dishes? I have to learn to cook for him. He says you're the cook in the family."

I twirled Della for the final turn and the music stopped. "Sure, Della, I can do that."

"Thank you, Dan. I know we can be friends." With that she spun on her heel and skipped to the side where Alonzo waited.

A few days later, I pulled out the cookbooks and looked up the recipes for the stews my father liked best. My mother's note in the margin read *No peas*; my father never liked peas. When I wrote out the recipes on cards for Della, I left the peas in.

CHAPTER 19

Summer, 1934

A stand of hemlock trees, survivors of the smog and hard-blowing winter winds, flanked the grave's end where Grandma's head would rest. The new-growth bright green branch tips brushed against the minister's back as he waited for us to lower the coffin. I shifted my strap end to balance George's on the other side, Papaw and Uncle George manned the second strap, and one of the gravediggers guided the edge into the hole. We let down the pine box inches at a time, taking care to settle it as if we laid her on a pillow.

The minister intoned prayers thanking God for sparing Grandma prolonged suffering, and we breathed out our amens with sniffed tears. After the minister blessed the grave, the cluster of ladies who had made their way to the cemetery in testament to their friendship with Grandma ambled away.

Having been a rock for us throughout the turmoil before the

divorce, Grandma began falling apart when we settled into the two-house arrangement after Alonzo and Della married. With my father gone, Grandma could have resumed her everyday presence in our house again. Nedda had always appreciated Grandma's help, though they were not close as they might have been, with Hattie looking over Nedda's shoulder. But Grandma did not set foot in our house again. Grandma's arms were always open to us but she closed herself off from the sad reminders of Lillian's absence. She never asked me about the trunk, and it stayed hidden.

Lillian's shadow hovered over Grandma's days. Uncle George carried out his intention to try to ease Grandma's mind about her daughter. He continued searching for Lillian, traveling alone to Ohio and then on to Nebraska, when he picked up a lead about her from someone he knew who had relocated there. An undercurrent of gossip in town had the Feeke brothers cooperating with George, to find Roy. Nothing came of the hunt. Grandma passed without having heard from Lillian again.

Unable to make peace with her daughter's absence, Grandma took up my mother's long walks. Grandma trudged to the post office Monday through Saturday, no matter the weather, to pick up her mail, explaining the habit as good exercise. I handed her the bundles with cheery snippets of conversation and winced at seeing pain and disappointment crinkle her face when there was nothing from Lillian. She nagged Papaw to get a telephone installed, then nagged the operator with her repeated inquiries about missed calls. If I called their house, the expectation in Grandma's hello made me almost apologize for not being the one she wanted to hear from. Papaw fretted, "She's wearing herself sick," and no matter how he or any of us tried to ease her distress, she was like a snail winding inside its shell.

The walking stopped when she collapsed along the road. The physical troubles with her heart forced her into bed but the heartache could not be treated. When I sat by her sickbed and took hold of Grandma's hand, she would open her eyes and smile to see me there. Propped against the lamp on the side table was an old photograph of Lillian and Uncle George perched side-by-side on the gate of a farm truck, Lillian's arm around her younger brother, broad smiles for the camera. Grandma could gaze on it and imagine them in that happier time.

I prayed at the grave for her to carry that comfort over the threshold into heaven.

Papaw fell to his knees at the graveside, murmuring goodbyes, asking her to save him a place. The haggardness in Papaw's face, his stooped shoulders, and a shuffling stride, had worn into him in the weeks since Grandma became ill. His tears fell onto earth so dry they formed little beads rolling away. Uncle George helped Papaw to his feet and stepped him back. Neither would leave Grandma until the men filled in the grave.

The gravediggers waited under a tree, ready to put the dirt piled to the side over the coffin. At the undertaker's signal, the men tipped their hats in respect before taking up the shovels. The same men who had chiseled through the icy ground to make a place for Lonnie now wore kerchiefs across their noses and mouths to avoid breathing the dust as they picked and shoveled into the ashy soil.

Jane threw the last of the flowers she held into the grave and turned away. Toward the end, Jane was at Grandma's side with the rest of us, holding back tears with that way she had of pulling herself in. But she and Grandma had not reconciled over the different feelings they had about my mother. They treated each other kindly, and Grandma reached out to bring Jane closer many times, but Jane kept a limit between them which Grandma regretted.

Nedda waited for us on the gravel path that wound amidst the graves, holding Ollie's hand. She motioned for George and me to follow her toward the cars parked behind the undertaker's van. My sisters walked ahead of us. At the cars, Oscar was unloading baskets. Grandma's wish was for us to have a picnic like the ones we used to have at the farm instead of going back to the house for a gathering.

The air was warm, and we unfolded the blankets under one of the big maple trees. Uncle George and Papaw made their slow way over. We set out the food, and when we were assembled on the blankets, Papaw said, "We won't cry now, because your Grandma wants us happy. She only wanted us happy." And that made us cry. Nedda started passing the plates and hunger persuaded us to eat, not much talking, no rush. The cake was

Grandma's favorite, lemon poppy seed, and we perked up reminding each other of the many times we had enjoyed her cakes.

When I got up to walk over to Lonnie's grave, my brother George followed me. I carried flowers set aside from those placed with Grandma and laid them on our brother's grave.

Gazing at Lonnie's headstone, George confessed, "I used to think he was lucky to die, and I wished I had died, too."

Startled, I turned to George, now close to my height, trying to keep my voice soft. "You used to wish for that?"

"When Mama wouldn't get up in the morning, and when she left, yeah."

I flashed on the nights when he cried himself to sleep. "You feel that way now?"

"Naw, not anymore. I'm grown now." He was twelve. "I'm going to get more cake."

Watching George trot back to the family on the blankets, I took in what our teachers would call the "tableau" before me. Up on the cemetery hill was one of the few spots where the valley was visible enough to follow the course of the river and the ribbons of the roads for miles around. The blankets seemed to float my family above it like a lifeboat on an ocean. Nedda with Ruthie and Annie leaning on her, relaxed into her welcoming arms. Oscar and Ollie rolling a ball back and forth with Addie, now six years old. Uncle George propping Papaw back-to-back, and my brother plopped in front of Papaw. Jane sat at the edge of the cluster on the blankets, gazing off across the hills toward the river.

In the movies the shipwrecked were saved from the merciless waves by reaching a deserted island just as they lost hope, grateful for ground beneath their feet. We had been rescued by Nedda and Oscar.

Uncle Charlie had coached Oscar in negotiating with the Feekes to buy the house next door to us, where Marion and Roy had lived. Daily life between our two houses had melded into a predictable, smooth rhythm, especially for Addie, who did not remember before with my mother the way the rest of us did. Nedda and Oscar treated Addie like a big sister to their son, and Addie enjoyed bossing him and playing with him like he was one of her dolls. But she had a streak in her that believed she was right, no matter what. At least once a week, she spent time on a stool facing the wall in the corner of Nedda's kitchen to think about her misbehavior. Addie collected resentment of her punishments like a gunnysack of grudges. When she was reprimanded for one thing, she wailed about old wrongs against her, covering her ears to not hear what you were trying to tell her about managing herself. Her face would go dark, she would hide, and later come out so quiet we were mystified about what calmed her mood, wary about trusting it to continue.

Maybe it was our exhaustion with managing the tantrums, but when Della began asking for Addie to spend days with her and the baby, we allowed her to go. None of us visited my father's house, and he avoided coming to ours, the extended family meeting in the neutral territory of Uncle Charlie's house for holidays.

Maybe Della was lonely, alone most of the time with her baby daughter while my father was on the road. Or she needed help that a six-year-old girl would provide without complaining like an older child would, if asked to fold laundry or run upstairs to get something. But the special treatment Addie enjoyed in Della's house made it harder for her to conform to the rules at home that she chafed at. We did our best with Addie but it was easy to fall back on feeling sorry she had no mother, let her wheedle us to give her what she wanted to calm her down.

Grandma's passing meant the loss of her steadying hand with Ruthie and Annie. They gravitated to her for help with problems and the private talks they were uncomfortable going to Jane or Nedda with. Ruthie was fourteen, the age Jane was when my mother left. And Annie was sixteen, same as I was then. They had grown beyond being lumped together as 'the girls' who would do as they were told. They usually stopped at Grandma's house on the way home from school, often staying there for supper, or even the night. Relying on Grandma to guide their girlhood and settle their fears was past. Seeing them on the blanket wrapped around Nedda made me realize they would feel Grandma's loss hard.

That night, muffled voices in the bathroom woke me. I listened for a minute, then let myself fall back asleep until my alarm rang. In the kitchen, Jane had the coffee ready.

"Ruthie's monthly started last night," she said. It was unusual for Jane to include me in intimate details.

I had no idea what I should say. "Is everything okay?"

"Yes, but she cried a lot." Seeing my unease, Jane went on. "Ruthie worries over every little thing. She thinks kids at school talk about her, that nobody likes her. She has trouble concentrating on her schoolwork. Now she feels like her body is … different."

"All this came up last night?"

"It's been there, but now she's feeling it more. She knew this would happen but she wasn't ready. She has to get more confident."

"You're the one to help with confidence."

"I don't know how to give it to somebody." Jane listened for sounds on the stairway. "When she comes down, be nice."

"I *am* nice to her."

"Yes, but most of the time we don't pay her enough attention." Jane was good at picking up what bothered her sisters but not at helping them handle it. Their relationship with Jane was fraught when her bossy side took over, which it did more often than not. For her to spend this much time on Ruthie's needs was unusual.

"What about Annie helping her?"

"They have different friends now—Annie's crowd is driving and going to dances."

"When you were sixteen …" I left my thought unfinished. We looked at each other.

"Annie's not going wild."

"How do you know?"

"People would tell me."

"I don't want to wait for that."

"What are you going to do? You aren't their father."

"No, but we have to watch over them. Or their father will step in."

Jane put down her cup. "You'll be doing that without me. I have a job."

She chuckled at the stunned look on my face as Ruthie, Annie, and Addie came into the kitchen in a burst of morning wants.

"What did you say?"

"I am moving to Uniontown. I have a job."

Talk around the table stopped, the three younger girls' eyes moving from Jane to me. Nedda came in the kitchen door with eggs.

"It's too quiet in here," she said.

Jane blurted, "I just told Dan."

Between them, I confronted Nedda. "You know about Jane's job, her moving?"

Nedda flushed, set the eggs on the sideboard, reached for my arm. "Dan, let me explain ..."

Nedda and Oscar were in on the secret. My old anger gushed through my body, found the muscles of my neck and arms too comfortable, tensed them hard, clenched my fists.

"Explain blindsiding me." Facing Jane, who held herself rigid and haughty, staring at me. "After all we've been through, the risks I took, you decide to leave."

"No, Dan, *you* decided you *wouldn't* leave. I never planned to stay!" Jane stomped out of the room.

Hurting from their deception, I refused to meet Nedda's eyes and left for work by the back door. After my father's wedding, I had lulled myself into believing we had crossed through the hard times. For two years, we had lived in relative calm, made the new routine normal, shared everything. At least I thought so. For Nedda to hide Jane's plans from me was hurtful, but I blamed Jane.

Since her graduation from high school, I had assumed Jane would find work when she wanted to. We had enough money to allow her to take time to decide. She did not seem interested in much beyond her social life. She occupied herself going out with friends most evenings and weekends. She treated the family as a distraction from more interesting company. But, as I learned, the source of her distraction was not her town friends.

Ferrying Addie back and forth to my father's house, Jane had become friendly with Della, gradually moving from polite chats in the doorway to having lunch, to staying whole days, talking with Della while the children played. Lonely Della confided to Jane about missing her working life and its satisfactions. Della's wistfulness for the independence and accomplishments she had left behind provoked in Jane a different view of her own future, dressing like Della used to, making her way in the business world. Maybe Della saw a bit of herself in Jane. She at least saw Jane's potential, and she told my father as much.

Through her contacts in Uniontown, Della heard of an opportunity in the office of the highways department. Never mind that Jane had no interest in the highways of Pennsylvania or office work in general; the lure of being on her own reeled her in. Convinced by Della to put aside her resentments and let them help her, my sister, accompanied by our father, went for an interview. When he was satisfied with the respectability of the position and the head of the office had looked Jane over, the men shook hands and Jane got the job. The matter of where she would live was settled through Della, too. One of her friends lived in a women-only rooming house, and my father secured Jane's place there.

The office expected her to start in a few weeks. Lost in the dream of getting out on her own, Jane shrugged off the details of brushing up her typing and shorthand. Nedda gave Jane a pass on most of her home duties. Most days she went to my father's house, where Della refitted and tailored some of her suits as a start of Jane's business wardrobe. Jane tossed her old clothes in piles for Annie and Ruthie. They loved watching Jane practice different hairstyles to complement her new array of hats. Often skipping dinner with us, in the evenings she went out with friends.

Nedda got Ruthie and Annie involved in planning a surprise goodbye party for Jane, and the three of them corralled me one afternoon to discuss the set up. With my eyes on Nedda, I said, "So I am included in *this* secret." Nedda sighed and looked away.

Ruthie stage-whispered the details until Annie reminded her

Jane was not in the house. "I know, I know," she said, "but it is so much fun to give Jane the best party. She is so lucky!"

"How is she lucky?" I asked.

"She gets to start a new life. Her own life. No one will know about us there."

I took Ruthie's arm. "What is bothering you, Ruthie?"

"Nothing! Let's plan the party."

She twisted her arm away from me, and my mind flashed on the photograph of Lillian at Grandma's bedside. Ruthie's resemblance to my mother was striking. The same tilt of the head, the profile, the petite frame. Nedda turned the talk back to the party plans and the moment passed leaving me with an ache.

With Grandma's passing, I had stumbled back into loss, like traveling a path through a forest that dead-ended in thick brush. I went from home to work and back again. The loss compounded with the sense that everyone was whirling away from me. Jane was leaving, and Ruthie as much as said she wanted to. Annie was spending half the nights at Papaw's house to keep him company and, despite Nedda's rules, ran around with her friends as much as she could get away with. I expected George to go on the road with some baseball team when he finished school. What did I want for myself, with everyone hewing out paths of their own?

Sorrow weighed on me. I fumbled around Jane, not knowing how to start the conversation I wanted to have with her before she left. And it appeared that Jane had no need to talk to me. She was so eager to go.

The days until her departure dwindled, with our contact limited to breakfast before she rushed off most mornings to take care of last-minute needs. Two trunks packed with her new clothes sat by the front door, waiting for the final items to be put in just before the journey. Flowers sent by friends wishing her well filled the front room with fragrance too reminiscent of Lonnie's funeral for me to appreciate the good-luck sentiments. Frantic that Jane would simply leave me, I berated myself for wanting something from her that I could not name.

If Jane suspected the ruse the girls used to get her over to Nedda's house for the party, she hid it. Streamers festooned Nedda's front room. Ruthie and Annie screamed "Surprise" louder than anyone, and Jane threw her hands up in delight. Her closest girlfriends and their mothers came, filling the front room with bedecked ladies. Oscar signaled me and we busied ourselves with refilling punch cups and keeping the little ones out of the way. Della arrived carrying her little girl. I hadn't expected to see Della, but Jane greeted her with an easy hug. Della stayed long enough to pick over a slice of cake and give Jane an envelope from my father. He intended to check in on her when she got to Uniontown.

When the party ended, as we were cleaning up, Oscar asked, "Jane, tell me again which train you're getting tomorrow, so I can get you there in time."

"Oscar, I'd like Dan to take me, if you don't mind."

My heart turned over.

"Yes, sure. Dan, how's the truck running?" I had bought one of the old pickups from Uncle George.

"Fine, fine. I can drive Jane to the station, no problem." When she heard this, Jane smiled.

The next morning, I loaded Jane's trunks into the bed of my truck. Inside, breakfast was finished and Nedda and my sisters scurried to add the last items to Jane's traveling case. Leaning against the truck while I waited, I gazed at our house as the sun brightened behind it and the river glistened below. Next door, Oscar was in the midst of painting the outside of their house, ladders propped in front and on the side, the new color slowly replacing the old. He had been urging me to help him and then together we would paint our house, too. High on the ladder, or on the roof, the view would be far and wide on a clear day. Picturing us side-by-side on the ladders, slapping paint on the eaves, joking, talking, I warmed to the idea. My concern for so long had been to keep us safe inside, as if our house was a cocoon wrapping us together. Maybe I could see it differently, as the place where each of us found our way.

Commotion on the porch pulled me out of my reverie. Nedda, Jane, George, Annie, Ruthie, and Addie tumbled through the front door, all talking at once. Nedda instructed Jane about avoiding strangers on the train. Annie rolled her eyes and handed Jane the lunch they had packed for her, giving her a hug and kiss. Ruthie followed with an embrace around the neck that had Jane gasping and laughing. George stuck out his hand, and when Jane looked from it to his face he wrapped both arms around her. She rubbed his hair and kissed his cheek, told him to hit the ball good for her. Jane stooped to hug Addie tight, kissing her over and over, until Addie squirmed out of her arms. Jane straightened her skirt and jacket, grabbed her handbag and lunch in hand, and skipped down the porch steps to the passenger side of the truck. George brought the traveling case to me. The family yelled their goodbyes and Jane turned in her seat waving as we pulled away.

Up the road we stopped in front of Papaw's, where he was waiting at the gate. Jane opened her door, stepping into his arms.

"You make us proud up there, you hear?" he whispered into her ear. Jane nodded and hugged him again. "We will miss you, Jane, and you know your Grandma loved you, and I love you." This was a lot of emotion for Papaw to put into words. Jane's tears oozed from the corners of her eyes onto his shirt.

"I will come back and visit you, I will," she said. He nodded and prodded her into the truck, closed her door.

"Go on now, get her to that train, Dan. Don't let her be late."

I put the truck in gear and we pulled away. In my mirror, I watched Papaw take out his handkerchief and wipe his face. This time Jane did not look back. I glanced over at her dabbing her eyes, then resettling herself in the seat with a sigh. "That was harder than I expected," she said.

We pulled off River Avenue to head through town. Silence in the truck, Jane staring straight ahead. She had asked for this ride with me but I was unsure how to tell her that I understood she had to go, yet it pained me to let her go.

Then in a quiet voice, she rescued me. "I am so sorry, Dan. I haven't known what to say to you."

Glancing at Jane, I flashed back to the day I sat in the truck with Roy, hearing how my mother talked to him when she couldn't talk to my father. Somehow the effort got so hard for my mother, she didn't talk to any of us, and left us with nothing. I did not want that silence between Jane and me.

"Jane, say what you feel. I can take it. You and me, we got ourselves this far."

Pulling the truck into the train station parking area, I turned off the engine. Jane grabbed my arm. "No, Dan, you're the one who got us this far. I wasn't brave like you, and I'm not brave now."

I put my hand over hers. "What you're about to do takes a lot of confidence."

"It's not the same. I use people, I know that. I'm like Dad that way, that's how I get along with him. But you did what was right for all of us."

Shaking my head, I smiled at my sister. "When we all get to wherever we're going, we'll find out if it was right."

CHAPTER 20

Fayette County, Pennsylvania, 1985

The sting of my mother's abandonment faded with the old wallpaper in our front room, the vibrancy washed out, the hint of her imprint traceable in us.

Annie declared she most resembled my mother, with the same petite frame, and for years kept her hair styled the way Lillian did when we were young. Primping in front of a mirror, she would demand we recognize the likeness, calling on Papaw as judge when none of us would satisfy her demand. Only one of the photographs of my mother, taken by my father, remained in our house, and Annie longed for more evidence of her mother's looks, but refused to ask my father if there were others. Papaw soothed her with the gift of the photo of Lillian and Uncle George that Grandma had kept at her bedside.

Annie's frequent allusions to Lillian pained Ruthie, who cried at the slightest mention of our mother. After Jane left,

Ruthie regressed in longing for my mother. When she found out that Uncle George had searched in vain, she started a personal vigil, insisting we leave the front door unlocked on the chance Lillian might appear when we were out.

George hardened into a young man by toughening his body, concentrating any sad or angry feelings into muscle strength and stamina on the baseball field. He could not cope with the girls' fixation on our mother. Using any excuse to leave, he would stay away from the house for days at a time, camping in the woods or going to the farm. Although he remained easy in manner when we were alone, he turned away from my efforts to draw him into talking.

Addie's tenuous connection to my mother dissolved. If Grandma had lived, Addie would have learned about Lillian as a little girl, been told and retold the story of the day Lillian gave birth to Addie with Grandma at her side. Maybe I should have given Addie more of my memories of my mother, gotten Uncle George involved, taught her about Lillian's childhood at the farm. But it was Della who mothered Addie.

Spending time in Della's house was like discovering a desert oasis for Addie, and I admit she thrived in certain ways under Della's care and teaching. But Della also indulged her, too quick to excuse Addie's sassy behavior and give in to her stomped-foot demands. When Addie was twelve Della had her second child, a son, and Addie half moved in to help Della with her girl and boy. Sibling relationships with Della's children were easy for Addie, who relished being their older sister.

Papaw was a daily fixture in our house from breakfast through supper during his last years. I reclaimed Lillian's cookbooks and experimented with the recipes. Without Jane there to mock my attempts, surprising Papaw and my brother and sisters with the dishes I concocted and seeing them eat gratified me. Papaw enjoyed watching me cook and chatting about nothing. In the hours between meals, he would read until his chin fell forward into a nap, then rouse himself and check the hour the day had come to. "Don't know how long I was out," he would say to whoever walked in on him.

Papaw insisted on sleeping in his own bed every night, so one of us would help him up the road in the evening and back down before breakfast. Most often Annie walked him back, then she moved into the spare room in Papaw's house, keeping watch to prevent his failing joints causing him to fall. She encouraged and abetted him in his two favorite pastimes: reminiscing about Grandma and Lillian, and town gossip.

Firm in his belief that Grandma waited for him, Papaw was not afraid to die, and his death was merciful—one morning when Annie went to wake him, Papaw was gone. Burying him next to Grandma, close to Lonnie, spreading flowers over the graves, we held onto each other but cried little. Papaw had left nothing unsaid or undone with us. But I missed him deeply. Turning from the stove, my mind would catch a glimpse of him slurping soup at our table. Once, he was sitting on the end of my bed when I woke in the night.

The loss of Papaw pushed me further into silence. Routine saved me or sank me, depending on how I turn it in my mind. I went ahead with each day's work, sat with the family, cooked as usual, but my heart froze and I had no desire to do or think anything more than what was required. Annie inherited Papaw's house, and on her own there, she took up the care of older folks in town.

Della had been true to her promise to ensure my father continued the weekly allowance. He calculated reductions but maintained the regular drop-offs over the years, until only Addie was left with me at home. One Friday the driver did not arrive and after that I did not expect any money from my father. Combined with my post office salary, it had been sufficient to see us through. And there was the bonus of Uncle George's contributions. It turned out that he correctly judged the increased demand for his beer with the end of Prohibition. The legitimate business grew fast and, as he expanded, he continued to set aside my mother's percentage of the profits. I opened savings accounts, and my brother and sisters each had a nest egg.

I have stayed in our house all these years, even after Nedda and Oscar sold their house next door to move to Pittsburgh. Maybe I didn't push myself enough, maybe having the money kept me still. I think back and can't find the spot where I went blank on myself. Before he retired, Mr. Kegg prepared me to take over in the post office. His confidence in me substituted for Papaw's missing presence. He was like Papaw in his advice to me, too; Mr. Kegg stressed that I should find someone to love and make a life with. He had cherished his wife and wanted that blessing for me. For a time, the casseroles from several young ladies appearing on Saturdays were directed to me and I suspected Mr. Kegg had something to do with that. But I did not feel a response to those gestures.

Jane married for the first time about two years after she left home. As I predicted, the job at the highway department had no appeal for her, but one of the men working there did. Older by twelve years, Jane's husband had family money and the benefit of his knowledge about where the planned highways would create business opportunities. They bought a roadhouse on a spur of the National Pike, guaranteeing a steady stream of car travelers and truckers for years, until the state redirected the new super-highway to bypass the outskirts of the old towns. But Jane had her own timetable. As soon as the place was profitable, she divorced and bought out the husband. With Jane as the sole proprietor, the restaurant thrived by offering evening dinner service when people in the area had no respectable options for a night out.

The dining room seated a hundred guests, and the kitchen gleamed with oversized stoves and refrigerators. A bar next to the dining room served beer and liquor, with music and dancing on weekends. Bossy Jane was in her glory, decked out to greet the customers, overseeing the chef and cooks and servers. Her pride in the property enlarged her goodwill toward the family, with invitations for holidays and birthdays in the dining room, and overnight stays in the private quarters on the second and third floors. Jane arranged for my father and Della to visit separately from the occasions when Addie, George, and I came, along with Papaw in the first year. Jane hosted the dinners when Nedda and Oscar were visiting in town, and at Jane's restaurant we celebrated a small wedding for Annie and a send-off for Ruthie before she left to find a job in Detroit.

Jane was a good businesswoman, correctly judging the time to sell, before the war years and the diversion of the car travelers dried up the profits. Wealthy and young, Jane attracted plenty of men who noticed her looks and her savvy, but I was surprised when she married a second time. "He'll be there if I need him," she said about husband number two, a handsome but meek man who waited for Jane to speak first. My sister was true to herself, always.

Wartime service propelled George into the world beyond the baseball field. Enlisted in the Marines, he was spared the worst of the action in the Pacific when his penmanship and affable way of relating to his fellow soldiers caught the attention of an officer that landed him a post in the communications pool. When he shipped back to California, he rented places in different beach towns until he decided on newspaper work in San Francisco.

The Army had rejected me due to my eyesight, but when the military expanded the overseas postal service, Mr. Kegg used his connections to get me into home-front service, training recruits in sorting methods and postal codes. Addie graduated from high school as the war ended and followed Ruthie to Detroit for work.

The last time the six of us were together was my father's seventieth birthday.

It was Addie who persuaded us to attend the celebration Della planned for my father. "Della has put so much effort into the party, and she says it would mean the world to him for all of his children to be there," Addie cajoled on the telephone.

All of his children? Addie was still in the dark about my father's two children with the boarding house widow. Jane and I had buried our knowledge of them with the damning photographs, stashed away with the deed to the house. Revealing their existence to my brother and other sisters never felt necessary. As much as I had struggled with the lies early on, as the years passed I ceased reckoning with them. If Della knew about the other children, she surely did not mean to include them. It was the six of us that Della wanted there, for her invented portrayal of family togetherness. One by one, Addie worked on us, wore down the excuses, got us to agree.

I had not seen my father since Addie's graduation, and then had not spoken to him. Jane urged forgiveness. "He's an old man, what does it matter now?" and I shrugged. No point to argue it with her. My anger at my father had a permanent home inside me, had become easy company.

Della's daughter hosted the party at her house, a big noisy affair, with assorted friends, old gas company cronies, and many of Della's multitude of relatives, kids running through the house and yard. Jane was sitting with her arm around my father when I arrived with a reluctant George in tow. It was strange to see my father aged, the only glimpse of the forceful baseball player he had been still evident in the way he wore a cap. I greeted Della and my father with a perfunctory birthday wish that Della thanked me for. George mocked him with a salute and my father grunted.

After retiring from the gas company, Alonzo had transferred his photography studio to his garage. Hobbling with a cane, he went on his own to shoot crime scenes and took the prints to the police station, and the old boys there were gracious in accepting them though they had long ago hired their own people for such work. Della and her son had arranged photos my father had taken in displays in the garage and yard. It was easy enough for George and me to roam around the yard and say hello to folks without engaging too much. We settled in a corner where Annie and Ruthie had claimed several tables and a circle of chairs.

After dinner, Della's son corralled us for taking a family picture. He had learned photography at my father's side. With his modern equipment and lights, he posed us for the shot and timed it so he could jump in before the shutter clicked. In that photo, I see our pain preserved. Della and my father sit in the middle of the sofa, she with her hand on his arm, flanked by their daughter and son. The six of us stand behind the sofa, George angled at the left as though he walked himself into a group photo by mistake, Ruthie smiling too brightly, Addie looking startled, Annie poised to puff on a cigarette. Jane stands with her hand on my father's shoulder, gazing down at him with a half-smile. And me, looking beyond the camera at the children and friends in the room yelling for us to smile. As soon as the flash disappeared, Della shooed us away from the sofa and directed her son to continue taking shots of her and my father with their children and grandchildren.

At my father's wake, an enlarged print of that family picture sat on an easel near the coffin.

Jane took charge of the funeral arrangements for bereaved Della. When I entered the stately old funeral house, where the undertaker readied bodies in the basement and consoled mourners in the parlors, Jane was stationed in the hallway, greeting those arriving to pay respects. Some of the old-timers he had worked with or played ball with survived Alonzo, but not many. Exchanging nods with Jane, I entered the parlor where my father was laid out at the far end of the room. Just inside the door, Della sat on a settee to the side. Seeing she was alone, I wondered where her daughter was but took the moment to speak with her.

Della turned red-rimmed eyes to me. "Dan, thank you for being here. Your father would be pleased."

"Della, I am sorry for your loss." Wooden words like I reflexively said to postal customers were all I had. When I sat beside her, she took my hand, dabbed at her eyes with a handkerchief.

"He loved you, Dan. You have to believe that."

"Della, we don't need to pretend now. You loved him, and if you were happy in your life with him, that's good enough."

She sat up straighter. "I know it was hard between you. He regretted that."

"Not to me, he didn't."

Della sniffed back her tears. "He was a proud, proud man. When the stroke made his arm limp, when he couldn't hold a spoon, had almost no speech, he moaned his regrets."

My eyes floated over the family picture, and beyond it, rising just above the edge of the coffin, my father's gray stubble of hair, the ruddy high forehead. I had not let myself have a direct look at his body when I came into the room.

Neighbors approached Della, and I stood to let one of the ladies sit and murmur condolences. She clutched a rosary. Flooded with the sensations from Lonnie's funeral, I stumbled out to the porch. Hearing Jane calling me, I kept going to my car, sat there for a time, drove home.

That night at our house, Jane said, "You don't have to come to the funeral. But Della would appreciate you being there."

"I don't need your permission." Harsher than I intended but Jane was more attentive to choreographing the event than to my state of mind.

The next morning, by the time I made my way on the stone path to the grave, most of the mourners were heading to their cars. Coffin in the ground, gravediggers shoveling back the dry earth, Della at the graveside propped against her children. Under one of the big trees, Jane talked to the minister. Annie was herding her brood toward Lonnie's grave, Ruthie and Addie stood smoking with Nedda and Oscar. George had refused to come east; his words to me on the telephone, "Let him rot."

I stood in Della's line of vision long enough for her to acknowledge my presence, and her son led her away. Dirt covered the entire coffin, only the last few yards of earth were left for the men to shovel in. Grabbing handfuls of flowers from the bouquets lined up to top the grave, I visited Grandma, Papaw, and Lonnie. The cemetery quieted to its natural sounds of birdsongs and rustling leaves.

The family had left. Coming back along the path toward my father's grave, I noticed a man standing by the fresh mound of earth, his back to me. Hearing the crunch of my steps, he turned and looked at me with those eyes I had seen in the photograph thirty-five years earlier—of him with his mother and baby sister. Staring, both of us frozen, he broke the spell.

Turning back to the mound, he said, "God damn you," and spat on the grave. Then he looked me in the eye again, his hard glare daring me to protest. I did not. Kicking stones out of his way, he marched to a car, drove away. Never having had the courage to acknowledge him or his sister, I could not fault him.

Della sent me ten sealed cartons of photos my father had taken before she knew him, the dates on the labels written in my father's scrawl. My angry impulse was to tear open the boxes and discover the full proof that my lying father was a despicable man.

But the wounded son cocooning in my heart was too fragile still to embark on that hunt. I stacked the boxes in the cellar opposite the furnace, where the darkroom used to be. When I went down to stoke coal in the firebox, I imagined throwing the boxes into the flames and erasing what they contained. But I let the boxes reside under me in the cellar, like a dank burial ground whose spirits were kept at bay as long as I did not disturb them.

Eventually the old coal furnace died, the cellar was cleared to install the gas, the boxes carried to the bedroom that used to be the girls' room upstairs. Maybe the instinct that kept me from burning the boxes guided me to open them. One day when I went into the room for a blanket, I unsealed a box at random, and started on an odyssey. With the photos in my hands, the memories flooded through me, and I wrote what I remembered.

In the good weather, I wrote sitting on the front porch. Marion used to complain she never could make much of the hardscrabble yards around our houses, the dirt so compacted and full of coke dust that almost nothing wanted to grow. I have settled for pots on the porch and window boxes to enjoy the blooms and color of flowers in the spring and summer. The town widened and paved our rutted road, bringing the curbside and a sidewalk halfway into the yard. Some neighbors have moved or passed on but most stayed put, having no resources to do anything much different than work at the edges of the mining and the coking as it petered out to a fraction of what it was in the old days.

The day Jane arrived back in town, I waited in the reception hall of the old hospital, now a nursing home for local sick and elderly folks. I doubt she would have come back if she'd had a say. Jane's third husband managed to amble in, supported by a cane and clutching the ambulance gurney she lay on, as the attendants pushed her through the doors. Her blue eyes were clear and shining and thick white hair surrounded her gaunt face like a cotton ball. I longed to see her smile though I knew her condition meant she probably could not. Stiff like a mannequin while the men moved her into a wheelchair and the aides arranged her arms and legs, once placed she sat with the stately bearing she had as a young woman. Not long after he signed her into the home, her husband passed.

When I sit with my sister in the afternoons, I sense we find each other somewhere in our memories. Showing Jane the old black-and-white photographs, I ask, "Do you remember this day?" to bring back the times when we stood posed in a row with George and Lonnie and our sisters, Addie in the pram, with Grandma and Papaw. In the few photos there are of my mother, she is smiling. With Jane, I relive our life before Lonnie died, when we thought we were a happy family.

Once, when we looked at the photographs, Jane cried out, "Mama, Mama." At that moment, the picture in my hand was one of the older six of us, before Addie was born. My mother is not in the frame. She was, as I recall, standing by my father, who was shouting at us to smile and stand still as he prepared to take the shot. Lonnie was giggling and fidgeting from leg to leg. You can see the camera caught his pose in the fraction of time to freeze him between giggles. My mother applauded when the shutter clicked, and then we split apart, shoving each other.

They tell me a person with dementia has lost their memories, but I see Jane grasping for hers when she listens to my voice explaining the photographs. Her breathing quickens, her knuckles tighten with clutching her skirt or my hand. She mumbles or slurs if she tries to form words, and when she is quiet her face is a mask. She cannot interpret the clock to know when I will arrive or how long I am there, or if I miss a day. The aides tell me that after my visits she lets them spoon some soft food into her mouth without fighting. Maybe I help ease her distress.

I have no power to understand what Jane feels or knows or can think, but she is the only one who can look back into our story with me. After all these years, I am less certain of what I remember. Looking into the images fading on crumbling paper, I plead for the ghosts to tell me what I have missed. Or lied about. Most nights, in my mind's eye the ghosts unfurl the past, and I am unable to turn away, one scene after another, running with no end.